The Loss of Heaven

THE LOSS OF HEAVEN

JACK WARNER

CHARLES RIVER BOOKS

BOSTON

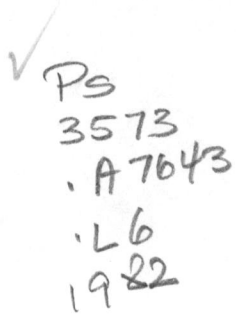

Library of Congress Cataloging in Publication Data
Warner, Jack D.
    The loss of heaven.

    I. Title.
PS3573.A7643L6   1982   813'.54   82-9573
ISBN 0-89182-062-0

Copyright © 1983 by John D. Warner

Published by
Charles River Books, Inc.
One Thompson Square, Charlestown, MA 02129

All Rights Reserved. No part of this work may be reproduced in any form without written permission of the publisher, except for brief passages quoted by a reviewer.

ISBN 0 89182 062 0
Printed in the United States of America

To my Mother and Father—
I wish he were here to read this

Author's Note

The places mentioned in these pages are real, the people are not and never were—although I must admit I wish that were not true of all of them.

Many people have encouraged me in this effort. They know who they are, and I am grateful to them. I would especially like to thank Gene Prakapas of the Prakapas Gallery in Manhattan, classmate and comrade in Wolf's Head, for his valuable criticism of my first efforts on this book.

Having your first book published is quite an adventure. I have been extremely fortunate in having Dennis Campbell as my editor and to lead the way for me—every author should be so lucky.

The Loss of Heaven

SOME MEMORIES

IT happened during Hitler's war. Dan Conway remembered how the old man would sit with his father in the kitchen far into the night and he could hear them laugh and shout and occasionally whoop a joyous curse on the nights when they learned that the Luftwaffe had pasted some English city. They called them English in those days, not Brits, but it was the same feeling.

He would lay wide-eyed on his back in the dark and hear other sounds, strange voices, sometimes knowing they were not Irish, from the crackle of a radio he didn't know they owned. Some nights, he could sense a muffled flurry of activity through the thin bedroom wall and he would slide off the edge of wakefulness into fuzzy dreams of himself leading heroic charges against an English army that eventually surrendered to him, rank after brown uniformed rank going down on one knee to him in disciplined obeisance as he accepted the teary eyed English general's sword.

He was bouncing a yellow ball off the chipped brick front of the house the day the English came. Belfast was busy with all kinds of military activity. He didn't turn at the noisy racket of the Army lorries until they squealed to a stop beside him and then suddenly the street was full of English soldiers in baggy battle dress.

A fat-bellied officer with two red pips on his shoulders led three big fellows with their tilted, flat tin helmets up the steps and into the hall. He remembered squeezing the ball as hard as he could and how dry his throat got.

His father came out of the door first. A soldier pushed him from behind and his momentum carried him past the short rise of steps until he fell hard onto all fours. Two of the soldiers were dragging the old man, holding him by the elbows. They stumbled on the steps and let the old man fall on top of his father.

The officer kicked at the two of them as they struggled to untangle themselves and rise. The point of the officer's boot caught the old man in the side. Dan saw the old man's mouth open wide with pain, so wide that he could see a couple of black teeth left in the ruddy gums.

Dan rushed at the officer and punched him as hard as he could in the belly. He heard laughter over the sound of the officer's grunt and then the butt of a rifle smacked him full in the face. The crunching sound of his nose breaking was very loud to him.

As Dan knelt on the sidewalk, the puke and blood and tears came out of him, and he watched while his father and grandfather were manhandled into the back of a lorry.

Some History

IN 1945 TO THE astonishment of much of the Western world, the class ridden people of England swept the Coalition Government led by the heroic Winston Churchill out of office and installed a Socialist government dedicated to the creation of a Welfare State.

A wispy little man named Clement Richard Atlee became Prime Minister of Great Britain and Northern Ireland for this first majority Labor Government in English history, and in doing so he became custodian of the dreams of his long suffering Socialist cohorts. They were a contentious lot, these Socialists, for they had spent their lives in opposition, but now having reached the top of the greasy pole of political power they were agreed on their basic objectives. They would nationalize certain industries such as public utilities, coal and steel. Free medical care would be provided for all the King's men and women and children, and there would be broad based relief programs for the underprivileged.

Somewhat to the surprise of Mr. Atlee he found that his long time colleagues in Northern Ireland were dragging their feet implementing these cherished goals, especially that of monetary relief for the underprivileged, dragging their feet in a way that exceeded even the legendary stubborness of those citizens of Northern Ireland who have referred to themselves for centuries in Ireland as Loyalists to the Crown.

On a sunny autumn afternoon in 1946, when London's parks were velvety green again and new bright spots of flowers were healing the scars of recently dismantled gun emplacements, Prime Minister Atlee received at his Downing Street residence a trusted associate just returned from the city of Belfast in the Province of Ulster, Northern Ireland.

As they settled into their elegant burnished leather chairs Clement Atlee wondered fleetingly how many British Prime Ministers over how many scores of decades had flexed their mental muscles to prepare for yet another discussion of whatever particular aspect of the Irish question was vexing the English government.

His visitor, a tousled haired one time Oxford classmate of Atlee's with a widespread reputation as a chatterbox, sat silent with evident embarrassment on his face when the Prime Minister asked bluntly why medical care reform was proceeding so slowly in Ulster and why there seemed to be no discernible movement on matters of enrolling the underprivileged for Welfare aid.

Finally after some very theatrical throat clearing the man spoke. "It's the Catholic thing, Prime Minister. There is strong feeling in Ulster that if a Welfare program is established, those receiving the dole will be Catholics, for they certainly make up the bottom rung of society there and most assuredly will qualify as underprivileged. The government there does not want to subsidize these people." He paused, seeming to hope for an interruption and when none came he continued. "It seems that they feel that giving these people help will keep them in Ulster. They leave now at the slightest opportunity because there is nothing for them there. Our people will be paying them to stay and sit in the pubs and drink which, as we know, they are the acknowledged world champions, and talk sedition against the Crown, which is never out of their thoughts, and of course breed like rabbits, which they do." He made a bridge out of his fingers and smiled down at it. "Simply put, I guess one would say that the Protestants of Northern Ireland do not want to subsidize sedition and sex on the part of their despised, scruffy Catholic countrymen." He was pleased with himself until he looked up and saw the grimmer than usual mouthline under Atlee's precise black moustache.

"You're to go back to Belfast at once and tell those people that this government's programs are for everyone and will be implemented as such with all dispatch or we'll send some other civil servants over there to do the job."

After a heavy silence the man spoke. "May I say something further on this, Prime Minister?"

"What is it?"

"Do you really think it's wise to hurry Northern Ireland into this program, I mean it's . . . "

The intensity of the Prime Minister's stare closed the man's mouth. Atlee's voice was harsh and the words even more clipped than usual. "You mean you're infected with that disease of those people in Ulster. It didn't take long to get you into their thought process obviously. They want whatever plusses they can find in union with the Crown but they want to continue to run that province in their own bigoted way, even if it means defying the Crown they make such noise about being faithful to." The Prime Minister relaxed now and his words lost their sharpness. "I don't know if this course is the wisest. We all know how many marvelous people there were among the Northern Irish during the War, and we owe them a great deal, but if we don't push the Protestants into dealing fairly with the Catholics then we will most assuredly face another three hundred years of grief and madness over there. Grief and madness that we'll have to pay for one way or another." The Prime Minister stood up signifying the end of the interview.

"Well, sir," the man continued, presuming on their years of friendship as he retrieved his gloves and walking stick from the butler, "I don't know about three hundred years. I just hope we're not going to be paying for Catholics sitting in their pubs forty or fifty years from now, drinking and scheming to drive the British out of Ireland."

"If they are doing that forty or fifty years from now," Atlee said wearily, "then I'm afraid the whole country will be close to blowing up."

Some Business In London

"You know we could walk," said the short man as he paced back and forth in front of the fat lumpy-faced man and tall blonde woman. His extra high, hard leather heels clicked out his impatience.

The tall blonde woman looked down at him and said, "I never walk if I can help it."

"I'm sure," he said.

"It's quite a bit after eight, your Lordship. We asked for the car at eight," the other man said. "Shall I call it?"

With a set face, the top hatted doorman stood listening. He smiled briefly and spoke in a clipped English accent, "I believe this is your car, sir."

The Rolls Royce glided around the curve of the small green park in front of the Dorchester Hotel and came to a smooth stop in front of them. A small blue and gold triangular flag was attached to the gleaming right front fender.

A tall, square shouldered man wearing a black chauffeur's cap and jacket got out of the car in one easy motion.

"Lord Agstar?"

"Where's the other driver? What's his name?"

"He was taken ill, sir."

The short man grunted something. The chauffeur held the near door open. Lord Agstar got in last.

"You're Irish, eh?"

"Yes, m'Lord."

"I knew it. I'm awfully good on accents, always have been. I spotted the brogue. Even one or two words and I can tell." Agstar settled into the back seat. The blonde woman worked at the folds of her dress as the two men stared at her legs. The chauffeur turned his head towards them from the front seat.

"Where will ya be goin', Sir?"

"We're going to dinner at Stuart's. You know the place?"

"Yes sir, right here in Mayfair."

"That's it," came the short reply.

The car smelled clean and rich and the blonde wriggled her shoulders against the soft nubby grain of the upholstery as they moved through the disciplined London traffic.

The fat man let out a sigh. "Oh, it's good to be back home. New York is so hectic." He took a deep breath, then said, "And London is . . . ah . . . you know."

"And it's so clean," interrupted the blonde.

The short man was gazing out the window.

"Civilized, that's what it is."

"What, Harry?" asked the blonde.

He didn't look at her. "I said it's civilized, the most civilized big city in the world."

"That's right," said the other man, "that's the word, it's civilized. It really is."

The big car eased to a stop. The short man stared up at the chauffeur as he held the door for them. The man's long high cheekboned face was accented by a badly broken nose. His eyes were a faded blue.

"A prize fighter, too, eh Irish?"

"No sir, just an accident."

The short man laughed and said, "Must have been some accident."

The chauffeur watched the thick oak door with its leaded circular window click shut. Then he leaned against the side of the car. Violin music came faintly through the broad curtained windows of the restaurant.

A dapper man in a bowler hat accompanied by a much younger lady in a fur coat went into the restaurant. Her laughter hung in the air after the door closed. An old lady talked loudly to herself as she walked past led by a balding cat on a thick leash.

The chauffeur took a brightly wrapped package with a large red bow from the trunk of the car. He walked into the restaurant and stood just inside the door.

The maitre d' came over to him with a questioning smile.

"Yes?"

"This package is a surprise for Lord Agstar. The blonde lady will come and get it during dinner. It's a surprise tho' so don't say anything."

"Of course. I'll put it here by the cash register where she can see it."

"That'll be fine." The chauffeur tightened the red bow on the box, gave the man a nod and walked out. He took off his cap and his black jacket and tossed them into the Rolls Royce. Then he walked quickly down the street past the lady with the cat who was retracing her steps.

The explosion was so powerful that the back of the cash register was carried through the window. The old lady never knew what took her head from her shoulders. The cat was quietly lapping from a sticky puddle that had formed on the sidewalk as the dazed survivors stumbled moaning and screaming from the shattered wreckage of the restaurant.

Part One

One

It was two o'clock in the afternoon. Dan Conway stood motionless just inside the entrance to the noisy smoky pub. He looked the room over with a slight turn of his head and as he did he rubbed two fingers over the twisted cartilage of his nose. The gesture was part of him; there were times when he resented the habit almost as much as its cause, but now in the familiar dinginess of the section of Belfast always known to him as the Short Strand, his mind was on the men he saw at the far end of the crowded room.

A badly scratched record of the Clancy Brothers singing "The Wild Rover" surged unevenly through the room. Dan walked past the afternoon regulars bellied-up to the bar and felt their awareness of him. A thin pasty faced bartender nodded once sharply and kept his eyes on Dan while he muttered something to one of the drinkers. Then he raised his voice, "All right now, lads! Who's for another jar?"

Two men sat at a table set against the far wall. One with rust colored hair and skin pitted with acne scars laughed an exaggerated loud laugh as Conway sat down at the table.

"Christ, does that mean he's gonna buy a drink? You aughta come in here more often, Dan Conway. It looks like the cheap bastard likes havin' a celebrity in this dump or else he's scared shitless."

"Take it easy, Red," said the other man at the table. His name was James John O'Connor and he was always a very serious man. The redhead's remarks had increased his usual intensity. "Keep your voice down, man," he continued, "what's the matter with you?"

"All right, all right," Conway said quietly, "I got word to come back here because Jerry Regan wanted to talk to me about something big. Where is he?"

"He's in his room over the White Swan, I hope," said O'Connor. "He asked us to explain this thing to ya."

"Why isn't he here?" Dan asked in the same soft voice.

"Well, ya probly know he got picked up by the Brits a couple of times since the bombin' started again over there in England and the last time they grabbed him, after Lord what's his name was knocked off—"

"Yeah, what was his name, Dan?" the redhead interrupted with a snigger. "You know the Minister of Defense who got blown up," he grinned.

Dan turned his head and stared full into the redhead's eyes and the grin went away at once. Red looked down at the table and his belly sent him a warning that caused him to shift himself in his chair. Dan turned his attention back to O'Connor whose voice ran quicker now. "Well, anyway, they banged him around pretty good before they let him go and he's been sort of layin' in up there over the Swan since."

"What he means is he's on the juice again," Red said defiantly without looking up.

"Ahh," Dan sighed. "Well, let's hear about this business, whatever it is."

James John O'Connor licked his lips and then began to speak slowly in a rolling brogue, enunciating each word. "Red here has met a fella who says he can make a deal with a British soldier to get a truckload of automatic weapons."

"Who is this fella?" asked Conway.

O'Connor waited while the bartender placed three unasked for pints of foam topped stout on the table. The redhead jumped up and looked anxiously around the room, shading his eyes like a sailor at sea searching the horizon. The bartender squinted a cold look at him and O'Connor growled, "What is it, Red?"

"What is it?" answered Red in a taunting tone. "For the love of God, man! Don't you realize? It must be the Second Comin' of Christ himself. Where is he? He must be here for this grog to appear like this on this table. It's a bloody miracle!"

"It's a bloody miracle you haven't had your fuckin' head blown off yet," snapped the bartender.

"All right, that's enough. Sit down, Red," Dan said, adding a "Thanks," as the bartender trudged back to the bar.

O'Connor shook his head in a weary gesture. "Well anyway, Dan, Red met this fella at the races, and he . . . well . . . Tell Dan how it went, Red. But stick to the story."

"Shure," said the redhead. He hiked his chair closer to the table and his body seemed to swell a bit as he prepared to savor this time when these men must pay attention to him. "Well, this bloke comes up to me at the races from time to time and talks about the dogs. Good dogs, lazy dogs, you know the usual chatter."

Conway watched the redhead and he slumped in his chair and let his long legs stretch under the table. He knew these men, had watched their posturing as long as he could remember and he settled himself now to endure this Irish drama that made the telling of a story as important as the story itself.

"He's a real plunger," intoned Red, "always bettin' big, and a spender. Not so close with his money he wouldn't buy a drink now and again. Well, one day we're havin' a few jars and he says to me would I know anyone who might know what to do with a truckload of automatic weapons." Red looked round the table with a feral grin that displayed his remaining discolored teeth. "I played it very cozy, a course."

"Umm," grunted O'Connor with his lips pursed.

Red darted a look at him. "I did. I told ya I did. I said maybe I knew somebody, maybe I didn't. 'N I asked him just what he had in mind. That's when he said he knew a sergeant in the Royal Marines who was in bad need of money and could set up a deal for somebody to get their hands on automatic rifles and ammunition. So I told him I'd see what I could find out and I'd be in touch with him."

"How would you go about doing that?" Dan asked.

"Doin' what?"

"Getting in touch with him."

"Oh, well. He's always at the races," Red answered.

"You've been goin' for years haven't you, Red," Dan remarked in a casual conversational tone.

"Shure, shure, I have. I know the dogs as well as anybody in this bloody country, North or South. I'm a regular and why not. There's no fuckin' job for us to be at," he said defiantly.

"And what about this fella? What's his name?" Dan asked.

"McMahon," said Red.

"McMahon," continued Dan, "is he a regular at the dogs like yourself?"

"Well, no." Red paused briefly and then continued. "He's just gettin' into followin' the dogs he told me. That's how we got talkin' the first time. He asked me what I thought about the dogs in a certain race." He shrugged. "What the hell, people know I know the score on bettin' the dogs. They know that." Without glancing down and in a seemingly reflex action, Red placed the palm of one hand over the threadbare elbow of his jacket.

"All right, Red, finish it up," said O'Connor.

"Okay, Okay," Red grumbled. "So I been keepin' James John up to date on all this and he's been talkin' with Jerry. Right?" he said looking at O'Connor who nodded slowly. "And then he said Jerry wanted me to take James John to the track to point out McMahon to him and I did. And McMahon gave me the soldier boy's name and phone number. Which I got right here."

"You never met this Marine?" Dan asked.

"No, Jerry said no meetin's. Nothin'. Waitin' for you, I suppose." He pulled a badly wrinkled piece of paper from his pocket and smoothed it by running the edge of his hand back and forth across the pencilled numbers. Then he presented the paper across the table to Dan.

"I'm out of touch with the Belfast phone numbers now," Dan said. "Where's this fella live?"

"I dunno," Red said.

"He lives in a little odds and end shop on the Crumlin Road. Tells the neighbors he's moved back home here from South Africa," O'Connor said with a pleased look.

Red was staring at him slack jawed. "For Chrissake," he said.

"Jerry had me follow him there, the last few days."

"You never said a bloody word to me," Red said harshly.

"Take it easy, Red," Dan said.

"Security, security," O'Connor rumbled.

"Security, my ass," the Redhead said.

Dan let his exasperation show in his voice. "Don't talk nonsense, Red."

"Well don't ya trust me?" Red asked plaintively.

"We don't trust this guy, McMahon. You goddamn fool," O'Connor growled.

Two

THIS WAS SPRING, but the wind was left over from winter. It had no softness in it as it came slicing at them, carrying the chill of the Hebrides, full of sharp, stinging rain. The two men flanked Conway as they pushed along the street, heads bent, scraps of paper and dirt gusting around them from time to time.

"What do ya think, Dan?" asked James John.

"Let's go over what you found out about this McMahon."

James John cleared his throat before he began. "Well, he's been telling folks that he left here years ago and worked in South Africa. Made some money. Doin' what I dunno."

"Not bettin' on greyhounds," Red said in a sullen voice.

"He's got a shop on the Crumlin Road," James John continued, "sells religious stuff. You know, junk. Jerry had a couple of other fellas watchin' im too," he said, ignoring Red's glare. "And they said that this fella is some kind of a religious nut. Carries a bible in his pocket, I guess. And spends time everyday at church, usually that Protestant church on Woodvale Road. In fact, the fellas watchin' him were goddamn unhappy about the time they spent in church."

"Serves the bastards right," snapped Red.

James John plowed right on with his recitation. "He's one of those people that stay there kneelin' with their hands up to their face while everybody else is up and gone. You know the kind, Dan. But as far as politics go, we can't find out anything. He never talks about those things, but he does talk like he knows what God is thinking. In fact, so far Jerry Regan says he seems to be one of those people who talks all the time and sez nuthin'."

"He aught to be right at home, here then," said the redhead.

Dan grinned at him through the rain.

The brick and stucco walls of the grim houses that bordered the sidewalk were marred with occasional oversized letters of graffiti. "God Save the Pope" followed by "Fuck the Queen" in tall white letters stretched the length of a brick wall. Further along the treeless street a gutter had overflowed—the water swirled with aimless bits of trash. The wall nearby carried the message "No Pope in Belfast." Below this someone had scrawled "Lucky Old Pope." The redhead pointed at this and said, "Sure, that's what this country needs, a good sense of humor. I bet you're glad to be back in this happy-go-lucky place, eh, Dan Conway?"

Dan turned and led the way up the steps of the White Swan Pub, a two-story stucco building edged with faded grey paint, its front windows painted over a dark green. Cigarette butts littered the steps and trickled out bits of tobacco into the puddles.

A tall, chestnut haired girl with high cheekbones stood behind the bar, her hand on the worn brown stick of the beer tap. She pushed the handle up when the three men entered and was motionless, staring at them. She came out from behind the bar and walked slowly across the room, full of herself, shoulders back and breasts very proud. A card game was in progress at one of the tables she passed, and a man about to play a card stayed his hand in mid-air. His opponents didn't notice him. The chatter in the room softened.

She came close to Conway, a big woman, only half a head shorter than he.

"You're back," she said, her eyes full on him.

"It would seem so," Conway said.

She put a hand out slowly and touched his arm. "You're alright, Dan?"

"I'm fine, Moira, just fine."

She jerked her hand away. "Goddamn you, couldn't you write or call or something? I see things in the newspapers but I'm not sure if it's you. I don't know what you're doing or where you are."

Conway's words were quick and hard. "Not here, Moira, not here."

"Will I see you later?"

"Yes."

Her body lost its tenseness. "I suppose you're lookin' for Jerry."

"Him too," said Conway, and she smiled.

"He still keeps the room upstairs. I think he's up there now. Of course you know he was lifted and locked up for a time while you were gone."

Conway nodded and turned from her.

"Dan."

The sadness in her voice stopped him and he looked at her.

"He's different than when you last saw him, and it's not just the booze. He's old now. The last time did it. Those devils, they finally made him old.

They've had at 'im too many times."

Dan found the wall switch, but nothing happened. He moved carefully up the narrow stairway, his feet feeling onto the calloused steps. He remembered there were two high steps and then a short one, and his thoughts went to his grandfather and of how the old man had explained this to him one day years ago. Anyone not knowing these stairs would bump the high ones and come down hard on the short one. The old man had chuckled and said how most English castles had this and the Tower of London had the same setup on one of its circular stairways. He could see the old man's bitter smile and he tried to remember what his voice sounded like as he said, "Sure, we've learned some wicked things from them, but not enough or they'd be out of our country, off our Island," and he remembered the sound of his palm smacking flat against the table or bar—more often a bar.

The door to Jerry Regan's room was open. Conway stood at the threshold and looked in. Regan was settled back against the headboard of the bed, his hand on a book in his lap, his head tilted to one side, glasses just hanging onto the roundness of his nose. He had a grey stubble of beard that merged with his short, white hair, and his small shoulders moved in even cadence with his rapid snoring.

Books and newspapers were everyplace, some piled miraculously high. There was one chair just visible. On the table beside the bed was a half filled whiskey bottle, gold against the light.

Conway leaned against the doorway and watched Regan for some time. Then he made a fist and hammered the door casing once, hard.

Regan's eyes came open and at the same time one hand went under the pillows, bringing out a small pistol.

Conway spoke softly. "Jeezus, Jerry, that's quite a greeting."

Regan was using one hand to fix his glasses. "Mother of God, is that you, Dan?" His words were rubbery and now he put the pistol by him on the bed and reached down and picked up a glass from the floor. He took out a set of false teeth, shook them once and, covering his mouth with one hand, set the teeth in his mouth.

"Well, DanO, here you are back home and damned glad I am to see you." He looked around and said, "Ah, just push things out of that chair."

"How are ya, Jerry?"

"I'm alright, Dan—for an old man, I'm alright."

Conway tipped his head toward the door. "You've changed some habits."

Regan pursed his thin lips and nodded. "Ay, of course you'd notice. It's a thing I've got now. Since this time in Long Kesh in solitary. I can't stand bein' in a closed-in place. I'll get over it, I guess. I don't know why this time bothered me more than the others. Christ, I started out with your father. I should be used to it by now. Well, the hell with that stuff. Now you're back, there'll be some real grief for the bastards here." He sat on the edge of the bed and swung his feet onto some books and newspapers on the floor. He reached down and tossed a number of papers onto the bed, indicating headlines as he did. "See, I kept up with things over there. Of course, I got messages from the membership, but I love to have a drink up here and watch 'em squeal in their newspapers. By God, Dan, you've got 'em wild, and they're sick of it, the British people are. I can smell it now, they've had enough. If we keep the pressure on they'll get out of Ireland once and for all."

"Jerry, what do you think about the thing with this fella, McMahon?" Conway asked.

"Ah now, that's a good question. Ya mean is he an informer, a plant?" Regan asked himself. He stared at the ceiling, his fingertips moved against the stubble on his face. "Yes, a good question. Informers have helped keep the Irish race in subjagation to the British through all these centuries." He was silent for awhile. "Well, DanO, he seems old to be gettin' into that game, but ya never know." He looked straight at Conway. "That's one reason why we sent word that we'd like ya home. I can't make these decisions so well anymore. It's up to you yourself, Dan. The rest of the leadership will help and advise when we can." His hand moved reassuringly. "And we will, we will. But for real boldness, Dan, you're the man and if we could grab a truckload of weapons and explosives from the Brits it would be a grand, bold thing. But if it's a trap—if they've planted him here to trap us, to trap you—Jeezus that would wipe us out."

"Not forever it wouldn't," Dan said grimly. "This thing wouldn't end that easily."

"Christ almighty don't I know it and doesn't the whole Irish race know it," Jerry said. "But still," and his voice trailed off as he stared, unseeing past Dan who watched him with real fondness. "If it's a trap," Jerry said again and stopped and now his eyes fixed on Dan.

"If it's a trap and it didn't work it wouldn't be bad, either," said Conway.

"Sure, if it didn't work," Regan said, reaching for the golden whiskey.

Three

MOIRA'S HEAD WAS DOWN over the sink when Conway came back into the bar. She raised her eyes and watched him as he sat with James John and the redhead. She walked down the bar undoing her apron, her eyes never leaving him. She tossed the apron onto a newspaper a man at the end of the bar was reading.

James John stopped speaking when Moira sat at the table. She laughed quick and harsh and shook her head. "James John O'Connor, if you think I'm the least bit interested in whatever madness your schemin', then you're even crazier than I think you are."

"We know what you're interested in," the redhead said, showing his front teeth.

"Shut up ya little scut or I'll put another scar on that face of yours," she said.

The redhead's eyes narrowed and he glared at her. Moira wrinkled her nose at him.

"All right, I'll meet you lads tomorrow as planned," Conway said.

The redhead turned back to stare at Moira before he went out the door. She was talking to Conway. "No more work for me today, Dan."

"Good."

"D'ya mean that—are ya pleased?"

"I am." They sat unmoving, looking at one another. Conway spoke quietly. "Let's go."

Moira's eyes were bright. "Aren't ya even gonna buy me a drink?"

"Do you want one?" he asked.

"No."
He got up from his chair and looked down at her. "Let's go."

Moira was lying on her belly, her chin cupped in her hand. The bed was a tangle of sheets and blankets and she kicked her feet to free them. She was staring at Conway who was lying on his back, his head against the wall. His gaze moved the length of her body and he winked at her when his eyes met hers.
"Did ya miss me, Dan?"
"Umhum."
"Really miss me?"
"I missed you."
"That's it, tho', isn't it—ya don't *really* miss me."
"I miss you, Moira."
"And that's the best you can do, isn't it?"
"Yes."
"Well, you know how it is with me." She put her face into his chest and spoke the muffled words against him. "I ache for ya, Dan. That's how I miss you." She raised her head and turned so that a breast rested on his hip. They both looked at it. "And how are the girls in England? Are they as good as me?"
He shook his head. "I don't know."
"Ah, go away with ya. Ya don't know. Tell me, how are they?"
"I don't know, Moira."
"Truly, Dan?"
"Truly."
"Ah, Dan." She scrambled to her knees and rested her buttocks against her heels. There was no fat on her. "You don't trust 'em do ya? That's why you don't sleep with 'em. It's true, isn't it?"
"I guess it is."
"My God. I'd think that would be enough to get you out of this murderin' business you've spent your life in."
"Well, we're gettin' near the end of it."
"Dan, you don't believe that, do you?"
"I do."
"Well, then you're spendin' too much time elsewhere lately. You grew up here. You watched them destroy your father's life and so many others, half the time on nothin' but suspicion, years in and out of prison, no jobs, the Protestants havin' everything their way and scared to death that if they give up a little they'll lose it all. And the Catholics so predictable—so stupidly predictable—the whole goddamn thing—"
"Moira—"

"No wait, Dan," she said quickly, "you never let me speak on this, but hear me this once. Get out! For the love of God, and more important for your own self, your life, get out. I know things, Dan, more than you think. I know it's more and more you makin' all the decisions for your people and, Dan, if I know it so do others. They know you've been in England—they must know. You think you're safe in this part of Belfast—Ha!" Her words rushed out. "They'll get you. They'll kill you and that's why it's never the end of it in Ireland, cuz if they kill you you'll become a memory and somebody will kill some of them in your name. Ah Christ, Dan, nobody knows that better than you." She ran her fingers through her hair and put her head down. When she looked up her cheeks were wet. "You could have more than you've got, Dan. You're not one of these wild kids. Don't ya want some kind of life for yourself? You're runnin' out of years." She knelt there in front of him, her arms at her sides.

He reached out and pulled her to him. She turned her face away and spoke as he held her. Her voice was very low. "Stay here, Dan."

Conway put his hand on the back of her head and twisted it until she looked at him. "You know I can't do that, Moira."

She jerked herself away from him. "You mean you won't."

He grabbed her again, pulling their bodies together, his thumbs pressing on her hipbones. She started to speak but her lips were covered with a rough kiss, and he forced his tongue into her mouth.

In the morning it was still raining. A gutter close by was broken, and he awoke to the slapping sound of water dropping flat on stone. Moira was lying with her back to him. She didn't move when he swung his feet out of bed onto the cold linoleum. He pulled on his trousers and fingered into his shirt pocket for the crumpled paper Red had given him. He went down the hall in his bare feet to use the phone on the wall.

Someone who said he was Sergeant Murdock of the Royal Marine Regiment answered after two rings. The words rolled out in a short-breathed Scotch burr. "Sergeant Murdock here."

Conway's words were clipped and fast with only a hint of a brogue. He hung up without waiting for a reply.

The iron bed sagged and squeaked when Dan sat to put on his socks and shoes. Moira slid down toward the middle of the bed. She kept her back to him.

He sat still. The noise from the broken gutter sounded loud. Somewhere a baby cried. He turned and put his hand on Moira's shoulder. She didn't move.

"I gotta be goin', girl."

She didn't speak and he squeezed her shoulder. "Moira." He stared at a mole on her back and squeezed her again.

"I heard you."

"Well, I gotta go."

"Go then! For Christ's sake, go! I'm sure you've got wonderful things to be doin' to build the classless-socialist Ireland you've been talkin' about for so many years. Go! Build a new tomorrow for Ireland. Go blow up some pub or theater or hotel, go!" She twisted round and looked at him through the hair that fell across her face. "Go and get yourself trapped and killed." Her voice became wildly sing-song. "By the Paras or the Royal Ulster Constabulary or the Ulster Volunteer Force. You know those devils have a few good religious souls prayin' to put a bullet in you."

"Ah, don't talk that way. I'll see you soon."

"No, Dan, you won't see me soon. I've had enough. You've used me for the last time. Go find some whore to relieve the pressure for ya next time. I've waited and cried and held my breath for the last time." She put her head down and shook it, hard. Then she looked at him again. "And now your people are skulkin' round that creep McMahon from the Crumlin Road."

His voice jumped at her. "Who told you that?"

She tried to sound a laugh, but it broke in the middle. "Who told me that? You fool. You're back in Ireland. It may be the North of Ireland, but it's Ireland. Talk comes with the air and the water here. You think you and your group are so secret. Well, you're not invisible."

"Careful, Moira, careful," Conway said.

"Ha! You tell me to be careful. You better use that word to yourself. I know this, Dan. They want you bad and why not? You better be careful, not me. What's he doin' with your people?"

"You know I don't talk about those things, Moira, so don't ask."

"Sure, don't ask. All these years. Don't ask. Don't tell me anything. I let you inside me, but I can never get inside you, and that's all I've ever wanted. Well I don't really care anymore, and this time, finally, I mean it. Don't come back, Dan."

He got up and worked at a button on his shirt. Then he picked up his windbreaker from the chair, all the time looking at her.

"You do mean it, don't ya?" he asked.

"I do."

His eyelids almost covered his eyes. "Well then, so long, Moira."

"Goodbye, Dan." Her hand moved slowly to brush the hair from her face. She turned over and lay face down for a long time after he closed the door quietly behind him.

Four

THE COLOR OF JERRY REGAN'S skin matched his hair this morning. He rubbed his watery red eyes with a misshapen knuckle and lowered his mouth to the steaming mug of milky tea the old woman set on the table. She stood watching him, her toothless mouth sunk into her face.

"Shure the drink is punishin' your wild restless body, Jerry Regan, as I knew it would." She nodded and her tousled grey hair bobbed. "I often said it would!"

Regan raised his eyes and spoke around the edge of the mug. "Your money's on the table. Take it and for the love of Christ don't give us one of your sermons."

She put one hand to her mouth as she slid the coin off the table. "Ah, Jerry, the love of Christ indeed."

Conway waited until the woman shuffled back to the counter before he spoke. "Jerry, you're goin' to have to listen to a short sermon from me."

"Well, keep it short, DanO."

"I want you to lay off the grog today," Conway said flatly.

"Would that be for my body or my soul?" asked Regan, staring unblinkingly at Conway.

"I want you in good shape, Jerry. I've contacted that Marine sergeant and I'm setting up a meeting for tonight."

"Jeezus, that's quick, Dan."

"Well, if it's a trap, it's better we spring it. I've not told them where we'll meet. I want to hold that 'til the last minute. The only one who'll know is you. That's the way these operations have got to be run and that's why I want you dry today, and anytime we're workin' at this business."

"I'll be dry alright."

"The old farm outside Maghera near the Glenshane Pass is where we'll set up, Jerry. I figure we'll need eight men and a safe place for after."

"If there is an after," said Regan softly.

Dan looked closely at Jerry without speaking and Jerry Regan suddenly wondered at the magic of life, of birth. These were the same blue eyes, the same astonishing deep blue—almost violet—of Dan's father and for an eerie moment Jerry Regan was confused. Who was he talking to? Where were they? A strange trickle ran up his backbone and he hoped Dan didn't notice his shiver. God, a drink would taste good, he thought, then Dan's voice caught him up.

"I'll meet you by the small brook below the old farm, but have your men up round the farm by early dark."

"It'll be done, DanO, and done dry. What about McMahon? If he's helpin' bag us we shouldn't leave 'im walkin' round."

"Mr. McMahon will be with me. If it's a trap, I'll try and use him for barter with the Brits."

"Ah well, well. I imagine that'll be a bit of a surprise for Mr. McMahon," said Regan as he wiped his mouth with the palm of his hand. "And what about weapons, Dan? What d'ya think?"

"Well," said Conway, "our boys know enough not to hang around for a long firefight, but handguns won't do the job with the Army."

"Then you think it's a trap, Dan?"

"I don't know. But if it is, I think it's time we flex our muscles a bit more with their army, here on our island."

"Ah, DanO, that's grand. So we'll break out the new stuff. Ya know, we got some fine automatic rifles, M-16s, armalites and machine guns from America."

"The boys told me about it," said Conway.

"Imagine," said Regan, "we got the stuff right out of one of their armories." He chuckled. "They said we could've got more if the lads had a bigger truck. Of course, the Yanks have got so many goddamn guns they don't half know what to do with 'em, especially now their balls shrivelin' up the way they are."

"Ah, Jerry, the world is always short of balls," said Conway. Pushing away from the table, he walked to a dirt streaked window and stood looking out at the street.

A battered van lettered "O'Connor's Plumbing Service Ltd." backed into the alleyway. Conway spoke over his shoulder to Regan who stood behind him. "We'll see you tonight, Jerry."

"You will indeed, DanO," said Regan. He moved closer to the window and watched as Conway went out the side door and scrambled into the rear of the van. The rusty doors shut quickly behind him.

Conway was pushing through the last button on a pair of greasy coveralls when the van slowed to a crawl. James John O'Connor spoke without turning his head from the wheel. "There's a patrol stopping cars up at the intersection of the Antrim Road, Dan. There's a hatch under the tool chest for the pistols. Red, give him a fast hand."

The redhead swivelled around from his seat as Conway pushed a metal tool box to one side. He lifted a canvas cloth covering part of the floor and then tugged at a recessed handle. When the top came up Conway set their pistols into the small compartment, lowered the cover and pulled back the canvas. The chest was pushed back in the time it took for the van to move into place beside four black helmeted soldiers. They cradled their rifles, butts tucked into the tops of their bulging cartridge belts. Their faces were young and solemn above the shrapnel vests that covered their mottled camouflaged jumpers. Two of them moved to the passenger side, while a freckled faced soldier with corporal's stripes leaned toward the window to speak to James John.

"Where's this vehicle going?" he asked.

"A plumbin' job. Where else?"

"Where?" asked the soldier.

"Up the Crumlin Road."

"What number?" asked the soldier. He reached with his free hand and unbuttoned a flap on a baggy thigh pocket and pulled out a small notebook. He slung his rifle strap over his shoulder and unclipped a pen from the notebook.

O'Connor stared up at the soldier, a crooked smile forming on his face. "D'ya mean that the Queen's peace can be better kept by writin' down where our plumbin' job is?"

"O.K., Paddy, just give me the address and then get out of the van. I think we'll have a look at your tools," the corporal said loudly.

"The number is 1763. It's near the intersection with the Ardoyne Road, and we're late now."

"What a shame. Out," said the corporal, and he tipped his head toward the back of the van to his comrades.

James John and the redhead got out and lit cigarettes. They watched the rear of the van. Conway climbed out and walked to the driver's side and stood very close to the corporal.

"Lousy business, eh?" he said.

The corporal didn't answer. A soldier near him gave a quick glance inside a highly polished old Ford where two heavy, white haired women sat staring setfaced out the window. The soldier waved them along, and they drove off without changing expression.

A succession of crashing sounds came from the back of the van. O'Connor and the redhead moved to the open doors. Conway stayed beside the corporal.

The redhead's voice was almost lost against the next loud noise. "What the bloody hell d'ya think you're doin'?" A continuous harsh jangle of sound came from inside the van.

Conway spoke softly. "I guess your boys are havin' some fun."

The corporal walked slowly toward the noise, Conway beside him. O'Connor's face was pale as he stared into the van. One of the soldiers was sweeping his arm along the shelves and dumping tools, cans, boxes into a jumbled pile on the floor. Pieces of pipe and tools fell off onto the road. James John turned to speak to the corporal. He closed his mouth when his eyes met Conway's.

"And you goddamn people wonder why you have to drink alone in this country," said the redhead.

"Find anything?" asked the corporal.

"Nah. Junk, mostly junk," answered his mate.

"Not 'til you got hold of it," said James John.

"Alright," said the corporal, "let's go." He leaned into the van and slid a metal case from the corner. He pulled up the latches and took out the drill set in the recess. He held it up in front of his eyes.

"I guess you plumbers use these often."

They all watched him. He let go of the drill and it crashed on the roadway. The plastic handle shattered. James John and the redhead stared down at the drill and began to curse softly. The soldiers walked toward another car and didn't look at the men bent over, scrambling on the roadway.

The redhead continued to curse until Conway spoke, hardly moving his lips. "That's enough. Let's get this stuff back in and get goin'."

"My brother hates for us to use his truck for this business," O'Connor said as they tossed tools and metal fittings into the van. "He'll be wild about breakin' that drill handle."

"Maybe we'll put the drill to good use on McMahon if he's double-dealing with us—so your brother will know he's makin' a contribution to the cause," Red said.

"Ah, my brother's had enough of the cause I'm afraid," O'Connor said morosely.

The van moved smoothly with the sparse traffic on the Crumlin Road. Not far past a squat armored car parked with its back against a candy store, they stopped and backed into a narrow alley. Dan finished taping the handle of the drill with black electrical tape as O'Connor said, "This is it, Dan."

"Check it out from the front, Red. We won't go in unless he's alone," Dan said. "James John, is there a back door we can use?"

"I dunno, Dan."

"Go back and take a look. If we can go in and out that way, it'll be much better. Take something with you to work on the door."

O'Connor took an oil can and a screwdiver and walked in long strides down the alley. Dan pulled up the floor covering of the van and took out the pistols. He spun the cylinder on one and then slid the pistol into his jacket pocket.

James John opened the van's rear door and looked in at Dan with a satisfied expression on his face. "There's a back door and we can go in that way. I got the door fixed so we can walk right in."

"Good job," Dan said to O'Connor's evident pleasure. They both stared out toward the street where Red leaned scowling against a postal box. He finished one cigarette and ground it out while he lit another. He shook his head and hurried down the alley to them. "There's a bloody old hag in there. The two of 'em gabbin' a mile a minute," he said.

"Take it easy," Dan said. "You've got to learn patience in these things. Learn to do them right." The three of them looked out toward the street as Dan spoke.

"There she is," said the redhead, taking a deep drag and flipping his cigarette away in a long high arc that descended in concert with a sudden spattering of rain.

A round shouldered woman wrapped in a black shawl shuffled in broken slippers across the mouth of the alley.

"When we get inside, you walk in with a big hello, Red. That ought to put him off balance. Let's go," Dan said as he moved quickly toward the rear of the building. He edged carefully between overflowing trash barrels and scattered boxes and slipped through the half open door at the end of the building. He stood very still after his first few steps into the room and did not move until his companions were inside. Then he led them down a narrow walkway that was bound by floor to ceiling shelves. The shelves were empty and covered with a thick layer of dust. On one side, the space between two shelves was taken up by an intricate spider's web.

Dan looked up the stairs near the end of the room that rose to the second floor. The door at the top was closed. In front of them a large tarnished brass crucifix was over the opening to the shop. Dan stood to one side and motioned for Red to move into the shop area.

Cyril McMahon's back was turned to them. Mumbling to himself, he sat on a high stool with his head bent over a book. He swivelled round at the creak of the floor as Red entered through the back way.

Despite the gloom of the shop, Dan could see McMahon's face register an initial flush of surprise, and then as he and James John followed Red into the room, he watched the jolt of fear run through the man. McMahon slid down from the stool, the book forgotten in his hand, and stood wide-eyed for a perplexed moment. He was a round man. That was Dan's first impression and it remained so. Round baldhead, round eyes above a small O of a mouth, his belly, even his upper arms and legs, McMahon seemed a series of stacked circles.

"I've brought a couple of friends to meet you, McMahon," Red said as he swaggered into the small room which contained a jumble of religious paintings, poorly lit photographs and books with worn bindings lying in piles on top of and inside two fly specked glass display cases.

"What's goin' on here, Red? What are ya doin' here? Comin' in the back way and all."

"Hey! We come and go as we please," Red snapped.

"We're here to talk about the weapons that you and your friend Sergeant Murdock want to sell," Dan said as he leaned against the door frame.

"Well, you could of come in the right way or told me you were comin'."

"Oh shure, we always try to do that," O'Connor said.

"What's that you're readin?" Red asked and grabbed at the book McMahon held, but the man spun away with a nimble movement that surprised Dan.

"That's my business. What the devil's got into you, Red? I thought you and I were pals."

"Pals, my arse," Red snarled. "You been tryin' to make a fool out of me."

"Easy, Red," Dan said in a voice that turned the others' heads toward him. Then he continued quietly, "We want to know a little bit more about your friend Murdock. Where you met him and why you picked out Red as a man who might buy a truckload of weapons."

McMahon's eyes were on Dan as he spoke and when James John continued the questions McMahon still kept his eyes on Dan. "Yeah, you're just back here to Belfast, you say," James John growled, "yet, you've got all this goin' on and as a matter of fact, what in the name of Christ would cause anybody to come back here to retire? Have you got kith or kin here?"

"Well, now boys, wait a minute now," McMahon said in a voice that tried to be genial but lost that quality in its quaver. He began to speak again but before he completed a word the tinkle of a bell sounded as the front door of the shop opened.

A tall slim man came into the shop without pausing. He seemed to push up on his toes at the end of each step so that he pranced rather than walked. His hair showed strips of blonde as he removed a wet felt hat and knocked it against his raincoat with a chuckle. "My goodness, there certainly is no shortage of rain in this country." His accent was undistinguishable. "I hope I'm not interrupting anything, gentlemen, but I was told I might find some fairly old Bibles for sale here." He turned languidly while slowly peeling off calfskin gloves. His pale grey eyes took in each man as he moved. "And which one of you gentlemen is the proprietor?"

Dan's hand was in his jumper pocket gripping his pistol. He watched McMahon staring at the visitor. Suddenly, the man took a long stride to Dan's side and slammed the black snout of a pistol into his ribs pinning the hand Dan had in his jacket pocket at the same time.

His voice—now hard and clipped and British—cut through the room. "Don't move, any of you. I'd love to put a hole in this piece of filth. All I need is the thinnest excuse. Search those two clowns, Cyril. And remember both of you, one tiny mistake and your broken nosed hero here is a dead man."

"You Brit bastard," snarled Red. The man smiled and without loosening his grip on Dan's arm or releasing the pressure of the pistol muzzle, he shifted his weight and kicked the redhead, putting the point of his toe deep up into his crotch. Red's scream was short, piercing and shocking in the confines of the room.

"Now, there's one Irishman that really will be short of balls," the man said delightedly. "Anyone else care to comment," he asked without looking at Red who lay doubled up moaning and retching on the floor. "We have a problem you see," he said to Dan in a conversational tone. "Put that hand up in the air, please. Yes, that's it. Place the palm against the wall. That's fine. Now, we'll take that hand out of your pocket—without the pistol, please. If I see a glint of it or if you move quickly, I shall just kill you. That's it. Yes," he mused aloud, "we have a problem. We're supposed to be civilized and we have to live by some rules in dealing with you barbarians. We aren't supposed to do the kind of things," now he spoke slowly and distinctly, "that you fucking animals do." Still without looking at him he took a short step and kicked Red in the side to punctuate his words. His grunt was hardly audible beneath Red's abandoned cry. "Now both hands over your head, Conway. You too, there dumbo. That's it. Stay that way. Just toss their things there in the corner, Cyril. That's a good chap." He moved away from Dan in a quick backward step. "Now we'll call our friends and have these vermin taken out of circulation." McMahon was going through Red's pockets and it was obvious that the sobbing and retching redhead hardly knew what was happening.

"Quite by chance, I was checking on your situation, Cyril, and I saw the redhead outside. Waited a bit. Figured that if he was here that perhaps the mad dog himself might be in town. Nothing like a bit of luck, eh Conway? Especially after the times we've missed you in England!"

"I suppose," Dan said somberly. He moved forward a bit and the man raised the pistol.

"Get right back in that doorway and stay there. Keep your hands up and if you'd like to make a run for the back door, please, please, do. Take the pistol out of his pocket, Cyril," he ordered. Dan's hand reached the wall over the door and his fingers touched on the large brass crucifix hanging there. McMahon shuffled uneasily near him and reached gingerly toward Dan's jacket.

"For goodness sake, Cyril, I don't think he'll bite you. Now get the job done." The man nudged McMahon with an elbow as he bent to check Dan's pockets. In one furious sweep, Dan tore the crucifix from the wall and in a long savage downward chop sunk the end of the cross bar into the tall man's blonde head. A high pitched wheezing scream came out of the man's mouth and his eyes went still. The force of Dan's effort carried him across McMahon. Dan, McMahon and the dying man fell in a tangle on top of Red who groaned loudly. O'Connor stared immobile for a long moment. Then never knowing that he did, he quickly crossed himself.

They waited at Dan's command inside the rear door. The rain had stopped and the alleyway consisted of a series of connecting puddles with bits of wood and soggy paper on the oily surfaces. Red leaned, doubled-over against the wall. His face was the grey color of an overcast day. There was a sour smell in the air around him. His breathing was ragged. He managed to keep a pistol pointed towards McMahon whose hands were bound behind him. O'Connor was wiping perspiration from his forehead with the edge of a broken knuckled thumb. He and Dan had just deposited the body of the tall man in an upstairs closet in McMahon's flat.

"What now, Dan?" he asked.

"I want to ask your friend here some questions," Dan said with his head down as he looked through the tall man's wallet, "but not here. We've got to get out of this place. Untie him, James John. We can't have him tied if we get stopped again."

"Let me take the book with me," McMahon pleaded.

Dan looked at him in surprise. "What?"

"My bible, let me take my bible."

Red glared at McMahon and tried to spit at him. The mucus dribbled down his chin.

Dan shrugged. "Get it," he said to O'Connor.

"Bullshit," croaked Red.

"You can put that pistol away now, Red. You'll need both hands gettin' in the truck," Dan said.

The van nosed out of the alleyway and Dan spoke quietly to O'Connor. "We'll go out past the airport and then up to Maghera."

O'Connor turned and spoke in a rough rasping voice over his shoulder to McMahon who sat with his back against the bins of metal fittings, his eyes closed, perhaps to avoid Red's murderous glare. "If we get stopped, you're to keep still. Anything happens to us while we're with you and some one of our people will get you. Someplace, sometime."

"I know that," McMahon said without opening his eyes. "I know, the trouble and grief that God has sent to test me." His arms were crossed holding his bible against his chest.

"You goddamned hypocrite," Red forced out the words and made a lunge at McMahon, grabbing his arms, making a fumbling attempt to pull them apart. McMahon held tight to his bible, squeezing his arms to this chest.

"Get your Godless filthy hands off me," he snarled.

Dan spoke sharply, "Stop that, Red, and listen to me now. This is a military operation, not a wrestling match. Leave him alone. I don't want your hassling attracting attention. I won't tell you again."

Minutes later, O'Connor's short low growl signalled the presence of a military patrol further down the road. O'Connor slowed and drove at a cautious crawl between an armored car and a troop carrier parked at an intersection. Soldiers standing in attitudes ranging from boredom to alert tension watched the traffic. A beefy faced sergeant glanced at the cab and then waved them along. The van picked up speed and O'Connor eased out a long sigh. "Well now," he said, "I hope that's the last we see of the army of occupation for awhile."

"We'll go to Murray's garage in Maghera," Dan said and put his head back and closed his eyes. Red muttered an occasional groan from the back and then Dan heard a whispered mumbling. He turned his head and saw McMahon's lips working as he read his bible. Red seemed asleep, his head leaning against a cardboard carton. Dan glanced out his window and to the south he could see the late afternoon sun break through the overcast and change the color of the water of Lough Neagh. Three sailboats looked a starched white as they angled across the glinting surface.

Two young boys kicked a football along the slick stone block surface of Prince Albert Street in the village of Maghera. They separated when O'Connor's plumbing van made its rackety way up the street and turned into Murray's Garage.

Dan and James John O'Connor marched the mumbling McMahon between them into the littered office cubicle of the garage. Dan kicked a chair into the center of the room and swept some oily rags from it.

"Sit here, McMahon," Dan said curtly.

McMahon remained standing. He held the bible in front of him with both hands. "You might as well know right now, I have nothing to tell you."

Dan moved close to McMahon and the man tilted his head up to look at him. His round, red rimmed eyes did not waiver from Dan's glance.

"How this session goes, depends on you. You understand that, don't you?" Dan said.

"That's typical justification talk that your type uses, Conway. You are Conway aren't you." McMahon spoke the words in a cool, almost reflective manner. Dan knew as he watched and listened that there was no fear in the man now.

Red stood rubbing his crotch with both hands while he glared at McMahon. He rushed at him now, driving him back into the chair. "Sit down, goddamn it, he told you to sit down."

"What's your connection with that man in your shop?" Dan asked sharply.

"Why don't you say his name? You looked at his papers. I expect they told you his name was Booth. Can't you say the name? Is it possible there's some shame in you? You killed Booth with a crucifix, Conway."

McMahon's first words had been controlled and measured, but now each remark was at a higher pitch than the one before. "Killed him with a crucifix! You barbarians. His name was Booth and he died a hero's death at the hands of the anti-Christ. Died trying to rid our country of you savages."

"Whose country?" O'Connor bellowed.

"Our country. We're part of Great Britain and you are papist savages. That's what you are!"

"Wait a minute," Dan said. "I asked you what your connection with Booth was?"

"I volunteered to help him and his people and I'm proud I did."

"Who are his people?"

"They work for Her Majesty's Government."

"And Murdock? What's his role in this?"

"I don't know."

Suddenly, Red walloped McMahon in the face, a round house swing with his palm open. The sound was sharp in the room and a fiery imprint of Red's hand showed on the seated man's cheek in the garish light from the single unshaded bulb that hung from the ceiling.

"You were usin' me. Makin' a fool outta me."

"That happened when you were born," McMahon said, disdaining to touch his face.

"Yeah?" said Red as he stared at McMahon. "Oh yeah," he shouted suddenly and raised his arm, but Dan stepped in front of him.

"Who told you to start talking to Red," Dan asked quietly as Red stalked out of the room.

"No one told me to do anything. I was asked to help and I hope I was able to be of help."

"Who asked you to help?"

"People of conscience and goodwill. Christian people."

"And what were you supposed to help these Christian people do?"

"Put an end to this Catholic conspiracy to separate Ulster from the Mother Country."

"And you were going to do that by setting us up with Murdock and his people?"

"I don't know what's supposed to happen with that business with Murdock."

"You don't, huh."

"No! I don't."

Their heads turned for a moment to the clatter of sound from inside the plumbing van. Red's legs were visible at the open door on the passenger side.

James John O'Connor spoke. His voice was heavy and slow. "You know you're talkin' complete nonsense, man. Ya must know that. There's no more Catholic conspiracy in this country than there is on the moon."

McMahon just stared at him.

"We don't give a good goddamn for the Church," O'Connor added.

"Who'd Booth work for?" Dan asked.

"I told you, Her Majesty's Government. I don't know what branch. I never asked."

"Did he introduce you to Murdock?"

"I never met Murdock."

Dan put his face close to McMahon's and the man clasped both hands tight around his bible.

"Never met him?"

"No."

"Who pointed out Red to you?"

"Booth."

"Why did he? What did he say?"

"He said they thought Red would be receptive to buying arms and they wanted to find out."

"Receptive, huh? What's the story with you, McMahon? Where do you come from? What do you do for a livin'? It's not that phoney shop."

Red stomped back into the room. He held the electric drill in his hand like a pistol. "Let's get some real information out of this fresh bastard, Dan."

"I'd like to hear some of that, too," O'Connor said.

McMahon stared at the drill.

Red plugged it into a socket and squeezed the hand-grip, the whir of the tool filled the room. No one moved or spoke. They stared at the metal rod as it spun into a blur.

"Don't be a fool, man," Dan growled. "Tell us what you know."

"I've told you what I know. You people are going to do something savage to me anyway." There was a tremor in his voice now.

They spoke through the off-and-on whirring and whining of the drill as Red clasped and then released the grip. He grinned at McMahon and watched him with bright eyes.

"Listen to me, McMahon," Dan said. "Tell us what the plan is with Murdock and the truckload of weapons. Tell us who you work for. Who hired you? Who else besides Booth is involved with this and you'll be out of this country unharmed. I promise you that."

"Do you really think anybody would trust your word, Conway?"

James John O'Connor astonished his comrades as he suddenly roared, "Better than your word, you fuckin' spy. Dan Conway's words have been good for our people in Ireland all his life." His arm lashed out, his fist smashing into McMahon's face.

"Your people! Your people!" cried McMahon, ignoring the blood gurgling from his nose. "You and your people are a papist scourge on this land. Go down to the South with the rest of the rabble down there and have your babies and take the Pope's orders and chant with the priests and—" The words poured out of McMahon, tumbled out of his fat round bloody mouth.

O'Connor looked at him with surprise. "The man's balls are bigger than his brains," he said. Dan shook his head and said nothing as Red grabbed one of McMahon's hands.

"We want straight talk, you bastard."

"Get your hands off me, you filth!" McMahon held tight to his bible.

"Grab him, James John," Red grunted as he tried to pry McMahon's hand loose. He held the drill with one hand and pulled at McMahon with the other. O'Connor looked quickly at Dan and when Dan nodded, he put his big knuckled hands on McMahon's arm.

"You want to hold on to that book. Then hold on to it," Red snarled. The sound of the drill was loud. "Hold him," Red shouted as he aimed the shining point of the drill at the back of McMahon's hand.

"What's the plan with Murdock?" Dan asked in a loud voice.

"I don't know," cried out McMahon, transfixed by the drill. Its black cord made it seem an obscene snake in Red's hands.

"What's their plan, you son of a bitch." O'Connor's voice was shaking.

McMahon clamped his lips together and jerked away from Red's hand. O'Connor still held him but the sudden movement caused them both to sprawl onto the floor. McMahon held his bible now in one hand. With a furious burst, Red stomped his foot onto McMahon's wrist and with a bending, stabbing movement, he drove the point of the drill into the back of McMahon's hand. The whir became a tearing stutter as the bit ground through the flesh pushing in right up to the snout. Bits of skin and flecks of blood flew up from the drill head. A scream came out of McMahon's chest and filled the room. His eyes rolled back in his head and a line of drool ran out of the corner of his mouth. Now the drill sent a piercing whine to mix with the other unhappy sounds in the room.

"Ah, Jesus," Red said. "It's gone through and caught in the goddamn book." He twisted and shook the drill and McMahon's unconscious body jumped convulsively. O'Connor turned his head away as the drill, spinning out a brief fearful bloody spray, was yanked out of McMahon's hand.

"Red, get a bucket of water," Dan ordered.

O'Connor took the drill from Red's hand and held it down by his side. "I better, ah, better wash this, ah, clean this thing. I, ah, don't want my brother to . . . Well, you know." His words were directed at no one as he went out of the room.

McMahon whimpered and then Dan hurled water from a rusty can into his face. McMahon's eyes opened and focused at once on his hand.

"What's the plan with Murdock and the truckload of weapons as bait?" Dan asked as he knelt on one knee beside him.

McMahon's body began to shake. Words came from him in gusts. "Hear me, O'Lord. Rescue me from the wicked."

"All right, all right, man. Take it easy. Tell us what we want to know!"

McMahon's hand began to jump. He restrained it with his other hand. "I told you I don't know what the plan is. I've never met Murdock. We don't work that way."

"Who's we?" Dan snapped the words out.

"I'm sure you've already guessed. Special Intelligence. The only man in that operation I knew was the man who used the name Booth." Taking his eyes off his hand for the first time, he glared at Dan now. "Why don't you ask him?"

"What was your mission here?"

"To meet Red and pass the word about Murdock and the weapons."

"And then what was supposed to happen?"

McMahon sighed. "What was supposed to happen was—those clods would go to their boss, Jerry Regan, who's become a total drunken sot. They'd talk it over with him and there would be typical Irish Catholic confusion." His mouth formed a small tight circle and he grunted in pain. "I guess that's what was supposed to happen. Now for the love of God, leave me alone."

Red and O'Connor stood motionless watching McMahon. Suddenly, Red snarled and reached down and grabbed McMahon's mutilated hand. "Leave you alone, huh. We'll leave you alone, you son of a bitch. Just the way you leave our people alone." Red's acne scars grew intensely white as the color of his face rose to match his hair.

McMahon twisted and his scream became a moan. Dan pushed Red's hands away from McMahon and asked another question in a tired voice. "What else was supposed to happen?"

McMahon's eyes were closed and his voice was low. "You were supposed to happen. You were supposed to come back here to Northern Ireland."

FIVE

JAMES JOHN TURNED the key and nodded at the crisp tone of the engine. He pursed his lips. "By God, it's goin' to be a nice feeling bein' behind this wheel instead of wrestlin' with that van," he said.

The hood of the car reflected the wan streetlight outside of Murray's Garage as the Cortina moved out onto the street.

"Is the money for the car comin' from one of the bank jobs in the South?" asked Red. No one answered and he continued, "Maybe we could stop along the way somewhere and have a jar and, you know, toast the boys workin' the banks. It's nice to be able to go in style like this. We could lock the Reverend, here," he gestured at McMahon, who huddled in the corner snuffling and cradling his hand, "in while we have just a taste."

"Stop here!" Dan said and Red forgot about McMahon and turned quickly and looked at Dan.

McMahon raised his eyelids slowly, just enough to see, and watched Dan with total, breath-held attention as he got out of the car and walked swiftly to the red trimmed telephone booth. His tall frame filled the narrow structure and the three men stared at the patchwork geometry of his figure behind the neat rectangles of the glass as he bent his head to the phone. No one spoke or moved in the car. Red remained with his hand half raised. The rain returned in a quick hard surge but O'Connor ignored the need for windshield wipers. He did not take his eyes from Dan—none of them did. He had become a fuzzy watery blur, but they continued to watch him, not wanting even to blink. This phone call was critical to their lives. Each of them knew this and the knowledge filled the car with silent, almost bursting, intensity.

A gust of wind cleared the windshield for a moment and the sallow street light outlined the imprint of the imperial emblem of Her Majesty, Elizabeth II Regina, a faded black reminder of Empire stenciled on the desolate phone booth.

"McMahon, ya see that?" James John O'Connor's voice was gentle in the charged stillnes.

"See what?"

"The insignia on the phone booth, the Queen's mark."

"Sure I see it, it's on every phone booth."

"Every phone booth in Britain, yes, and here in the North. But this isn't Britain and we don't want it to be. That's what this is all about, man, do ya understand that?"

McMahon's answer was a long deep sigh that hung in the silence of the car.

"Turn right outside of town," Dan said as he settled himself in the car. "Head for the Glenshane Pass." James John glanced at Dan. "We're goin' to meet Jerry Regan and some of our people there."

"And then some other players?" asked James John quietly. He wedged a ragged thumbnail between his upper front teeth.

"I hope so," said Dan.

"I suppose that means no drink then," said Red.

A hard gust of wind shook the little Ford and a fusillade of raindrops burst on the windshield. "It looks to bein' a wild night, Dan," said James John as he leaned forward and turned the wipers on.

"In more ways than one," said Red as the car left the village behind.

McMahon groaned. His breathing was heavy. He began muttering. Lonely spots of yellow light shone through the rainy blackness from an occasional farmhouse, then there was just the night. The headlights flashed on shaggy cattle, heads down, massive rumps turned towards the wind.

Lichen-covered stonewalls glistened hard and green in the sweep of the headlights. Dan stared out at the night without seeing it. The warmth of the car, the drumming rain on the roof and the momentary sense of safety that he felt right now let his mind range freely and his thoughts went to Moira and he could see her body and remember the feel of it and then he heard her voice and her words and a wave of sadness washed over him with the certain knowledge that she was gone from his life. It would not be the same with her again. He knew her strength and pride and he respected it even as he knew that it would keep her from him. Their relationship was ended. He accepted this but the edge of sadness stayed, and as he watched the running, trickling, twisting, aimless lines of water on the window beside him he wondered if somewhere ahead of him could be a time of quiet, steady living.

James John grunted something and Dan saw the headlights catch the tumbling water of a narrow brook.

"This is it," he said quietly and straightened up in his seat. They turned off the road and stopped on a dirt path.

Dan got out and tightened the collar of his jacket up around his neck. He took only a few steps from the car and stopped. The sounds of the brook joined with the wind rushing off the mountains beyond. He waited and then returned the whistle that carried over the night sounds.

"DanO."

"Here, Jerry."

Regan's face and hair were a grey smudge against the darkness. "I've two of my men here with me. The rest are set up around the farm. Nothin' doin' yet," said Regan.

"I called him from Maghera not too long ago," said Conway. "That'll give us time to set up."

They moved back to the car, joined by two indistinct figures as they spoke. Regan put two automatic rifles and magazines on the roof of the car. He wiped his glasses, shielding them inside his jacket from the rain. "Jeezus, some night! I think I may be gettin' too old for this line of work."

James John spoke through the open window. "If they ever gave us a chance for proper jobs, maybe none of us would be in this line of work."

"What's that goin' on in the back?" asked Regan. "What is that I hear?"

"That's the Reverend McMahon sayin' his prayers," said Red.

"Is he needin' prayers then? Well if he is I think he may be a little late," said Regan.

"All right," Dan said. "I'll give you time to set up around the farm and then I'm goin' to drive up there with McMahon and wait to meet with Murdock."

"Ya figure to use him for a little trade, Dan?" Regan asked.

"I'm going to try."

"Well, I hope it works. We got a car near the brook and a truck parked in some woods near the farm," he continued. "James John, you know Quinn's farm outside Strabane, we can lay in there after if things get really hot."

"Good, Jerry," said Conway. "Check the men out up at the farm. I know it's a nasty night, but we'll see if we can make it nastier for the Brits."

"You think it's the army settin' this up, DanO?"

"We'll soon see," said Dan, taking an automatic rifle and stuffing three magazines into his coverall pockets.

Red pushed McMahon into the front seat and Dan slid into the driver's seat. "Good luck, boys," said Conway.

McMahon's lips shut and he stared at the automatic rifle lying on the seat. Rain striking the car was the only sound. Storm clouds covered the moon and Dan peered into the darkness. He looked over at McMahon, who raised his glance from the weapon and looked directly at Dan as he started the motor.

"Why don't you give it up, Conway?" Flecks of dried blood fell from his upper lip as he spoke. "You're not goin to beat the British Army with your gun or the British people with your bombs. It's not too late to make a deal. This is your last chance, man, get out now." His voice was hoarse and the words rushed out of the lumpy red circle that was his mouth. "Let me speak to them. I can talk to them, whoever it is. I'll tell 'em you'll make a deal. They'd take care of you with plenty of money and an easy life somewhere. You're important to them. You could do yourself some real good for once in your life. Get out now and all you'll have to do is feed them some information and you're away from this forever, nice and easy. These mates of yours, they're scum, you know that. They're slated for hell, all of em."

Dan exhaled a lung full of air and shook his head. "It never changes does it?"

"What's that?"

"Scum, that's the way you people see us and always have. Scum. It's been that way forever." His soft voice became terse and hard. "But forever is a long time, McMahon, too goddamned long."

"Agh!" McMahon grunted and looked down at his torn hand held against his chest.

Dan gave his attention to the car as they moved uphill, the crunch of gravel under the wheels joining the sound of the rain; from time to time his gaze swung to the open window at his side but there was only the deep black night. The headlights caught the fractured remains of buildings. Conway slowed and turned into a grassy yard. The drizzly sweep of the lights showed what was left of a stone farmhouse. Parts of a thatched roof remained; window openings, their symmetry lost to time, looked blacker than the night; the outline of a broken stone wall traced its way to decayed outbuildings and the tumbled mossy ruins of a barn.

Conway parked on an incline near the house facing out to the road with the motor running and lights on. They sat motionless. Dan stared down the path of light through the rhythm of the wipers.

McMahon raised his hand up to his face. Pieces of flesh hung from the puncture. Dark red blood welled out and trickled down his hairless wrist into his sleeve. He stared at the wound. Suddenly he intoned, "O, Lord, be not far from me; O, my help, hasten to aid me. Rescue my soul from the sword, my loneliness from the grip of the dog."

"Hey," Dan said sharply, and as he spoke a beam of light intersected the Ford's lights. Dan slammed a magazine into the underbelly of the rifle. McMahon jerked at the harsh sound of the metals joining. Conway flicked his headlights once, then again and again. The oncoming lights went dim, then bright. A long, black car rolled into the yard and stopped. Dan dimmed his lights. The black car didn't respond. Dan narrowed his eyes and a low growl came from between his clenched teeth. A man in uniform got out of the driver's seat. He moved sideways from his car with careful steps.

"All right, McMahon, get out of the car—slowly," Conway said, "very slowly." McMahon pushed open his door and sprung out of the car. He stumbled, then got his balance and ran shouting toward the other car. He held his bloody hand up above his head. A hammering burst of gunfire exploded through Dan's windshield. Uniformed men leapt out of the doors of the other car, automatic weapons bucking hard against their hands. Muzzles moved in searching blasts at Conway's car, at McMahon, at the rain. As his windshield shattered, Dan dove from the car and rolled behind the stones at the corner of the house. He scrambled to a gap in the wall. The grass looked very green in the headlights.

McMahon had fallen in front of the long black car. A soldier on his side of the car was pushing up to one knee looking at McMahon. The weapon in his hands jumped frantically. Dan's short burst caught the soldier in the side. The man's finger continued to squeeze the trigger, even as his body was thrown up and back. McMahon came to his knees screaming. He was staring at blood spurting from his stomach. He put his hands over the terrible wound and then held his crimson hands up before his face. He put his head back and cried out, the words lost in the racket of gunfire. Then he pitched forward, his face slamming into the velvet grass.

A staccato hammering of gunfire came from the other side of the soldiers' car. Dan's vehicle was erupting in small geysers of metal as bullets tore their way out. He heard firing from the field across the road. He went down on his stomach, weapon cradled in his arms. He worked his way over stones and rubble, keeping a fractured wall between himself and the soldiers' car. Alternating elbows and knees, he scuttled toward the pile of stones that marked what was left of a wall of the farmhouse. The noise of the gunfire increased. He could hear the sound of slugs smashing into the cars. He reached the pile of stones, swiveled the weapon up to his shoulder and raised himself up onto his elbows. One of the headlights on his car was unsmashed. On the edge of its beam he could see one of the soldiers, his beret pushed back on his blonde head, his young face sharply white against the night and the mottled dark jumper he wore. Dan pushed wet hair from his forehead and squinted along the barrel of his weapon. His first shots kicked up dirt. The soldier swung round. The next burst smashed into him, knocking him over, his eyes wide and searching. The whites of his eyes were very visible.

Suddenly from the black moonless sky, a roaring, whipping thunder came rushing at the farmhouse. One powerful hypnotic light cut out part of the night. Dan lay still, face against the ground, almost paralyzed by the intensity of the sound, shocked that this noisy, snarling, stuttering monster could overwhelm him so totally. He had not heard the helicopter until it was on top of them. Now its two heavy caliber machine guns were turning his car into scrap metal. Dan lifted his head and watched this for a moment, then he scrambled to a crouch and raced to a corner of the ruined house close to the copter, and flattened himself against the wall.

The machine pivoted in the air, giving its guns a different angle. Another searchlight snapped on, peered into the rubble of the old barn and then walked its dazzling way toward house. Tracers flashing streaks of brilliance shredded the night. Conway could see troops through the open door in the side of the gunship as he braced himself and his weapon against the stone and mortar of the house. He poked the muzzle through an opening that had once been a window. Bits of the ancient wood left in the frame broke like chalk.

He brushed his eyes across his forearm and then sighted deliberately on the copter's main rotor. He held the weapon tightly against his shoulder and slowly squeezed the trigger. Now the helicopter's guns searched for him, screaming ricochets deflecting off the stones nearby. He poured bullets into the base of the whirling blades until the firing pin hammered on empty. He kept the weapon at his shoulder, quickly worked the release, slammed in a fresh magazine and resumed firing. The helicopter seemed to lose its balance, tried to regain it, staggered, then fell over on its side, the blades still slashing the air in wild furious protest. Oily black smoke came from the vertical rotor and the motor began a piercing anguished scream. It made no further forward motion. The big-bellied machine fell lifeless out of the sky.

The helicopter struck the edge of the ruins of the barn. It twisted and collapsed onto its belly with a tremendous shrieking of metal. A low rumbling whooshing sound was followed by an explosion and a burst of wild flames that reached higher and higher into the black night. Dan turned his face from the heat and moved quickly through an opening in the farthest side of the house. He zigzagged away, flattened himself onto the spungy pasture, and watched the growing, searching inferno as it reached up into the night.

Soldiers emerged from the copter, one dragging another, others staggering or crawling. Conway tucked his left elbow under his rifle, took a deep breath and aimed short bursts at the dark figures outlined against the coppery fire. A soldier stumbled from the blazing mouth of the chopper carrying the sagging body of a comrade. Dan's shots knocked the man backward into the flames, his burden sprawled on top of him. Across the sounds of wind and battle and fire he heard the racketing noise of another helicopter. He got to his feet and went down the hillside toward the brook. He did not turn to look at the tower of flames behind him.

Dan heard the panting before the footsteps. He held the rifle waist high and waited. The words came in gasps: "Dan Conway—Dan Conway."

Dan gave a low whistle and slid the rifle bolt forward.

"Jeezus, oh, Jeezus, don't shoot. It's me," gasped Red.

"Right here," said Dan.

"Jerry Regan's been hit—hit bad I think. Everybody else—is okay, away in the truck. James John is helpin'—Jerry down here." Red stood head down, thin chest heaving, his mouth grabbing for air, phrases punctuated by deep breaths. "Mother of Christ—what a night! The Brits—the Brits'll never get over this."

"Wait by the car, Red. I'll go back and help with Jerry," said Dan.

The car lurched and a long low sigh came from Jerry Regan. He squeezed Dan's hand and spoke. "Well, DanO, I've been dry inside at least, this day and this night. I could do the right thing by a bottle of Paddy's."

"Jerry, you've got a belly wound. You know drinkin' is the worse thing you could do."

"The worse thing has already been done to me," said Jerry.

"Sorry about the bumps, Jerry. We're almost to Matt Quinns," said James John.

The car slewed its way into a muddy yard. The lights swung across the front of a small cottage. Geraniums in pots on the lower window sills were a quick flash of color against the drab stucco. Through the lines of rain, Dan could make out low stone outbuildings and a large barn beyond the house. Everything was in darkness. James John brought the car to a sliding stop. They rocked forward against the brakes. "Mother of Christ!" The words were a groan coming out of Regan, then a bubble of laughter. "You know, James John O'Connor, I don't think I'll ride with you again."

Dan was out of the car moving to Regan's door when a flashlight caught him full face.

"Who is visitin' Matthew Quinn on this wild wet night?" barked a voice behind the light.

James John spoke as he got out of the car. "That's Dan Conway in your light, Matt, and Jerry Regan here with us too, and he's bad hurt."

"Holy Mother, what's happened? Dan Conway is it? Ah, it's an honor, and I'll tell ya here and now," Quinn cleared his throat.

"For Christ's sake," interrupted Jerry Regan, "ya sound like one of the Abbey Players. Will ya help me out of this bloody car?"

"Ah, Lord-Lord," said Quinn bending to the car. "Ma! Ma! The lights—put on the lights," he shouted, pushing his torch into Conway's hands. He lifted Jerry Regan out of the car in one motion without even a deep breath and moved easily through the mud toward the lighted windows of the house.

An old woman stood inside the door. She peered closely at each face through shiny, bland eyes. Her sparse hair was white and stringy, a faded slip hung well below her dress above untied men's work shoes, and a heavy belt sagged round her thin body. She mumbled and chatted to herself. Quinn stood for a moment in the kitchen, a broad block of a man, with intense dark eyes rimmed by faint wispy blond eyelashes, the light reflected from a pink bald spot as he looked down at Reagan.

"In here," he said, shouldering a door open. A deep charred-black fireplace took up one side of the room. A long low divan draped with dust-bearded sheets was set in front of the fireplace. Jerry Regan's mouth hung open; his tongue moistened his lips. He did not open his eyes when Quinn laid him gently on the couch.

Dan put a palm on Regan's forehead, then parted his shirt and looked closely at the wound. "He's got to have a doctor."

"Oh Christ! That's dangerous," said Red.

Dan glared at Red for one intense moment and then looked at Quinn. "Can you get somebody?" he asked.

"I can surely try," Quinn said slowly.

"All right. First, I'll want blankets for Jerry, lots of 'em and a fire here would help, too. James John, you drive Quinn. Red, I want ya to go with 'em. James John'll drop you with our people in Strabane. Your face will be missed in Belfast, Red. I want you back there as soon as possible." Red fingered the pock marks on his cheek and stared out of the corner of his eyes at Conway. "Matt Quinn," continued Dan, "have ya a bottle of whiskey in the house?"

"I have, I'll bring it with the blankets," said Quinn.

"Shure, you're all they said you were, Matt Quinn, as good as the Quinns before ya," breathed Jerry Regan without opening his eyes. A grin or a grimace turned the corners of his mouth.

The whine of wheels spinning, the old woman's piercing giggle, a sharp, despairing moan from Jerry Regan. The noises came in the same moment. Dan's head snapped up. His face was warm from the heat of the glowing fireplace. He reached a long arm to the pile of coveralls and pulled a pistol from a wet pocket. Three smooth strides took him to the wall beside the kitchen door. He was flat against it when the knock sounded. He looked at the old woman and jerked his head toward the door.

She opened her toothless mouth and giggled. Dan watched her briefly and then reached for the latch. As he did, the door opened. The visitor closed the door and stood with a wide back to him, then turned slowly and peered at Dan. A tall, heavy woman, tiny eyes hidden behind hedgerows of fat, her glance went to the pistol in his hand. She wore a long dark cloak and a navy blue bandanna covered her hair. A half-moon shaped black bag hung from her shoulder. She swung it onto a chair now as she shrugged the cloak from her wide shoulders.

"I'm Sister Rose of the Nursing Sisters of the Sacred Heart. Matt Quinn asked me to help." Her voice was clear and high pitched. "Where's your comrade?"

Dan pointed toward the parlor with his pistol. The old woman laughed, a shrill sound that filled the small kitchen. Sister Rose shook her head as she moved across the room after picking up the black bag. "God help her, she never gets better. Matt is a saint to bear with it all these years, and no life of his own—except with you people, of course." She shook her head. "Like his father and grandfather. Aghh." She peeled the blankets off Regan and lifted the makeshift bandage.

Jerry's eyes came wide open. The nun put a hand on his forehead. She bent her head and looked into his eyes. "This man has got to be in hospital. At once!"

"You got the wrong man, sweetheart," said Jerry. "I'm not goin' to any hospital."

Sister Rose held a syringe against the light and pushed the plunger. She bent and angled the needle into Regan's thin arm. "You must. That's a bad wound."

Regan's voice got stronger. "Listen to me, my beauty. Hospital for me with this gunshot wound means prison, and a prison clinic where they'll kill me after tonight's business. You know that. I've spent too many years in them from Borstal to Long Kesh." He winced as he continued. "I left my youth in goddamn English prisons. I'm not goin' to die in one."

"Well, Bucko," she said.

"Jerry Regan," he interrupted with a sigh.

"Jerry Regan. I'm Sister Rose and it's a terrible wound ya have, and I'll tell ya straight, man. If ya don't go to hospital quick, ya won't make it."

"Then I'm a dead man," said Jerry. "Give me a drink, Dan." Dan held the bottle in his hand and looked at the nun.

"You're Dan Conway, are ya?" He nodded and handed the bottle to Regan.

"Your name's on the radio." She looked around. "I don't think the Quinns have a radio, much less a television, do they? Well, all of Ireland is hearin' your name tonight, and England, too, I'm sure. Matt told me there was trouble and asked me to come and keep quiet." She pointed a finger at Dan. "And I will, but, Mother of God! I didn't realize how much trouble. I was stopped twice comin' here. I would think Matt and them'll have trouble gettin' back here. The Army and the Royal Constabulary, shure, they're everywhere. I've never seen anythin' like it." She pushed another needle into Jerry's arm as she talked. "And they'll be here, shure they will. They know the Quinns have been involved in this madness forever." She put a hand on Jerry's brow again. "So, if ya don't come to the hospital with me Mister Jerry Regan, I'm afraid ya'll be goin' with the British Army, and that whiskey's the worst thing ya could do." She stood up, hands on her rumpled hips. "What's it to be, Dan Conway? You're the big boss. That's what they say on the radio. So what's it to be?"

Regan spoke intensely. "In everything else, Dan, you're the boss. But not this. It's my life. There must be someplace Quinn can hide me. I won't be taken." He pushed himself up on his elbows. "Dan, you know what it would be like. You know what they'll do to us after tonight." He coughed and lay back. "Jeezus," he said softly, "the English. The most civilized people in the world until it comes to Ireland, then they become barbarians."

The nun spoke sharply. "Don't ya understand what I'm sayin'? Ya must be operated on at once!"

"We understand, Sister," said Dan.

The back door opened. Dan spun around to see Quinn and O'Connor lean armalite rifles against the wall and stamp their way to the kitchen fire. He went in and watched in silence as they stood rubbing their hands. The wetness dripped from them, forming tiny puddles on the dull linoleum. James John turned to Dan, his round face was very pale. "Christ in Heaven, Dan. They're everywhere, Army and RUC. At one stop I thought they were gonna keep us. We left the car in the back field. How's Jerry?" he added.

"Not good. Sister is with 'im. He won't go to hospital," Dan said.

"No, of course he wouldn't," said James John.

"Matt, we've got to get out of this house," said Conway.

"Yes, they'll be here. No doubt of that," said Quinn. "We've a hidden room in the barn. Shure, my grandfather used it and my father," he added proudly.

Sister Rose filled the doorway. "It's too bad you don't have children, Matt, so they could hide out there someday, too." The old woman rocked in the corner puffing furiously on a cigarette. Suddenly she burst into laughter.

"Let's get into the barn," Dan said.

The soft light of the lantern sketched grotesque, fuzzy shadows, and the smell of animals and hay was strong. The room was a low ceilinged box with rough caulked stone walls. Straw covered the damp earth floor. Cattle shuffled on the other side of one wall where hay and feed bags were piled in front of the narrow entryway.

Jerry Regan lay on a pallet of hay and blankets. He reached up and grabbed the nun's arm. "Sister, I want a priest." His eyes moved back and forth, never still.

Dan spoke quickly. "We can't do it, Jerry. It's too dangerous for us."

"For you maybe, Dan, but not for me," said Regan. "I've known you since you were a kid taggin' after your old man and your grandfather. We both know how much we've all put into this idea of one Ireland. I'm not askin' you to stay. Get out of here now. There's great things yet for ya to do, but for me—no more." His mouth opened wide and he breathed deeply. "You can guess how long it's been, but it's time for me and Holy Mother the Church to be gettin' together again." He took long shuddering breaths. The nun looked up at Dan as she knelt wiping Regan's face.

"No," Dan said. "Not with the Brits all over the place. It's too risky just for that. And what's the point of it?"

"Dan," Regan spoke with his eyes closed. "It was you firin' into those lads crawlin' out of the chopper, wasn't it? There was only one weapon firin', and I knew it was you. It's made me think of somethin' I read, one of the Germans said it, and they ought to know. It was somethin' about a man who fights dragons becomin' a dragon himself, and that's where you are, DanO. You've become a bloody dragon." His body shook again and he quieted himself with a deep breath and continued. "And that's where I've been for a long time too, DanO. It's turned me into some kind of dragon, too, but I guess I don't want to end as a dragon and that's the point of it." As he finished Jerry opened his eyes and smiled up at Dan, a gentle smile that seemed to Dan to wipe the lines and the years and the pain from his face.

Sister Rose heaved herself to her feet. "Conway, I'm goin' to try and get a priest here." She moved close to Dan. He could see the shine of sweat on her face. "So what are ya gonna do now, put a bullet in me?"

James John O'Connor's cheeks bulged larger and larger, then his mouth flew open and a blubbery snore sounded through the room. Dan sat with his back propped against a wall. Jerry Regan lay dozing, muttering beside him. Dan pulled the blankets up around Regan's shoulders, and then put his own head back against the wall and closed his eyes.

The clicking, snapping sound was sharp. Dan opened his eyes. Jerry's teeth were chattering, now rattling. His body twisted up and down on the floor, the blankets slid from him. O'Connor stopped snoring. He sat up and stared at Regan. Dan put his long hands on Regan's shoulders. Jerry's eyes were wide and bulging. There was a sharp blow on the outside wall. Matt Quinn's voice was harsh. "There's an armoured car comin' into the yard."

Dan was on his knees holding the blankets on Regan, he moved closer to him and his trousers stuck briefly in wet earth and hay. He looked down and saw dark syrupy blood forming an expanding pool beneath Regan. The growl of a heavy engine vibrated through the walls and hard, quick shouts came from outside.

"Oh, my God!" cried Jerry Regan, "I am heartily sorry for having offended thee—" Dan slapped his hand over Jerry's mouth. Jerry pushed the hand away. "—I dread the loss of heaven and the pains of hell." Dan clamped both hands on Regan's mouth.

"Sweet Jeezus. We're done for," whispered James John, pointing his rifle at the hay-filled entryway.

Hobnailed boots sounded in the barn. Singsong Scots' voices just beyond the hay.

Jerry's body arched up. The soft, yellow lantern light reflected from his frantic rolling eyes. He shook his head. Dan had a forearm across Jerry's chest, his hands hard on his mouth. Jerry grunted, pushed, heaved. A cow bawled in the barn, a voice shouted. A rasping noise started in Jerry's chest. He pushed his mouth hard against Dan's hand. Blood squirted out between Dan's fingers and under his palm and he jerked his hand away. Jerry Regan stared at him, his face now chalk white and full of fright. The light went out of his eyes and his body jerked hard and fell back onto the hay. Dan stayed on his knees, his head slumped until his chin touched his chest. He breathed slowly in and out, long deep breaths. A shrill crackle came though the walls, more shouts. The heavy engine started, the room trembled.

"Dan! Dan!" James John rasped the words out. Conway didn't raise his head. The engine sound drifted away. A chicken squawked nearby.

James John crawled across to Conway. "Dan." He stopped and raised one hand and stared at the blood smeared on his palm and on the butt of his rifle. He wiped his hand and the rifle with hay and looked at Jerry Regan. "Is he," he started, "is he?" The jowls in his face sagged. He didn't look at Dan. Cattle stamped and snorted. James John's breathing was loud.

Matt Quinn's voice came through the hay at the entryway. "They've gone, lads. I'm comin' in with Sister Rose." His beefy red hands pushed through the hay. "What it was, Sister," he said as he tossed the hay aside, "is that Ma made them nervous."

"Why wouldn't she, the poor dear." The nun's voice sounded from behind Quinn. Sister Rose moved her bulk around Quinn, casting menacing shadows along the wall. "I've got bad news for ya, Jerry," she said softly.

"He can't hear you, Sister," Dan said.

She fell to one knee next to Regan and put out a hand to balance herself. She touched his brow and then grabbed his wrist. "Oh, Mother of God! He's gone, and no priest." She turned her head to Conway. Tears pooled up and ran over the roll of fat beneath her eyes. "The priest wouldn't come, Conway. He wouldn't come. He said you're Marxist terrorists destroyin' Ireland and ya must pay for it with your immortal souls. O, Lord God, I know this man wanted to save his soul."

"Indeed he did," said James John. "He, he said an Act of Contrition. Uh, well, well practically. Didn't he, Dan?"

"He did," said Dan.

"Ah, well then, there's a serious sin on the priest's own soul,' said Quinn somberly, "and I believe—"

"Matt Quinn, will you take care of Jerry's body for us?" interrupted Dan. His voice was harsh and loud in the small room.

"I will, and an honor, too, it will be," said Quinn.

"Sister, will you do somethin' for me, for us?" asked Dan.

The nun still held Jerry Regan's hand. "What is it now?" she sighed.

"Will ya give James John a ride into Strabane so he can talk to some of our people? We've got to get out of here."

"The Army and the RUC are gettin' wilder by the minute, Conway. He'll have to ride in the boot, but I'll take 'im and that's the end of it." She brushed at her eyes. "Father should have come. It was wrong." She looked closely at Conway. "You're a smart one not to go yourself. Shure, everyone in Ulster knows by now that you've got a busted nose. And I'm thinkin' you'll have more than that before you're through."

Dan pulled himself out of a deep sleep and put his hand to his face and scratched at the stubble of beard. He felt tubes of straw rolling under his hand and ran both hands through his hair. He pulled the blankets tight around his shoulders. The barn smell that had brought thoughts of golden moments with his grandfather so long ago had lost its charm. He stared at the rough chiseled cuts on the heavy, age darkened beams and his thoughts went without will or effort to the old man and in his mind he could see the hands, the crooked fingers, strong and bony, and he could feel the squeeze of his thumb as he wrapped his hand around his and the sound of the old man's voice was clear to him now as it always was. Where were they, he wondered, when the old man said it so many years ago. "All these timbers ya' see lad. They come from the great forests of Ireland. Forests that the English cut down as they pleased, leavin' us nothin' but the rocks and the hills." And he remembered the old man reaching up and fingering the wood with a gentleness and awe. "There were great forests of wondrous trees like this all across the land until the English slaughtered em," and then the old man's tone changed and he rasped out the phrase that had echoed in Dan's ears as long as he could remember any words. "The bastards."

The sound of a car cut through his thoughts and he reached for his pistol without moving his head. When the musical whistle sounded from outside, he got up slowly and went out to the yard with the blanket wrapped around his shoulders.

James John O'Connor's eyes were deep-set and ringed in an irritated red. He and Dan moved across the yard toward the house without speaking. Dan glanced at the grey Fiat sitting in the crusted mud—a black-haired fellow was sitting behind the wheel. Dan felt his eyes on him as he and James John went into the kitchen.

"Who's the kid?" he asked.

"A boy named Rooney—you know the family, Dan."

"One of Pat's boys?"

"Yeah."

"Pat and one of his sons are still in Long Kesh, eh?"

"Yes. This is the lad the Paras dropped out the window—named Eddie—remember?" asked James John.

"Oh yeah, I was in England then and the British got nervous about that cuz our American cousins made some noise about it in their newspapers. When the Americans get curious and act like they might get upset and nosy—the Brits get nervous."

Matt Quinn was pouring steaming tea into chipped mugs and looking out the window into the yard as he did. "He's the lad they dropped on his head from the roof or something, is he?" he asked.

"From the third storey of bloody Castlereagh barracks," said James John.

"They dropped the kid head-first—broke his skull like an eggshell—it's a wonder he's still alive atall," said Quinn.

"He's out of hospital only a couple of months," continued James John. "When he got out he came right to us and took the oath."

"It looks like he's a keen one," said Quinn, turning from the window and handing cups of tea to them.

"How's that?" asked James John.

"Take a look," said Quinn.

The boy was holding a long barrelled Luger in one hand, bracing his wrist with the other. He moved the muzzle slowly round the barnyard, stopping at brief intervals as he lined the pistol's sight on a chicken, a cow, or a fence post.

"Jeezus," said James John. "Well, they've wrecked the whole family, they have—it's only the mother home alone now and they tell me the Army or the RUC are in and out of the house more than the postman. The kid's bright enough—but he's like a bomb lookin' to explode."

"You can't blame him for bein' crazy for revenge on them," said Quinn.

"He knows the border here well, Dan," said James John. "The Committee thinks ya must hide out in the South for a while—the Brits are wild trying to grab ya—or any of us for that matter—but it's especially you they want. They gave me a plan for ya to listen to, if ya will."

"I'll listen in the car later," said Dan. He turned to Quinn. "You understand, Matt."

"I do. It's best if few know these things. It'll put a stop to problems that happened in the past."

"Shure, they've lived off goddamned informers in the past—how well you know, Matt," said James John.

"Bring him in for tea," said Dan, "then we'll get going."

Eddie Rooney came slowly and carefully into the kitchen. He turned in a part circle looking in every corner of the room—a young tense figure with a cap of wild curly black hair that was accented by a jagged scar that ran in a startling white Z across his head. His upper lip had what appeared to be a failed effort at a mustache.

"This is Matt Quinn, Eddie," said James John, "and uh, uh, his-uh,-mother, and this is Dan Conway."

Rooney stared with large brown bulging eyes at Conway. He did not look at anyone else.

"Congratulations," Rooney said in a voice that tried to be gruff and knowing. He took his right hand out of his pocket and offered it to Dan. "Too bad you didn't kill more of the fookers."

Dan winked at him.

James John put his cup down. "Dan, can we get goin'? I got to get word to my brother that I'm goin' to be gone for a few days." He shrugged. "Ya know he still raises hell about this. He keeps tryin' to make a go of the plumbin' business."

"It sounds like your brother's a fookin' bloody fool," Rooney said.

"What!" said James John O'Connor, narrowing his eyes. "What's that?"

"He's a fool if he thinks a Catholic can get a fair shake at bein' in business in this country," Rooney said and turned and stamped his way out of the kitchen.

Six

THEY LAY IN A small green saucer of earth on the hillside; a chest-high stone wall hid them from view from the road which they could see as it descended in lazy curves to the stream which was part of the border. The road forked there. One branch turned sharply and stayed on the Ulster side following the stream, the other was carried across a stretch of white water on a graceful stuccoed stone arc into the Republic of Ireland. In the distance a steeple and cross trimmed a disconcerting purple marked a village.

With a turn of their heads they could watch the road behind them as it worked its way around sharp-nosed rock and through speckled yellow gorse, down the side of the hill, always penned in by stone walls from which other walls angled away, forming the endless slate-edged patterns of green squares and patches and oblongs and rectangles that are the fabric of Ireland. Sheep with the muddled daubs of red paint of their owners on their backsides ignored everything but the grass in the yard of a ruined house on the far side of the stream.

Dan's eyes closed and he let the faint sound of the soft push of the river and Rooney's throaty whispering move over him. He opened one eye a tiny bit and the flash of a blackbird caught his attention and he watched it wheel in the sky and then swoop and brake to a balance on the sharp tip of a nearby hawthorn hedge. He studied it, a black smudge against the soft blue sky.

"Bloody hell," said Rooney. "I used to go back and forth across this foolish border all the time. I was steppin' out with a bird from Carrickmacross for a while. Sometimes I'd get hassled cuz they'd make the connection with my father and brother—but not bad—now I have to hide out and scoot across."

He ripped a handful of fern stalks out of the moss and stripped their lacework into small pieces. "Shure, now that they've given me this fookin' scar and a permanent headache—they can spot me easy. Did they bust your nose?" He looked over at Dan and waited. "Did they?" he repeated.

"What?" said Dan quietly. He had both eyes open; the blackbird was rubbing his beak on the point of a branch.

"They bust your nose?" queried Rooney.

"Yes," said Dan.

"You know my old man, don'cha—and the brother, too?"

"I do," Dan replied.

"Well, I'll tell ya somethin'," Rooney said, breaking the slim stem of fern into bits. "I never paid any attention to their gob about socialism and James Connolly and the heroes of the Easter risin'—one Ireland—shure, what am I tellin' you, you know that stuff." The blackbird flew away.

"I was a good student—the Christian Brother's School—you could check, you'd see—I was a good student—my father never had what you'd call a real job, but spent lots of time lookin'—the brother never tried—Ma got work cleanin' offices nights. 'Twas always the dole. The old man hates it. Me brother says, fook it—they keep us this way, they might as well pay us for it. The old man would be wild with him then, tellin' him it was just what the fookin' English wanted—but I was studyin' and was goin' to get away from the whole bloody business. The hell with that nonsense, I figured—get some good grades and get a job and get the hell out of it all." Rooney laughed, a low gargle of sound. Dan turned his head and looked closely at him. Rooney's head was down, staring at the fluffy green moss. There was no hair at all where the scar was; it was as white as any skin Dan had ever seen, whiter than the clouds he had been watching cruise the sky, as white as Jerry Regan's face with all the blood shot out of him, Dan thought as Rooney's voice rolled on.

"So I broke my ass for a job—an accountant I was." He looked up quickly and his voice rose. "You could check it out—I had a job and was doin' well." He tore a chunk of moss out of the ground. "Yeah, I was doin' well 'til they asked me one day—there was a promotion comin' up and I knew they had to be thinkin' of me for the job—they asked me did I beat the drum on the Bloody 12th of July. I told the old man and he yelled at me. He said I never listened or paid attention—my head in books, studyin'. He said what did I expect from the Protestant Orange Bastards—they don't want us Catholics to get ahead. He said they want to keep us taigs where we are—in the fookin' mud." Rooney nodded. "I didn't get the promotion—huh, they gave me the sack a week later—cuttin' back they said and I was redundant. Isn't that a marvelous fookin' English word they use to cut somebody's balls off—redundant—Christ!! It's probably the last chance I'll ever have for a real job."

"Listen, kid," said Dan, "we won't cross over for awhile. Why don't you take a nap; we've got to drive down to Dingle tonight."

46

"Shure, shure, I'll shut up," said Rooney. "I know ya heard all this before."

"Not only heard it before, kid, we've all lived it," Dan said.

"Okay, I'll shut up." He leaned back and pulled the revolver from his pocket and as he aimed it idly at a passing robin he did not notice Dan's sudden wariness.

"We meet O'Connor at the other side 'eh and then stay overnight in Dingle in Kerry, is that it?" His attention was concentrated on the black menace of his pistol and when Dan did not answer he continued, "Then down to Bantry Bay, right?" Rooney pocketed the pistol and after a lengthy silence he spoke very softly as though he'd forgotten Dan's presence and was speaking to himself. "It'll be safe down there won't it?" he said, and he could not keep the hope out of his voice.

They heard the armored car before they saw it, and lay flat and still behind the stone wall as it growled its way past them. Rooney glanced at his wristwatch as the machine rolled cautiously down to the bridge and then turned and followed the river road.

"Right on time, the dummies," he whispered. "Too bad we can't blow the bastards up." They lay waiting until the only sound was the lazy muttering of the river, then got up and dodged quickly across the fields, running stooped beside walls, clambering over two of them, until they reached the bridge. Then they stood and walked quickly across. As they reached the far side a man in waders that came to his armpits worked his way around the bend in the river and standing in midstream he deliberately cast his lure far upstream toward the bridge onto the edge of the shadow of a hazel tree that darkened an area of water. Rooney moved to the bank of the stream and watched the man reel the bit of color back against the current.

"Hey!" he cried out in a delighted yelp and as Dan looked at him he could see the youthfulness bubble in him. "I can stand here and watch the fella fish and I can yell and shout or piss or whatever I want and there's nothin' the Royal Ulster Constabulary or the Ulster Defense Force or," and now his voice rose to a shout, "the fookin' bloody British Army can do about it. Nothin'!"

The fisherman stared at Rooney long enough to let his line drift too far and then reeling furiously he quickly backed his way downstream. He floundered in a great wheeling splash and Rooney let out a cheer that was cut short by a curse from Conway. "Did they knock all the brains out of you, kid? We might as well send out a news bulletin that we got over the border. Now shut up and get moving."

They scuffed along the gravel road which lay between tall lush hedges. Birds chattered at the shadows cast by the now constant late afternoon sun. A drooping horse pulling a creaking, overlapping load of hay moved out onto the road in front of them. A stumpy man in a dark tweed cap and Wellington boots walked beside the wagon. He acknowledged them with a wave of his stick. A lean black dog with a white chest circled the load running in long leaping bounds. He turned when he saw Dan and Rooney and raced toward them. Dan went to one knee and the dog slid to a stop beside him. The dog's tongue was warm and prickly on Dan's cheek. He chuckled and roughed the animal's ears then got to his feet and met Rooney's puzzled stare.

"What is it, kid?"

"Nothin', just surprised I guess."

"Hey, I like dogs . . . and some people, too."

"You're lucky," Rooney said bitterly.

The village was a crossroads cluster of stone and stucco buildings dominated by the church. The Fiat was parked in front of a two-storey brown house. A sign on one window announced "Guinness Is Good For You"—underneath was the faded name C.C. O'Brien.

Dan stood for a moment inside the doorway, rubbing his eyes. In the gloom and over the heads of the half dozen drinkers he could see James John O'Connor leaning on the far end of the bar. Across from him was a wiry man with starched white sleeves rolled up. The man's grey head was bent close to James John. Both men straightened and turned toward the door when the busy conversation in the room died. James John put his hand up to his face and rubbed it slowly down across his mouth. The bartender kept both hands on the bar and stared at Dan with a tight smile.

"Welcome to the Irish Republic," he said.

"Welcome is right," said Rooney as he glanced slowly round the room.

"Ah! Dan," said James John, "here you are—grand, grand—give us all a drink, Connie, and I'll have another."

"Whiskey for me," said Eddie Rooney.

"Porter," said Dan.

"Now, Connie, here's a man you can tell your grandchildren about," said James John as he reached over and put his hand on the bartender's shoulder. Dan moved to one side and watched the weathered faces in the bar. They were all turned toward them. He took James John's arm and moved him toward a back table.

"Connie O'Brien, mark this day," said James John with a wavering finger pointing at the ceiling, "the day your establishment was honored."

"That's enough," said Dan through tight lips. "Take it easy."

The bartender poured whiskey from a bottle of Paddy's into a glass that he held in front of his face. He raised the glass high and tilted it toward Dan. "Here's to one Ireland and to all Ireland's great heroes past and present—and long life to yez, too," he added tipping the glass to his mouth. In the group of drinkers at the bar someone snickered.

SEVEN

THE FIAT PULLED OVER against the curb as a two-wheeled horsedrawn cart jogged past them down the dim street. The driver sat sideways, his eyes half shut under the peak of his cap, reins flopping from his hands which bounced in his lap, feet dangling by one of the rubber tires, his pipe turned upside down against the constant drifting rain.

"So this is downtown Dingle, the big city of County Kerry," said Eddie Rooney, drumming his fingers on the steering wheel.

"The hotel's just up the street," said James John from the back seat.

"Well, you've had quite a nap for yourself," said Rooney. "Are ya sure about this place?"

"What d'ya mean?" asked James John.

"What do I mean?" barked Rooney. "I mean can we trust this old fart we're goin' to meet here—is the hotel safe? And as a matter of fact, what about this old guy Dan Conway's stayin' with in Bantry? I haven't heard anythin' about him either—only that he's an old Sinn Feiner."

"Goddammit, man," said James John, "I told you I've met old Maurice here at Brennan's Hotel before and the Committee said the Bantry Bay thing is safe. Do ya think that with what's left of the bloody British Empire lookin' for Dan I'd be careless—why—"

"All right," Dan interrupted quietly, "relax. Let's get in here and get a decent night's sleep."

The clamor of voices and music hit them when they opened the door. James John stopped short as he entered the narrow lobby and Eddie Rooney bumped into him. The three of them stood motionless for a moment, Dan's hand still on the street door.

49

"What the hell," muttered Rooney.

"Don't be bashful, boys, c'mon in," the voice boomed at them from a doorway on the left. The man was bigger than Dan. He wore a brown checkered tweed jacket and dark tie that contrasted with his flushed cheeks and silver hair. One of his big hands was wrapped around a small glass.

"C'mon, fellas, we're teaching all you Kerrymen the delights of the Martini." He spoke with the distinctive arrogance of an American. His head went back, strands of silver hair slid down his forehead, and he laughed loudly. A fat face with thick metal-rimmed glasses peered at them from around the man's elbow.

"Some more recruits, Larry?—C'mon in fellas," the man said and giggled. "The water's fine—or rather the Martini's fine."

The big man put his arm around James John's stiff shoulders and walked him toward the noise. "We're from America and we love this country, but it needs one more thing to make it perfect—and we're bringing it to you right here." He lifted the glass high over his head. "Here it is. This will make Ireland perfection—the Martini, American style. C'mon along and we'll show you."

A tiny baldheaded man was working behind the small bar. His eyes widened over the starburst veins in his cheeks when he saw the big man propel James John toward him through the crowd of tweed jackets. The barman wiped his hands and ducked under the narrow counter opening. "Hold it, Maurice," cried the big man, putting his palm out, "I've got a new recruit here who's got to have a Martini."

"Certainly, sir," said Maurice. He spoke in a sibilant whisper. "But ya wouldn't want me ta not give a proper welcome to my cousin come all this way from Galway to see old Maurice, now, would ya now, sir?"

"Hell no, Maurice. I understand. Hell it's family that brought me all this way to see Dingle. I told you my grandmother came from here—did I tell you that, Maurice?"

"Ah, you did, sir. Indeed you did, sir." He looked at James John and moved his glance toward the door. "Will you help yourselves, sir, I'll only be a minute while I welcome my cousin."

"Ah! That's marvelous," boomed the big man. "That's what I love about this country—you'd never see that in the States. You people trust everybody don'cha? It's a wunnerful friendly country." He turned and plowed through the crowd as he headed for the bar.

They stood for a moment in the modest lobby. Sound from the bar hummed through the white plaster walls.

"Sorry about the gang here," said Maurice. "Yanks, of course. A bunch bought the place a year ago from the old lady. She couldn't believe the price.

Mother of God they must mint the money over there." Dan bent his head to hear the soft words.

"I've never seen so many at one time," said Rooney in a low voice, "except, you know, in the movies. We see a few, mostly news people, in Belfast, but that's it. They're too fookin' smart ta come ta Belfast."

"Oh," said Maurice, "you wouldn't credit it. They're in and out of here all the time now. You'd think they lived round the corner." He rubbed his skin on the top of his head. "Listen now, boys, go right in the dining room there and I'll have the girl get something together for you. Something—shure ya must be that thirsty with such a journey behind ya."

They sat at one of the chrome edged plastic topped tables. A lump of peat smoked on the black grates of a fireplace above which the button eyes of a massive stag's head stared at the room. No one spoke as a young girl placed a bottle of Paddy's and dark bottles of Guinness and glasses on the table. She did not raise her eyes from the floor from the moment she entered the room until she left, skittering out the door.

"Christ, what teeth they have," said Eddie Rooney.

"What's that?" asked James John, looking up as he poured drinks.

"Their teeth, the Yanks, they all have good teeth," said Rooney. "Even Germans I've seen, some had bad teeth—the few Americans I've seen up North—never any bad teeth and that gang in there—all of 'em—good teeth. Jeezus it's something."

"It's the money, isn't it, Dan?" asked James John. "They've got the money to take care of things like that—even the deodorants and such. It's the money."

Dan shrugged and sipped his drink.

Eddie Rooney was running the ball of his thumb inside his mouth.

"The pressing, too," said James John.

"You bet your ass it's depressing," said Rooney.

"No no," said James John loudly through Dan's chuckle. "Pressing, I said—their clothes—they're always pressed. They must throw away their clothes after they wear 'em once or have a cleanin' shop on every corner."

Dan took his drink and walked to one of the tall white curtained windows that looked out on the street. A man on a bicycle pumped his way up the hill, head down against the rain. The wet paving stones caught some of the street's soft glimmering lights. Dan watched the man until he disappeared from view.

"Well, there's no doubt of it," he heard James John say. "The Yanks have got the world by the ass."

"Shure they do," said Eddie, the gruffness back in his voice, "shure they do, but what the hell good does it do us? Christ, look at those stiffs in there.

Shit—they tell ya they're Irish but they don't give a goddamn what goes on in the North. Christ, they run all over the fookin' world lookin' for causes and they've got a goddamn good one right in front of 'em—and their our own blood, too—but they don't want to step on their British cousins'," he spat out the words, "toes—if it was Blackies, or Russian Jews gettin' treated the way the British treat us, they'd raise all kinds of hell."

The door squeaked at the far end of the room. Dan spun around from the window. Maurice was backing through the door. He turned, holding a wide silver tray in shaky hands. James John took it from him and set it on the table. Chunks of yellow cheese lay in rows against pink and white ham and fat grainy slices of soda bread.

"Ahh," said Eddie.

"Little enough for ya, lads. The girl is after cookin' up some chops an' potatoes."

"That's good of you," said Dan.

"Good of us, Dan Conway—Mother of God! The good things you've done for this Island, some of 'em lately, too, I think." He nudged James John. "None of us could repay you," he continued. "It's an honor to me and 'twill be so to the old lady to have you under this roof this night." He poured a small jot of whiskey into a glass. "*Slainte*," he said, speaking the Irish language.

"Cheers," said O'Connor and Rooney.

"Now, young fella'," Maurice said, looking at Eddie Rooney, "I've a question for you. Is it Pat Rooney you're related to?"

"The old man," said Eddie.

"Well, well, I know your father. He's been in the movement for years, of course." He turned to Dan. "I think maybe it was your dad gave him the oath."

"I don't know," said Dan.

"I think so," said Maurice. He turned back to Rooney. "And do the English still have him in the North?"

"The brother, too," said Eddie.

"Ah, Lord—will they never let us be," said Maurice rubbing his scalp.

Eddie Rooney's head was bent over the tray piling cheese and slabs of ham onto a slice of bread.

"Mother of God, that's a nasty scar you've got, boy," said Maurice.

Rooney looked up at him. "Ya know how I got it," he growled. Maurice looked at him and shook his head. "They dropped me out a window," said Eddie.

"Who did?" asked Maurice.

"The Brits."

"They dropped you out a window?" Maurice asked. He looked at James John who nodded at him as he chewed. "Mother of God, they're barbarians,

Protestant barbarians," sighed Maurice, and blessed himself with flying fingers.

"Christ, it was in the papers. Don't you people get the papers here in the West?" asked Rooney.

"We're out of the mainstream here, ya might say," Maurice said with a small smile. "There's a few television sets and some get the papers from Cork or Dublin a day or two late—we have our local weekly, *The Kerryman,*—and the radio with the news in English and in the Irish—it's alright. The big news we get, tho'. I mean—we heard all about the British helicopter and the soldiers gettin' shot up." Very softly he added, "And we know lots of folks up in the North would like to get their hands on the man who did that to the English Army."

"Well my thing was in the news," said Rooney, leaning back in his chair.

"What in the name of God made them drop you out a window?" asked Maurice.

"For the hell of it, I think," said Eddie. "For the hell of it they held me by my ankles and dropped me out of the third floor of the fookin' Royal Ulster Constabulary Barracks." He spoke with his head back, staring up at the stag's head.

Dan was looking out the window, chewing slowly on a sandwich.

"I was at a dance in Portadown—rock music—we like rock up there," said Eddie. "In they come, four Paras and two RUC bastards. They looked round—there'd been some trouble in the town that night. I wasn't in it—I didn't want any part of politics then. The old man and the brother in Long Kesh livin' like pigs—not me. I wanted no part of it. I kept on dancin' with this great lookin' bird. They moved through the crowd in pairs and people stopped dancin' and just stared at 'em. They'd almost walk over ya if ya didn't move for 'em. I kept on dancin'. Two of the bastards came up to me, and one says, 'You're a Rooney, aren't ya?' So what, I sez. 'You'll find out,' he sez. Fook off, I told 'em. One of 'em laughed—I shoulda known then when that bastard laughed—I shoulda known. I could feel the bird shakin'. They each took an arm and I asked 'em what the hell was goin' on. I told 'em I was goin' to take my bird home. 'Not tonight, Mick,' says one of the Paras—he was a big bastard. That's what they called me all the time they had me. 'Mick—Mickey Rooney,' they'd say and then laugh like hell."

The door creaked and Dan turned toward the sound. The girl came in from the kitchen carrying a bowl of steaming white potatoes and a plate piled high with thick moist chops. Maurice was staring at Rooney whose gaze was still fastened on the stag's head. James John forked potatoes and chops onto his plate. Dan moved to the table and sat down.

"So they took me to Castlereagh. I been there a couple of times before." He looked briefly at Maurice. "You know how they are—if one person in a family is political, they lift someone else in the family every once in a while and treat 'em like shit.''

He looked back at the stag's head and spoke. "What was goin' on was the brother had made a try to break out of Long Kesh. He'd had some outside help—they figured it was me. Hell, I hadn't even known about it. Well, they got started and after a minute if I known anythin' I woulda told 'em. I even made up stuff, which they figgered was phoney, so they got madder—Christ, rubber hoses on the kidneys, needles under my nails, electric wires on my balls.''

A gasp came from the end of the room. The girl was standing by the kitchen door, her mouth covered with her hands.

"Get about your business now. This is not for young ears," Maurice said to her in a throaty whisper.

"Ahh! Gowan wit' ya," the girl said, not moving. James John chewed slowly and poured more drinks.

"So then what did the divils do?" Maurice breathed.

"Ya know a funny thing?" said Rooney. "When I woke up in hospital I couldn't remember." He looked at Maurice again. "Faces were lookin' down at me and I couldn't figger out what the hell happened or where I was. Then an RUC inspector come in and told me I jumped out the window at Castlereagh. When he said it—well—I remembered—and—I guess I fainted—cuz when I came to a doctor and the constable were arguin', the doctor tellin' 'im to clear out. But I remembered then—the laughin'—the two of 'em holdin' me out the window by my ankles and shakin' me and laughin' and one of 'em sayin', 'So long, Mickey Rooney,' and they let go and I could still hear 'em laughin'.''

In the bar someone started singing "Danny Boy" in a high clear voice. Eddie Rooney reached for his drink. "I can still hear their bloody laughin'," he said and hurled his glass into the fireplace.

Dan moved through the silence of the room and put his empty glass down beside Maurice. "It's time for sleep for me, Maurice. Can you point me in the right direction?"

"I can indeed, we've a fine room for you, Dan Conway, with your own tub. Come on here with me now and I'll give you the key."

As they left the room Maurice glanced quickly back at Eddie Rooney who was sitting motionless, staring into the fireplace.

Eight

No one was in the dining room when Dan walked in the next morning. The smell of bacon mingled with the musty odors of the peat fire and he stood for a moment and listened to the rattle of pans and the murmur of voices from the kitchen.

Maurice came noiselessly into the room from the hallway and gave Dan a toothless grin. "I'll have the girl get a breakfast for ya."

"I know I slept late and if it's too much—" Dan began.

"No, no, no," Maurice said rubbing his hands. "Your comrades finished off a good feed and you'll be getting a good meal now. I'll tell that fresh sprout of a girl to get busy, and she will if she knows what's good for her." He headed for the kitchen, straightening his narrow shoulders as he did. Dan smiled to himself as he sat down and listened to the brief explosion of voices from behind the kitchen door. The old man was obviously locked in perpetual combat with the kitchen maid.

Maurice came out shaking his head, the veins on his cheeks now a cherry red, and he slumped into the chair opposite Dan.

"By God, I go to Mass every morning and sometimes in my prayers I say a word for whoever the poor devil is that's goin' to end up with that girl. Somewhere in Ireland I suppose, right now the poor fool is goin' to work or school or whatever, happy as a king, never guessin' the terrible fate that's in store for 'im." He massaged the skin on the top of his head. "We'll have a nice breakfast comin' up for ya. It's a sin a man such as yourself, a hero of Ireland, havin' to put up with that little scut of a girl. Thank God ya won't have to worry about such treatment down at Michael Dillon's in Bantry."

Dan edged forward in his chair. "Do you know Dillon?"

"I do indeed. I'm the one passed the message to him askin' if you could stay with him 'til things calm down up North. The young ones around here still come to me once in a while when they need somethin' for the cause. They're not running in an' out a here all the time so that the hotel has problems, but if somethin' special comes up they know they can count on me." He stared straight into Dan's eyes. "You know, I been in this since the beginning." He raised a small wrinkled hand and smiled at Dan. "Well, one of the beginnings anyway—1916." He lowered his glance. "Not carrying a gun like you and Michael Dillon, but I've helped whenever I could, like now. I wrote to Michael and asked him if he'd do one last thing for Ireland, like the boys said, no strings attached, would he let a man stay there in his cottage for a while. No questions asked. I got a note back from him. The writin' made me realize how old he is, how old all of us from the old days are. It's like Shakespeare's stages of life . . . we start out writin' badly as tots and we end up as old men writin' badly. The circle's complete." He sighed and his body seemed to become even smaller.

"Anyway, Michael said alright, one last thing he'd do." Maurice rubbed the top of his head again. "He said he promised his daughter this would be the last of it and there was a strong line underscoring the word last in his letter . . . looked almost like someone else drew the line under the word last."

The kitchen door creaked and they turned to watch the girl back through carrying a tray whose weight caused her arms to shake. She moved cautiously to the table and set her burden down with a crash, then without raising her eyes from her tray she off-loaded a steaming tea kettle, a jug of frothy milk, a bowl of cornflakes, a plate piled high with brown toast and a large platter with three rich round yellow egg yolks surrounded by thick red slices of blonde bristled bacon and a heavy scattering of slices of brown-edged potatoes. Maurice and the girl stared at the food for a moment, then he looked up at her. "Where's the sausage?" he asked with a growl.

"It's too late to be cookin' sausage now," the girl snapped. She shifted her glance from the food to the old man as she spoke and her eyes were gleaming as she gave a toss of her head.

"Mother of God, girl," sputtered Maurice and the veins in his cheeks began to glow.

Dan raised his hand and said, "This is fine, Maurice. I don't want any sausage."

The girl snatched the tray from the table and when Maurice raised his eyes to heaven she quickly stuck her dart of a red tongue out at him and wheeled and dashed from the room.

Maurice shook his head and opened his mouth to speak. Dan got his words in quickly. "I want to talk about that fella, Dillon, Maurice—you understand."

"I do," said Maurice, "and I'm sure you won't have to take that kind of guff from Michael's daughter, who's an educated, intelligent girl, the light of Michael Dillon's life that girl is."

"She lives with him?" interrupted Dan.

"She does," Maurice nodded. "Down there in the wilds of Bantry in West Cork she lives with her father. She came back from the University, in Dublin it was. She teaches school and looks after her father. A good Irish daughter she is, a good Irish girl."

"Is he sick?" Dan asked as he spread a layer of butter on his toast.

"Ha! Michael Dillon sick! I guess not, his bein' a fisherman all his life, guidin' tourists and makin' a livin' from the ocean. No, he's not had a sick day yet, I don't think, and he was a terror against the English and the Black and Tans. A young lad, but he became a Company Commander. Ah! The stories I could tell you about what a terror Michael Dillon was," he stopped short and rubbed the top of his head. "Ah. I'm sorry, Dan Conway, there's nothin' you wouldn't know about bein' a terror."

"If I'm going to stay at Dillon's, can I trust this daughter of his to keep quiet?" Dan asked sharply.

"Oh. You've no fear in the world on that score, Dan Conway. She's her father's girl. Michael married late and the wife died bearin' the girl. There's been just the two of them from the beginning. Ah, if Michael Dillon says ya can stay, ya can stay in safety, believe me. The girl, Kate's her name. Katherine, after her dear mother. She'd never go against the father, believe me."

"When's the last time you've seen Dillon to talk to," asked Dan, chewing slowly on a cut of bacon.

"To talk to," echoed Maurice. "Why let's see. I suppose it was about ten years ago!"

"Ten years ago!"

"Well, he's way down in Bantry."

"That's less than a hundred miles from here," Dan said.

"I know, it's funny isn't it. Our people leave Ireland and wander all over the world. The phrase should be the Wanderin' Irishman instead of the Wanderin' Jew. But here at home, out here in the West of Ireland we stay in our villages. But the gossip, Dan. Ah, the gossip travels from village to village like magic. And for some people it's as delicious as magic. Maybe it is—who knows? But be that as it may, Michael Dillon, I'm sure, knows how I'm doin' and I know how he's doin'. And you'll be all right down there in his cottage on Bantry Bay, Dan, believe me, as safe as," he stopped short and his eyes widened.

"What is it?" Dan asked.

"By God, I was goin' to say as safe as the Pope of Rome, but you'll be safer than that, believe me!"

"I hope so," Dan said dryly.

Dan pushed his chair back from the table and surveyed the empty platter for a moment, then he reached forward and lifted his cup for one last swallow of tea.

"We'll need a good map on how to get to Dillon's house, I expect," he said.

"I've a map in my coat here and a sketch with it to show ya Michael's place," Maurice said as he produced a map so worn that the folds had almost become individual tattered squares. "Ya see here, I've marked a circle in ink right along here on the edge of Bantry Bay," and tracing the road with a tremulous finger, he started at the town of Glengarrif and moved cautiously around the head of Bantry Bay, past the village of Ballylicky. "The road is easy to follow along here to Bantry Town," he said, "then head out along the coast toward the village of Ahakista. This sketch will show you the way from there," he added briskly, placing the piece of yellow paper between the sheets of the map as he refolded it. "I went over this with your lads earlier so they'd know it to drive it, but you'll want to hold the map yourself."

He held the map in both hands for a moment and began to speak in a halting tempo, his eyes on the map. "Ya know—I said that it's been some time since I saw Michael Dillon." Dan watched the old man closely but did not answer, and, still staring at the map, Maurice continued. "And you know how I said that he knows how I'm doin' and I know how he's doin'—you remember I said that, don'cha," he said with a rush of words and suddenly looked up at Dan. "Well, I do know Michael's mind pretty well after all these years and I was wonderin' if you were plannin' to have the boys go in with ya when ya get to the Dillon cottage?"

Dan's puzzlement formed a furrowed line across his brow. "Why were you wondering about that, Maurice?"

"Well, as I said, I think I know how Michael's mind works and I told ya what a terror he was back in the rebellion against the English and later in the Civil War. He's tough and—"

Dan raised his hand, palm up. "Hold on, Maurice. What the hell is this all about?"

"I don't think ya should bring the Rooney boy into Dillon's," the old man blurted.

"Why not?"

"Well, it's too different now—it's not the way it was. The men of 1916 and the twenties were different. I mean no disrespect to you, Dan Conway, but the Rooney lad seems to be the way the whole business has become. Before it was hard and tough and cruel, too, of course. We wanted the English out and by

God they should get out and I believe they will get out—but now it seems like the whole thing has poisoned so many people. And Rooney—he's been poisoned by it all, Dan, and Michael Dillon won't like to see somebody sick like that in the cause. Rooney's just a gunman now, Dan, and he'll get worse. He's not like they were before—poets and writers and dreamers of one Ireland. That lad's only dream is killin' and that's not the kind of people Michael Dillon began his dream with."

"Well, Maurice, you'd better know that the only way to make the dream come true is to make things a nightmare for the British," Dan said, and took the map out of the old man's hand.

Nine

"Stop here," Dan said quietly as he folded the map. James John O'Connor eased the car over to the side of the road and for a moment the three of them sat still, their attention captured by the grey gusty water of Bantry Bay. A flight of petrels flashed across their front, whistled over the tips of the waves and quickly became tiny dots on the horizon and then just as quickly whirled in a barely visible about face and sped back toward land.

"By God, they're really free aren't they," murmured James John.

Rooney shifted in his seat and pulled his revolver from his pocket and trained the front sight on the swift birds. "Free, ha! The dumb fooks, they don't know where they're goin'."

Dan reached over the seat and grabbed the young man roughly by the shoulder. "God damn it, put that pistol away and keep it away while you're on this side of the border."

Rooney gave Dan a surly stare and slowly worked the pistol into his pocket.

"We're near the place right now aren't we, Dan?" O'Connor asked hurriedly. "I'll drive ya right up there. We'll make sure everything's all right."

"No, I'll walk from here. I'll see you someplace else one of these days. Tell the committee I'll be in touch one way or another."

"Good luck, Dan," James John said.

Dan winked at him and swung his rumpled leather bag over his shoulder. He stood for some time staring out at the Bay, hearing the car back and turn and the sound recede from him. After a bit he looked back in the direction the car headed and a flash of reflected sunlight caught his eye and for a few moments he watched the Fiat move noiselessly along the road that twisted its lonely way beside the Bay. At the head of the harbor the car, very small now, turned north and was lost from view behind the boulder strewn green hills that plunged down to the sea. He swung around and walked easily along the road that dodged in and then away from the touch of the ocean. Somewhere ahead of him on his right would be the single lone roadway that led up into the hills and Michael Dillon's cottage. A rush of water broke on a massive shoulder of granite on the edge of the road and a wisp of the brisk and salty spume touched his face. He licked his lips and stopped to watch the water as it slugged against the stone and curled and leapt and retreated and then slugged again.

He looked out across the water searching for the birds, found them and smiled. Then he turned and strolled slowly along the verge of the narrow roadway. Occasionally a gull cried and some unseen bird made pure melody in a bosky thicket on a small promontory that nosed out into the Bay. He tarried there on a strange and sudden impulse, searching the grass in a desultory way with the tip of his shoe, looking for a four-leaf clover. He had never seen one and his glance passed over the mossy little mound twice before recognition caught at him. He put down his bag and knelt, stared at the irregularly shaped little plant and then fitted his long forefinger and thumb on the base of the stem and snapped it cleanly off. He studied the clover leafs for a moment and then carefully placed the plant into his shirt pocket.

A sudden surge of wind caught at him as he stood up and he could see in the distance a low formation of dark clouds scudding in from the Atlantic. They moved at a speed that surprised him and seemed to drive a squall ahead of them. Two yellow-slickered figures in a dory on the far side of the Bay pulled with hand-over-hand tugs at ropes trailing from the stern and then headed the boat's nose into the wind blown chop.

Despite the wind, the first rain came in slow fat drops that soon became a mesh of soft clinging wetness. Dan turned off the road onto a gravel track wide enough for one car that led up into the hills that dominated this shoreline of the Bay. In a narrow gorge where a brook tumbled downhill to the ocean he paused for a moment and took his revolver from his pocket, broke it open and spun the cylinder checking the cartridge load, then he resumed his way up the track, leaning forward against the rise of the hill.

At the top of the hill the path branched in two directions and ran along the spine of this high land that gave a full panoramic view of the tossing white spotted Bay that stretched out to the grey, heaving mist covered ocean beyond. He could make out tiny cottages and the rock walled geometry of their farmland across the Bay in the sharply creased hills to the south.

He paused by a grey stone wall at the edge of a green stretch of lush meadow to survey the cottage that was set on the point of the hill at the end of a grassy pathway that carried the indented evidence of its use as a driveway. The whitewashed stone of the low two storey building was pale and clean even in the soft rainlight. Roses were bright patches of red and yellow that climbed their way to the slate roof. Small recessed windows looked out toward the bay, with pots of bright geraniums set on the indents of those on the first floor.

As Dan started toward the house a shaggy, black dog stepped out of the open front door, sniffed the air, stiffened, then moved rigidly with a low growl into the yard.

"C'mere boy," Dan called. The dog growled his way slowly toward him. "C'mon fella. Take it easy," Dan said softly. The dog nuzzled his outstretched hand and his bushy tail started to swing.

"It looks like you've made a friend." The voice was hoarse yet musical and the man stepped out of the doorway, and they stood motionless for a moment and studied one another, Dan with his hand touching the dog.

"Michael Dillon?"

"At your service," the man said and took a black bowled pipe from his pocket and studied it for a moment, turning it over in his hands. He was a small gnarled root of a man. His baggy trousers, pulled high up on his waist and belted lower down than the belt loops, could not disguise his bowed legs. His face was a ruddy pink, not a drinker's rouge red but the healthy color that Dan guessed was earned from the wind and sun. He wore a frayed tweed cap whose peak was set close over his eyes that peered up at Dan now, green and bright and sparkling with life as his closed and somewhat sunken mouth turned up in a grin.

"You can see why we call the dog Bluff," he said and his brogue was heavy, "and you'd be a fine, courageous fella that I been expectin' to visit us from the North named—" and he paused now and squinted a bit.

"Dan Conway," Dan finished.

"Exactly," Dillon said and he smiled freely now, showing a toothless mouth.

"Just tryin' to be careful, Dan Conway, just tryin' to be careful. Welcome, welcome. Come in out of this fine soft weather." He offered Dan his hand as he spoke and his handshake was quick and firm.

Dan stooped to follow Dillon through the doorway and once inside the old man turned and looked up at him. "You'd be a hard one to hide up North, that's for sure, what with the size of ya and the nose and all."

"Will it be a problem here d'you think?"

"No, I don't think so. I'm aware because of my friends in the organization and expectin' ya an' all, but people here in the West don't pay much attention to that business, although the latest fight with the Army has made everyone pay attention. Ah, that was a grand thing, and I'll take my hat off to whoever was in that operation. And that's the way it ought to be. Men to men. None of this bombin' and killin' poor, helpless women and children. Let the men—the soldiers—fight it out."

Dan did not answer. He put his bag down and turned to survey the room. A small fire burned in the fireplace and a dented dark copper kettle hung from a bar over the flames. The musky smell of burning peat seemed part of the house.

"Will ya have a cup of tea?"

"I will, thanks."

While the old man lifted the kettle and poured the tea into heavy ceramic mugs, Dan noted the wooden rocking chair that flanked the fireplace, its back ribs and arms worn to a shine. On the other side of the fire was a sagging, splayfooted easy chair with a low table next to it, piled high with books and newspapers. Set beside this was a waist high radio cabinet with additional books balanced precariously on its arched top.

One side of the room opened onto a small kitchen and a long, straight-backed couch with a scattering of books took up most of another wall. Dan tossed his bag onto the couch and as he did he noticed that electricity had been added to the house by running a metal tube along the base of the walls.

"You'll be sleepin' in the other room in there," Dillon said. He had a mug of tea in each hand and as he offered one to Dan he pointed his bony chin at a doorway next to the stairs at the far side of the room. "We've one of those pull-out things in there, just like the city people. Another invention of the Yanks, I s'pose. Kate got it. She has her school pals droppin' in from time to time."

"Kate's your daughter."

Dillon nodded to him with a mouthful of tea.

"Will it be all right with her, my being here?" Dan asked.

"Oh, sure, sure," the old man said fumbling with his pipe with one hand. Finally he put the mug down and took a penknife from a deep pocket and stood by the fire scraping the bowl of the pipe. The dog flopped down by the fire with a luxurious groan.

"I want to be sure," Dan said flatly.

"Well, I'll tell ya, Dan Conway, Kate is not what you'd call a supporter of the or-gan-i-za-tion," the word came out in pieces, "but she knows how I feel and she agreed that we'd do this and it would be my last involvement, so to speak, and that's the fact of it. She's away now for a few days but you've no need to worry when she gets home. You'll be welcome with her too."

"There's nobody else here is there," Dan asked, "or anyone else involved?"

"Nobody. And nobody knows anything about ya here. I've said there's a fella comin' for the fishin'—I'm still a guide, ya know, and I still have folks comin' to fish with me. So that's it. I have to explain a bit about any stranger here in the West because some people here are a mite gossipy. Ah, you wouldn't believe how gossipy they are, but your secret is well kept with me. Believe me."

They stood side by side in front of the fire, sipping tea in comfortable silence, each with his own long thoughts. The dog uncurled himself, growled and bristled his way out the front door.

Dan looked at Dillon who spoke heartily to the question on Dan's face. "You'll have to get used to that—he always starts off with a growl and ends up with a welcome wag. I said he isn't called Bluff for nothin' and remember, Dan Conway, you're in Bantry Bay in the West of Ireland. It must be one of the most peaceful places in this whole crazy world," he moved slowly out the door as he finished speaking.

Dan stood half-turned from the fire and listened to the old man's voice raised in greeting in the yard.

"Ah, Father. How are ya this fine soft day? Set your bike down there, Father, and come in for some tea and a biscuit."

Dan turned to the fire and then stiffened as he heard a strange voice say, "Any news from the North about the big fellow, Michael?"

Dillon's voice was low and quick-paced. "Come on in now Father and meet a fella who's come for the fishin'."

The priest stopped briefly on the threshold, looking back over his shoulder. "Is it himself come down to show our people what a real man looks like?"

"Father, Father," Michael Dillon's words came out in an anguished sigh.

Still standing in the doorway the priest bowed his head briefly and spoke aloud the ancient Irish phrase, "God Bless all in this house." His hair was the color of carrots. His long black cassock contrasted sharply with his white collar and very pale skin which was dotted with scatterings of tiny cinnamon freckles. He stood brushing his hands down the swollen midsection that bulged under his cassock. Dan noticed a ring sunk into one of his pudgy fingers. The priest's watery blue eyes were wide and round now as he stared at Dan.

"In the name of Almighty God, can it be," he spoke reverently, moving toward Dan with outstretched hands. "Is it, Dan Conway? Is it Michael?" he asked still staring at Dan.

"Ah, Father," Dillon said plaintively.

"It's alright, Michael, I didn't realize Mr. Conway was here. It is Conway, isn't it?" he cried, grabbing Dan's right hand in both of his. "Don't worry, Dan Conway, don't worry. Your presence here is safe with us. It's an honor to meet you, an honor believe me, no one here will breathe a word of it." His boyish face beamed.

"I'm glad to hear that, Father," Dan said, staring at Michael Dillon, whose head was down looking after the cleaning of his pipe, "very glad because I have been told there are a lot of gossips here in the West of Ireland."

TEN

SOMETHING WOKE HIM. He lay very still and wide-eyed, staring at the ceiling, remembering where he was. He heard it again, a rooster announcing another day's authority to his flock and to the world.

The memory of last night's events crowded his mind. The priest, Father Devoy, pushing off hard on his bicycle for a surprise, returning with a bottle of Jameson's. The kitchen table covered with oilcloth, dominated by the kerosene lamp and the whiskey bottle which seemed to achieve nobility as the night drifted on. The scattered detritus of bits of cold chicken, yellow cheddar and soda bread which grew inexorably as the hours passed.

Michael Dillon's old tongue showed the effect of the whiskey after the first drink and his mind drifted back to his youth, the rebellion against the English, and times of fearless comrades who—Dan knew—never were and always would be.

The priest's fancy cloaked Michael and Dan in suits of white armor in which they contested the evil Protestant anti-Christ for the soul of Ireland. The kerosene lamp light flickered on the low smoke-darkened ceiling and the kitchen seemed to glow with the fervor of the young priest as he called the wrath of God down on "the Brits." Late in the evening he stood unsteadily, a flush of excitement on his pale face as he unrolled a couple of newspapers and read the headlines in boisterous bursts. "British Army Seals Border," he shouted, "Manhunt Continues," he cried with a sideways glance at Dan who sat fingering the glinting crystal pattern of his whiskey glass. Finally the priest drew himself to attention and announced in a sonorous voice, "London Prepares Military Funeral for Slain Soldiers."

"I'll drink to that," he said and watched the old man as he slowly rose from the chair, one hand holding the edge of the table.

"I'll drink to *them*." Dillon emphasized the word and the priest watched him with a startled expression as Dillon continued. "I'll drink to their poor young souls. What do you say, Dan Conway?" he asked as he raised the glass to his lips.

"I'd say it's a tough life," Dan said. He finished his drink and stood up. The priest's puzzled glance went from one man to the other and finally he raised his glass to his lips and sipped at the whiskey. When Dan announced quietly that he was headed for bed he had felt the priest's eyes on him until he closed the door to what Michael Dillon referred to as "the other room."

Dan drifted back into a half sleep, his consciousness nudged from time to time by the occasional early morning chatting of birds that seemed just outside his window. When he came fully awake he swung his legs out of bed and sat for a moment looking at the small room. He had merely unfolded the couch and covered himself with a blanket the night before and now he realized that this "other room" was the formal room of the cottage. A bookcase on one wall showed no slice of space for another book. A heavy legged dark table and four matching chairs were aligned along another wall. Over the table were a colored photo of a rosy cheeked John F. Kennedy and a painting of Christ bearing his bleeding heart. The drops of blood were fat and very red. A large silver crucifix hung between the two pictures. Dan stared at this montage feeling a strong urge to look more closely at the crucifix. The rooster screeched again and he stood up and fitted the rollout section back into the couch.

He settled onto the bench set against the front of the cottage, twisting a bit until he fit himself into one of the bevels worn into the wood. The dog came around the corner and poked his nose up into his lap. Dan scratched the dog's head and leaned back to let the high morning sun warm his face. Rust colored cattle, burly and ragged, stood nose down in one of the sections of pasture that sloped toward the Bay and across the water thin black lines of smoke rose straight in the air from some of the cottages. Dan thought they might be cooking fires and suddenly he was hungry. He gave the dog one last pat on the head and rose and went into the house.

Michael Dillon was moving cautiously, fitting each foot onto the next lower step as he came down the stairs. His cap was not on and except for a fringe of curly white hair on the back of his head, his skull was smooth and hairless. He looked up at Dan in an appraising way as they headed for the kitchen. "By God, you look fit today," he said faintly.

"Absolutely," Dan said with a grin. "And you?"

"Ah, Mr. Jameson has left me with an awful head on me. It was too painful for me to put my own cap on my head and I'll tell you the truth, I'm not too keen about showing this bald pate of mine." He lowered himself slowly into a kitchen chair. "I'll get some food for us but I'll just get my breath here for a minute."

"If you don't mind, I can put something together," Dan said.

"Fair enough," said Dillon, leaning back in the chair. "I've no objection at all to that. Kate's been gone a few days. I'm not sure what food's left. If there's no eggs there I'll go out to the chickens and see if they're gettin' their job done."

"No, there are eggs here and some bacon—and ham too," Dan added as he bent over and poked at items in the waist-high refrigerator.

"Is there milk there for tea?" the old man asked as he gingerly placed his cap on his head. "I can get some from the cow in the shed if need be."

"There's some in this pitcher," Dan said, gesturing with a knife as he cut thick slices from the ham.

"Katey'll be back today maybe," Dillon said with a sigh. "I hope so anyway."

"Is she the cook?" Dan asked as he broke the egg yolks with the tines of a fork.

"Sure, she's the woman of the house," Michael Dillon said. "She loves doin' for me," he added proudly, "always has."

Dan cut the ham slices into bite-sized pieces and tossed them into the egg batter. "Tell me about Father Devoy," he said, suddenly turning to look squarely at the old man.

"Well, he's been here about three, or no—let me see—is it four, yes it would be four years. Come right from the seminary. Right from his ordination. I guess the Bishop thought it was time to give the old Monsignor a helping hand. He's been here for years. Funny, he had some kind of disease, the Monsignor did. I forget now what it was. Came here to die. You wouldn't usually see a Monsignor here in this part of West Cork but he fooled 'em, the Monsignor did. Got better instead of worse. He often used to fish with me but he's gotten quite feeble so Father Devoy does the running for the old man. The Monsignor just does Masses in our village now. Father Devoy takes care of the other little parishes out along the peninsula for the old man."

"Are you sure he'll keep quiet about me being here, Michael?"

"I'm sure as can be." He accepted the plate from Dan.

"How come?"

"Because of the Monsignor," Dillon said with a grin.

"What do you mean?" Dan asked as he settled himself at the table.

"If the Monsignor knew you were here and that Father Devoy knew about it and helped you in any way or didn't report you, it would be hell on earth for the young Father, believe me. The Monsignor may be physically feeble but his tongue still works and he's a terror with it."

"Not friendly to us, 'eh?"

"No, I wouldn't say so."

"Devoy must have to be careful."

"Yes, he does and it must be difficult for the young fella. I feel sorry for him." He pushed at his food with a shaky fork. "It's a terrible shame."

"I don't know that he could do much good for us politically out here anyway," Dan said.

"Ah, that's not what I mean," the old man said softly.

"What is it then?" Dan asked.

"It's the hate. That's what it is. To see a man of God like that hatin' anybody. It's wrong. A young man like that. A priest." Dillon was almost muttering his words. "It seems like he's planning a lifetime of hatin', and why? For what? He's never had any personal dealin's with this business. It's a shame. If the men of God are haters, who's left to make peace?"

Dan looked up from his food. "Do you read these books I see around the house?" he asked.

"Most of 'em."

"The history books?"

"All of 'em."

"Did you ever read of any religious man stopping a war?"

The old man stared at him for a moment and then tugged at his cap and turned his attention to his food.

Dan stood in the front yard searching the grey skies for the missing sunshine. Michael Dillon drew deeply on his pipe before he spoke. "Well, Dan Conway, you're supposed to be here for the fishin'—how'd you like to do some?"

"I'd like it."

"Ever done any?"

"Never."

"Well then it's time ya did—C'mon." He stopped short. "Got any rough clothes with ya?"

"No."

"We'll get ya some at Cronin's then."

"I've not got much money."

"Don't worry. I been swappin' fish for life's staples at Cronin's since before you were born. C'mon now."

Dan followed him around the house. A low hut of caulked fieldstone stood near the rear of the house. Chickens squabbled and rushed out of the open doorway as Michael Dillon stepped inside.

"The poor devils think I'm after having chicken every night of the week," he said with a wink. "But tonight, Mr. Conway, we're havin' fish—if we're lucky. C'mon, Dan," he continued, "I keep the fishin' gear in here."

Motes of hay freckled the air where light filtered into the shed through chinks between the stone walls. Part of the roof had fallen in and a pile of hay was stacked up through the hole. A cow with a swollen, sagging belly was tied to a post and it twisted its head to stare at them with large, liquid brown eyes. A calf came out from behind the cow's rump to look at them for a moment and then tottered back to the safety of its mother's girth.

Four fishing rods leaned against a ladder that led up to a narrow loft. "Take the longest rod, Dan, you could manage more, but it's the best I can do."

Dan stood with a hand on one of the rungs of the ladder. The middle was worn into a curve and he rubbed the smooth hard wood with the ball of his thumb. Michael Dillon watched him.

"Shure, I know the feel of that wood like I know my own skin," he said as he took his pipe from his mouth. "This is where I was raised." He looked up at the loft. "For over a hundred years my family lived in this place. No better than the animals who live here now." He slapped an affectionate hand on the cow's rump. "Ah, that's not true. These beasts have it better than many of the Dillons did. They're sure of their grain and hay. Not so with us Irish animals in the old days." He bent his head as he lit his pipe and then spoke around the stem as he took a fishing rod into his hands. "There's a mass grave marker near the church, Dan. It's from the times of the starvin'. I don't think anybody knows how many bodies were tossed in there." He was silent for awhile. "Anyway, we kiddoes slept up there. Six of us. Me, the youngest. But, I ended up with this land. My oldest brother couldn't stay to take it—there was not enough for him to stay for then. It should be his by rights, ya know, being the oldest."

"What happened to him?" Dan asked softly as the old man continued to gaze up at the loft.

"Ah, they all left. All of 'em. To America. Never came back." He shook his head. "Never heard from any of 'em. I may be the only one left. I dunno. Maybe some of their children or children's children might come by some day. That would be a grand thing." He seemed to have forgotten Dan now and his voice quivered with emotion. "I could tell 'em about the American wakes. That's what we called 'em when people from the Village left for America. And the word was right. They were wakes. Because we never saw any of 'em again. It was as tho' they joined the dead lyin' in the church yard. All we had of 'em was the memories. I can remember those wakes cuz' even the tiniest tot would stay up all night. The women wailin' and keenin' and the story tellin' and the dancin' and shure, shure the drinkin'—to kill the pain, I s'pose. I still remember how my mother would hug me so tight on those nights. So tight it would hurt and when the dawn came we'd walk down to the Village. Everybody would be there, the whole village. And whoever it was leavin' for America would go and I remember those times now when it's dawn and the first soft light has come. I remember how it was in the dawn those days when I was just a tot and I'd see the folks cryin'. Those dawns were full of tears. Even the men. My father too. Even my father. I can still remember watching my father cry."

"And don'cha hate 'em for that?" Dan asked sharply.

"Hate 'em?" Michael Dillon repeated blinking quickly. "The English, ya' mean. I dunno," he said, "if hate's the word. God knows they've given us generations of reasons. And I suppose there's plenty of reason for hate in all of it. But ya' know," he said suddenly, as he whipped the tip of his rod out through the doorway, "it goes to show ya' how smart the English are."

"Smart?"

"Shure. Look at the Germans spendin' all that money on ovens and showers and barracks and all to kill the Jews. The English didn't have to do a thing. It was perfect for them. They just stood around and watched a couple of million Irishmen starve to death. They almost eliminated the Irish race and it didn't cost 'em a shillin'."

Dan stared at the old man and he shook his head. "For God's sake, Michael, that doesn't make any sense."

"I know it doesn't make any sense, Dan Conway, but ya' know what?" He bent to pick up a tackle box and then stepped out into the yard. "You may find out if ya' spend much time out there on the Bay that hatin' the fish doesn't help ya' catch 'em."

Eleven

THEY WALKED UP the sharp rise behind the shed, fishing rods swinging with their movements, and soon reached a narrow track that ran along the spine of the ridge and twisted its way between sharp outcroppings of rock and bushes of bright yellow gorse. To their left beyond the house was a thick stand of pines, the only tall growth in this sweep of land.

The track descended to a scatter of houses grouped on the edge of an inlet dominated by a long stretch of shingle strewn beach. A modest whitewashed church sat on a knoll near the beach. The gold cross above it was bright against the slate colored sea. A rock wall enclosed barely discernible nubs and Celtic crosses and occasional more pompous reminders in a cemetery beside the church. The black clad figure of Father Devoy, very swollen at the waist now by his hitched up cassock, cycled leisurely on the church road headed for the village.

The coast road bisected the village and Dan guessed that if the Guinness signs were an indication, four of the dozen or so buildings they strolled past were pubs. In front of one stood a public phone booth and a gas pump.

Two men with weather worn faces crossed the road in front of them as they came into the center of the village. They wore the ageless uniform of the Irish farmer—black suits and mud spattered Wellington boots. The two offered respectful nods and greetings to Michael Dillon while quick-eyeing Dan with sly country curiosity.

Dan accompanied the old man across a gravel parking area bordered by broad leafed palm trees. Two dusty cars were parked near the doorway of an austere two storey stucco structure and beside them stood a sturdy pony, head down between the shafts of a rubber tired milk cart.

Dan leaned his rod beside the old man's and as he did he tilted his head toward the palms.

"That's a surprise."

"Never been down here in the South West before, Dan?"

"Never."

"The palms. I think the numbers and the size right here along the coast do surprise visitors. Even our own people. It's the Gulf Stream. It catches this part of Ireland the most. That's what gives us so many fish and so much rain."

"And not so many people."

"No, thank God." Dillon removed his pipe and rubbed a hand over his mouth and looked up at the small hand lettered sign over the doorway announcing P. J. Cronin's in red script. "We'll see what herself is up to today," he said with a wink. Dan followed him inside and stood by the doorway and surveyed the interior.

Cronin's was a pub, grocery store and clothing emporium. One end of the long room contained the bar, four oilcloth covered tables and a scattering of chairs in various stages of disrepair. The rest of the room was an admixture of crowded shelves and jumbled boxes of clothes, shoes, boots, canned fruit, vegetables, bread, even a hanging side of beef. A stalk of green bananas was set on top of an unopened box of work sox.

A short squat woman with grey hair pinned back came out from behind the bar in a rolling walk that caused her massive breasts to shift from side to side under the apron she wore over her dress. When she stopped in front of Michael Dillon, most of one breast bulged outside the edge of the apron. With her hands settled on the curve of her wide hips she looked up at Dan with lively grey eyes.

"Well, where'd ya' get this one, Michael Dillon?" she asked and then, not pausing for an answer she continued. "Did ya' bring some fish?"

"We're goin' not comin'," said Michael, walking past her to the bar.

"Ah, well, someone mentioned the lights were burnin' late up on the hill. I suppose it takes a bit of doin' to get goin' in the morning under those circumstances, and especially with the prettiest girl in all of Ireland not there to keep an eye on an old man."

Michael Dillon puffed on his pipe so fast that it sent off quick small balls of smoke. Four other men were in the bar—one at the dart board held his hand on a dart as he began to pull it out of the target, three with their heads together at the end of the bar near the window. Their faces were all turned watching this with obvious pleasure.

"We'll have a glass of porter if ya' have any," Dillon growled the words around the stem of his pipe. "And this fella needs a heavy sweater for the fishin'."

"A sweater is it?" she said as she moved behind the bar and worked the stick to begin to pour a tall chocolatey glass of Guinness. "Will you have something?" she asked Dan as she watched the creaminess in the brew slowly become a milky white cap.

"Humph!" said Michael with triumph in his voice. "I said, we—We, Mary Cronin. We'll have porter. The years are catchin' up with your ears."

"The man can speak for himself, can't he? God knows he's big enough."

"I'll have the same," Dan said.

She levelled the foam on the top of the glass with the edge of a flat stick and then began the ritual with another glass.

"A sweater is it?" she said again, looking up at Dan. "I think we might have just one big enough for ya." She placed the two tall dark glasses on the bar and headed quickly down the room.

Michael Dillon greeted the other drinkers with quiet hellos and a wink.

"How's Jack today?" he called to the unseen figure of Mary Cronin who could be heard behind one of the shelves.

When no answer came, one of the other men at the end of the bar snickered and muttered, "Feelin' poorly again from drinkin' too much of his own stuff."

"What's that?" roared the woman's voice.

The man buried his face in his glass. Mary Cronin came round the corner of the shelf, carrying a sweater; she glared at the other men as they stared into their drinks.

"Here we are," she said, holding the heavy blonde knit sweater up in front of Dan. "Here we are, try this on." She shook her head. "I don't get to sell many sweaters nowadays, the way things are with the tourists afraid to come."

"It fits fine," Dan said as he pulled the sweater down to his waist.

"Shure, it does," she said as the old man watched with nods of approval. "That's knit by Brigid," she said directing her words to Michael Dillon.

"Nice job," Dan said.

"Where d'ya hail from?" she asked Dan suddenly.

"I'm from Dublin."

"Dublin is it? It doesn't sound like Dublin, does it?" she said, again directing her words to Michael Dillon.

"Well, I was born up North but I moved to Dublin a while back."

"And who would blame you with the murderin' madness goin' on up there. I don't blame you. The fools up there with their shootin' and bombin', killin' innocent women and children. And for what? To drive out the English, they say. Ha! Why don't they leave well enough alone. We've no need for it. Do they think things will be fine and dandy up there in the North with that gang running things? They're murderin' gangsters. The I.R.A. The Provos. The this, the that. Scum, all of 'em—whatever the name. They should be in prison, every one of 'em. Or blown up like they blow other people up. They're ruinin' the North and the South." She stopped to get her breath and her breasts rose and fell, straining her apron. Michael and Dan, solemn faced, mouthed their drinks.

"Oh, shure, Michael Dillon was a hero in this country years ago but that was a different time and different men. Different men altogether. But what good did it all do? Answer me that."

"Did ya say it was Brigid knit that?" Michael Dillon spoke quickly into the silence in the room.

"Yes, and isn't it a lovely stitch?" Mary Cronin asked, her smile showing the few remaining teeth in her mouth.

"Each woman has a different stitch for her sweater, ya know." Michael said to Dan.

"I didn't know."

"And do ya know why?" Mary Cronin asked and she looked at Michael Dillon with a quick softening of fondness on her features. "Will you tell 'im, Michael Dillon?"

"I will indeed," Michael Dillon said slowly as he packed his pipe. "Well Dan, the sweaters were first knit long before anybody's memory by the women in the Blaskets and out in the Aran Isles and then here on the coast for the men and boys doin' the fishin'. The women know all too well the savagery of the sea and what it can do to a body that's spent time in the water. So they each have their own special stitch in these sweaters so that no matter what's happened to the body the stitch in the sweater will tell who it is."

Dan fingered the intricate twisting in the fabric of his sweater.

Mary Cronin sighed. "God knows it's the way of things in this country. The way it's always been. Even in the knittin' of a sweater. The Irish people are always livin' on the edge of sadness."

Twelve

DAN STEPPED CAREFULLY as they walked across the rock strewn beach heading for the float that moved just perceptibly with the impulses from the rippled water in the cove. His eyes were picking out his next footing when a shout caught him in midstep. He turned quickly and almost lost his balance.

Father Devoy stood on the other side of the stone wall that separated the road from the beach. He leaned his bike against the stones as Dan watched and then climbed awkwardly over the low wall, toppling a couple of stones as he did. Dan ignored Michael Dillon's muttered curse and kept his eyes on the priest whose flushed cheeks and stumbling attempts at speed on the beach caused Dan to tense and turn his head quickly searching for any other movement on the beach or road. His glance returned to the priest and he watched him with narrowed eyes as he slid to an uneven stop in front of him.

"Michael! Dan!" he said hoarsely. His breathing was short and quick and he paused for a moment and made an obvious effort to calm himself. His pudgy fingers smoothed the cassock over his heaving belly.

"For the love a God, Father, what is it? Is Katey alright?"

"Yes, yes, it's not that. It's Dan. There was a stranger in a car asking about Dan."

"Did he ask for him by name?" Michael asked quickly.

"No, no, he didn't. He—"

"O.K., wait a minute, Father, take it easy. Start at the beginning. Where did this happen? What did he look like? What did he say? Nice and easy now."

The priest threw his shoulders back. "Of course, Dan. I'm only out of breath a bit because I stopped in Cronin's looking for you after this man stopped me and asked his questions and they told me you fellas were going fishing and I wanted to let you know before you got out on the water. That's all. I'm certainly not losing my cool as the Yanks say in their movies."

"I'm sure you're not, Father. Now exactly what happened?"

"Well, I was on my bike just comin' on to the main road and this grey car, a Ford it was, a grey Ford, I checked it thoroughly. Very thoroughly."

"What were the license numbers?" interrupted Michael Dillon and the priest's cheeks got even redder.

"Well, actually, I didn't have a chance to check the plates. I realized that on the way to Cronin's but I could recognize the man anywhere. Anywhere."

"First, what did he say?" Dan asked over the sound of the old man's noisy sucking on his cold pipe.

"He asked if I knew where a friend of his was stayin'. Described you as a big fella with a busted nose. He said he was a friend of yours and had lost the letter from you describing where you were staying."

"What did the fella look like?" Dan asked.

"Oh I'll remember him. Heavy. Burly. Bald head and tiny eyes like glass beads in his round face, bald headed and nasty looking man. But, is he someone you know, Dan?"

"What did you say when he asked you?"

"Ah, not to worry. I figured if he was a friend of yours he wouldn't be running around asking questions like that. I assumed your organization is better run than that, so I told him nothing. In fact, I said that I didn't pay attention to who was or was not visiting in this part of the country but that I had not seen anybody of that description. I'm sure there's no sin in my sayin' that."

"And that's all, no more questions from him?"

"None. Well, he started to say something but I told him I had a busy day and had to be moving along and I left him sitting right there."

"I see."

"Do you know him, Dan?" the priest asked anxiously. "Do you know who he is?"

"No I don't. Did you get an accent, Father?"

"I couldn't quite tell if it was Ulster or Dublin or what. I've been thinking about that and I'll get it yet, but what will you do now, Dan?"

"First, thank you for bringing us your news and then I'll go fishin' if Mr. Dillon here still wants to do that."

"I do indeed," the old man said brightly.

"Is there anything you want me to do, Dan?" The priest's voice had a rising of hope in it.

"No, Father, there isn't. Please don't do anything or say anything."

"Well, of course I wouldn't without your direction," he said, avoiding Dan's eyes.

"We'll see ya later, Father," Michael Dillon said gruffly and turned toward the water.

The float sagged and swayed under their weight. Dan stood looking down into the scarred bottom of the half-moon shaped dory that swung easily on a limp line tied to the float.

"What do ya think, Dan?" the old man asked gently as he too stared at the boat.

"The important thing about it is you and your daughter and how you feel about it."

"What d'ya mean?"

"I mean it might be better if I clear out of here right now."

"Better for who?"

"Better for you and your daughter."

"D'ya really believe that, Dan?"

"Michael, I don't know. I don't know what's best for you right now. I don't know who this character is and I don't know what he wants, but I sure don't think he's lookin' for me to tell me I've won the Sweepstakes."

"I suppose that's a fact." The old man paused and turned to look up at Dan. "But ya know, it puts some pep into things here doesn't it. Kind of gets my old ticker pumpin', like the old days. I'll tell ya what," he said brightly, "you talk this over with Kate when she gets home and we'll abide by her decision. I'd like ya to stay on if it's up to me. Alright Dan?"

"Well then," he continued, "are ya still up for some fishin'?"

"More than ever."

"Ah, that's a good lad. Come on now." With the quick sure movements of a young man Michael Dillon stepped into the dory and, balancing himself with easy shifting of his feet, took both rods and laid them lengthwise on the side of the boat, then he unwrapped the line from the cleat and holding to the float with one hand spoke to Dan with his eyes sparkling. "How about you doin' the rowin'?"

"I've never done any. I don't know how."

"Would ya like to learn?"

"Well, I hope I'm not too old to learn something new." He stepped cautiously into the boat and sat abruptly on the nearest seat as the boat tipped.

"You'll get the feel of it soon, Dan. There's nothin' to it, believe me. Now just turn yourself around there, so you're facin' me here in the stern and take those oars. You see those oars?"

"I do," Dan said dryly as he slowly twisted round on the seat and wrapped his long fingers around the oar handles.

Michael Dillon shoved the boat away from the float and Dan chopped the oar blades into the water.

"Goddamn!" he grunted.

"Take it easy, we've nothin' but time."

"This is crazy. You can't see where you're goin', you only see where you've been," Dan said twisting his head for a look forward.

"Shure, Dan it's just like life. You'll see what I mean."

Dan grunted again as one oar came out of the water and the dory zigged.

"Bloody Hell!"

"Easy, Dan, easy. Remember the ocean's always underneath ya and always stronger than you are, so just set the blades in the water straight down, like you're slicin' firmly into a cake and pull evenly. Ee—ven—ly. That's it. Ah shure, you'll be skimmin' round the bay on your own pretty soon. Whenever the fancy takes ya."

The day had been grey and overcast with a steady breeze that sometimes carried a wispy wetness from the low hanging clouds, but now the sun came out. Dan rested the handles of the oars on his knees and watched the sunshine change the slate dull water to a glinting blue and out where the bay met the ocean he saw the roiled waves along the rip become a tossed frothy white.

"Tell me a little about Kate, Michael."

The old man leaned back and cupped a knee in his hands. He puffed hard on his pipe and for a moment his face was obscured.

"A little about Kate is it?" he said crossing his legs now and moving the pipe stem in his mouth. "Well, her mother, God rest her soul, died bringin' her into the world and it's been Katey and me ever since. She went away to University in Cork and travelled around England and Europe the way the young people do. The Yanks with all their money taught 'em that too, I suppose, but she's never been far from me really and she came home a few years ago. She teaches in the village school and she's writin' a book."

"What's the book about?"

"It's goin' to be about Yeats and his poetry. She's doin' it with a professor from the University in Cork. That's where she's been the last few days while school's out."

"And how does she feel about the idea of one Ireland?"

"Well," he said and chuckled, "I won't try to deal with that one. I think you'll find out soon enough from her if the subject comes up. But, you know what I told ya, Katey and I are a team and there's no problem with you stayin' here. About this new business tho', this fella askin' the questions, I don't know what she'll say but you understand, we'll have to go along with her on that. She went along with me on the first part of it."

"I understand," Dan said as he picked up his rod. "Now let's see if I can understand how this thing works." He turned the handle of the reel. "You said you swap fish at Cronin's for goods so maybe I can pay my own way here. I'd like to do that once in a while."

"Good, we'll give it a try then, DanO."

Dan's head snapped up and he stared at Dillon in a strange and gentle way, and as Michael Dillon looked at Dan he knew with an old man's knowing that Dan Conway's thoughts were a long, long way from Bantry Bay.

Michael Dillon picked up his rod as the dory drifted with the tide. He turned the rod so that the reel was facing Dan.

"Now, we hold it like this. Ya see. This attachin' arm that goes to the rod, we hold in between the second and third fingers. This heavy curved piece of wire is called the bale. I don't know why. Never could figure it out. Ya hold the line tight against the rod with your first finger and push the bale over. Til' it clicks—like that—then your first finger holdin' the line here is the only thing that keeps the line from runnin' free from the reel—if it does get away from ya, and starts to run free, ya first turn the handle of the reel, a bit sharp. Like this. And the bale snaps down—see—and keeps the line on the reel from runnin' out—but what ya want is like this—with your finger on the line ya bring the rod back to about where three o'clock is on a circle and then snap it forward and at about, ohh, eleven o'clock, then ya take your finger off that line and, ya see, out it goes. And remember—always keep your eye on the lure—always."

The line sailed out on a lazy arc, the red feathered tail of the lure became a gay spot of color against the diamond dancing waves.

"Then when your line hits the water, ya turn the reel handle back—like—that—like ya did before to stop the line from foulin'. Then ya bring the line back to ya—see—quick—quick—then sometimes slow—then quick again—the fish must think that the lure is a small fish in trouble—ya know—thrashin' for its life on the surface."

"The big fish eat the little fish that are in trouble. Can't protect themselves. Is that it?"

"That's it, Dan."

"I wonder if they learned that from us or we learned it from the fish."

He never saw the fish, he felt the sudden surge of strength against the line and the tip of the rod bent and he was surprised.

"Alright Dan. Alright, man—keep your tip down for a bit, just a second more. When ya bring it up, don't jerk it. Strong but not a jerk. That's it! That's it! You've set the hook! Now let's bring that beauty to the boat—easy man—easy—don't lose 'im."

The fish broke out of the wave twisting, leaping, silver and black above the exploded water.

"Ah, that's it—now—Ahh! Isn't that a beauty?"

The old man's voice was strong. He put his pipe in his pocket and stood holding the gaff, staring intently into the water at the side of the boat. His cap was pushed back and his eyes were bright. The fish was a blur of silver arrowing into the dark water as it dove beneath the boat.

"Shure, he sees the boat—he knows now—this is the time—his time has come—he'll fight it! God love 'im! Move toward the bow, Dan, that's it, keep that tip up but don't jerk it. That's it!" He lashed into the water with the gaff. "Ahh—there ya are, ya beauty ya."

He swung the gaffed fish out of the water; the hooked point of the gaff had gone through the fish but with a mighty twist it tore free and landed in the boat.

The silver symmetry of the struggling fish was strangely alive, clean and bright against the chipped, faded wood of the dory. The fish leapt and flipped, its mouth opened wide and snapped shut again and again. Each time less wide. The boat drifted as the two of them intently watched the fish. Finally the old man picked up his rod and whipped the lure out across the water. Dan continued to stare at the gasping fish as it struggled to live. After a few casts Dillon turned and put down his rod.

"Dan, there's somethin' that needs to be said. That fish is caught cuz he couldn't keep his mouth shut and I should've kept my mouth shut. I know it and I'm sorry. I shouldn't have told Father Devoy about you comin'. He didn't handle himself well with that man. Folks here don't shut people off in the middle of havin' a chat. They don't nick off like that. If the man's got a nose, he smelled that. You know it, Dan. I should've kept my mouth shut. You know it, don'cha."

"I do, Michael," Dan said, his eyes still held in fascination with the sad beauty of the fish lying exhausted, quivering, opened mouthed. "But don't worry about it. Things will be all right."

Thirteen

THE DOG CAPERED with delight on the float as Michael Dillon leaned from the bow and knotted the line around the cleat. Dan stepped from the boat and the dog nudged Dan's leg and his nose found Dan's hand. He bounced around the two men, sniffing briefly at the fish Dillon carried.

"C'mon, Bluff, stop it now. Ya mustn't let him get away with too much with ya, Dan."

"Why not? It's not like with people. You can let a dog take advantage of you and enjoy it. I like to fool with him. I had a dog for a little while once when I was a kiddo."

"Ah, they make great pals don't they? Katey and I, we'd be lost if anything happened to Bluff."

They crossed the road and headed up a worn path across the meadows; a stile walked them over a stone wall.

"Katey built this for me, believe it or not."

"This stile? She did?"

"I was a bit miffed at first but I didn't let on."

"Why?"

"Well, I didn't want people to think I was too old to climb over that wall. She was after me for years to put a gate in there. This is my path, ya know. I mean, it's my feet that wore it down all these years goin' to the fishin'. And I'd climb over that wall at least once a day. I didn't want a gate. I don't know why. Just didn't, and then a couple of years ago on my birthday I came back from fishin' and, bang, there it was. She built it at one of the neighbors' houses and all the neighbors got together and put it up while I was out fishin'." He smiled at the memory. "We had quite a party that night."

Dan watched a towering formation of heavy looking grey clouds that blotted out the sun. They stretched in a tumbled mass out to the horizon where sea and sky lost their identities. He felt the first tentative drops of rain.

"You been fishing here all these years," he said, still watching the cloud formation. "Have you ever got tired of the scenery?"

"Never, Dan, never. It's the finest life a man could want."

"Can you really make a living at the fishin'?"

Michael ignored the rain as he relit his pipe; his eyes were on the match as he spoke. "I did make a livin'. I don't now, of course. We need Kate's wages. But I always had one of the young fellas in the village workin' for me, helpin' with the scallopin' and lobsters and I made a good livin'. A course, life is simple here. We don't need what you city folks need."

The old man's breathing was labored when they reached the top of the hill. He shook his head and looked at Dan. "Those are long legs for a little fella like me to stay up with."

Dan reached over and took the rod from his hand. "You go in the house and take it easy. I'll put this stuff away."

"I'll take ya up on that offer," Michael said wearily.

The dog followed Dan into the shed, darting under the cow's belly and then standing out of reach of the cow's hooves, it snapped a short bark that was sharp and harsh in the confines of the shed.

"Bluff c'mere." Dan scratched the dog's ears but suddenly the animal's body tensed. His head cocked and without a preliminary movement he raced out of the building.

"Bluff, hey, Bluff!"

Then Dan heard the car. He walked out of the shed and stood by the corner of the house and watched a white Volkswagon come into the yard. The car door opened and the dog leapt in, a flurry of black. A ringing burst of laughter carried across the yard. A woman got out of the car and looked at him, the laughter still on her face.

When he saw the woman he smiled as he thought of one of the old man's speeches about the English, how he would curse and say, "The bastards are so arrogant, they really believe God is an Englishman," and how, as he did so often, the old man would talk of historical events as though they had happened yesterday. "Christ," he would say, "they believe that to protect England God sent the great storm that wrecked the Spanish Armada off the West of Ireland," and how the old man wondered aloud with a rare chuckle if the British were aware that the coffe-skinned, hot-blooded, shipwrecked Spanish sailors had lain with the milk-white Celtic women and produced the phenomenon known as the Black Irish. "Do they know their English God created those Black Irish beauties," he would say. Now Dan knew what the old man had meant.

This woman was one of those, mellow dark skin with raven black hair to her shoulders and eyelashes so long he was aware of them even across the space of the yard. She was wearing a bulky turtleneck fisherman's sweater and jeans. She walked toward him, fending off the dog who frolicked joyfully around her feet. When she reached Dan she offered her hand and looked up at him with the greenest eyes he had ever seen. Her face was somber now.

"Are you our expected visitor from the North?" She did not have her father's brogue, but her handshake was quick and strong like the old man's.

"I am. My name's Conway, Dan Conway."

Drops of rain in her hair shone like tiny beads of crystal.

"Welcome, Dan Conway, I'm Kate Dillon."

The dog leapt against her. "You've met Bluff I'm sure."

"Yes."

"Well, he doesn't bluff when he tells you he's glad to see you." She bent to pat the dog and her hair cascaded around her face. She brushed it away with one hand and looked up at him. "Where's himself?"

"He's in the house. We went fishing and he was a bit winded when we got back."

She gave the dog a final rub, stood and headed for the cottage. At the doorway she turned and spoke. "I guess these places were built for people the size of the Dillons. Does your head hit?"

"Not quite."

She smiled briefly and he noticed her teeth were even and very white. Michael Dillon's chin was on his chest. The peak of his cap moved up and down to the burry cadence of his snoring. Kate watched her father with the full tenderness of her love showing on her features, then she tiptoed across the room and went to one knee beside his chair and kissed him on the cheek.

The snoring stopped. Michael Dillon spoke in a raspy whisper, without opening his eyes. "Well now, who is it this time sneakin' in stealin' kisses? Is there no rest for me from you wimmen?"

Kate laughed and the sound warmed the room.

"Oh Pa, you're terrible." She turned her head quickly, her hair shimmered and she looked up at Dan, her face flushed. "Has he been deluged while I've been gone?"

Dan stared at her. Their glances held. He could see tiny crows feet at the corners of her eyes; there were no other lines on her face. He knew she had asked him a question and he wasn't sure what the question was. He nodded and turned away hearing Michael Dillon's voice.

"How are your pals in Cork City, Katey? And how is the business of the book comin'—are the university people happy with it?"

"Oh," Kate said and rose to her feet, "they're fine, Pa—things look good. They like the changes we've made in the manuscript and they think a publisher in Belfast may do the book."

"Belfast. That's strange," said the old man, stretching his arms and yawning, almost losing his cap.

Dan turned back from the window and watched them.

"Not really. I guess Belfast has a couple of fine publishing houses and there are some Yeats fans in one of them I'm told." She looked at Dan. "Our book is about Yeats. Yeats and the women in his life."

Dan's response was another nod.

"But Belfast, Katey," the old man said querulously. "Is there no one in Cork or Dublin to print the book?"

"Oh, Pa, not that! We're not going to get into that even in the printing of the book, are we?"

"No, Katey we're not. It's a grand thing, the book. Imagine a Dillon. In this house. Havin' their name on a book. And a girl at that."

Kate shook her head and smiled and winked at Dan and they broke into easy chuckles that grew into hearty laughter as they continued to look at one another until they stopped short, embarrassed, when the old man looked from one to the other and said, "What in God's name is so funny?"

"You are, Pa," Katey said. "You are. Like all Irishmen. This part of the twentieth century is not quite what you had in mind."

"Oh, the wimmen's business is it? Humph! What d'you think about it, Dan?"

"Not much, Michael. I mean," he said, rubbing his fingers on the crook in his nose, "I don't pay much attention to it. I guess it's a real revolution tho'."

"A lot more real and reasonable than the other so called revolutionary activities going on on this island," Kate said sharply. "And a hell of a lot less bloody."

"Now Katey," Michael Dillon said, rising quickly from the chair. "Tell us when do ya think these people will be publishin' the book?"

"I don't know, Pa. Kevin Duffy drove up to Belfast from Cork a couple of days ago. He said he'd stop here tomorrow and let me know what they say up there."

"Ah, Duffy, the Professor eh? His family has a lovely place near Glengariff, Dan. A wealthy family from Cork. Piles of money and he's doin' the book with Kate."

"Well," Kate said briskly, "what about some supper. Did you fellows get any fish?"

"We did. Dan got a beauty."

"You're a fisherman are you?" Kate asked with surprise.

"No, not a bit. My first time."

"He's goin' to be a good one," the old man said.

"Congratulations! Like it?"

"Very much. I'd like to go again tomorrow."

"Oh, I dunno if I'm up to it tomorrow," Dillon said, rubbing his lower back.

Dan looked at Kate and spoke quietly. "Would you come with me?"

A faint flush of pink showed on her cheeks. "Well," she said, and then she started again. "Well, Kevin may stop in—I'm sort of expecting him—but—yes, yes, I will."

Fourteen

Dan watched Michael Dillon fillet the fish. Despite the fatigue on the old man's face that had worked the lines around his mouth into clefts, the knife in his hand moved in swift skillful slashes.

"When it comes to fish you do it all, I guess," Dan said.

"It's a thing I really know and it makes me feel young—even when my back is tellin' me the truth."

Dan was aware of the sound of Kate's footsteps in the bedroom over their heads.

"Well, Michael, there's a thing I really know or at least I know better than fishin'."

"What's that?"

"I'm a pretty fair cook."

"Aha! You are, eh?"

"So I'd like to do the supper for ya."

"Fine and dandy. That won't make Katey mad either, I don't think. I'll go put on the radio and listen to the news."

Dan took the bowl of eggs from the little refrigerator. He heard footsteps on the stairs and Kate came into the room. She had replaced her sweater with a man's blue work shirt that was many sizes too large for her. Her sleeves were rolled up and she carried some notebooks under her arm and a couple of pens in her fist.

"What's this?" she asked as Dan cracked an egg.

"This is me preparing supper."

"Well, this is me being surprised. Mind if I sit here at the table? I've some work to do and I might even watch this performance a little."

"Why not?" He jiggled the egg in his hand until the white dribbled through his fingers.

"Are there any onions?" he asked as he cracked another egg.

"We don't have onions but there are leeks in the garden. I'll get some." She went out the back door and quickly returned. She stood beside him for a moment and washed the stalks and put them on the sideboard. There was a wispy fragrance about her. He had no idea what it was but it was pleasing to him.

"Does my father know you're doing this?"

"Yes."

"Was he appalled?"

"I don't think so. Why?"

"I think he believes that you are some sort of a true Irish hero and I thought he'd be upset at your doing woman's work." She sat down at the table and spoke to his back. "Just exactly what is it you do, Dan Conway?" The sound of a practiced radio voice and occasional static came to them from the living room. Dan kept his back to her as he poured small dollops of oil into the bowl.

"You mean with my cooking?"

"Please, no games. My father said you're involved in some way with the movement against the British in the North. With his old organization I gather. But, he was very vague. He always is if it's something important. He said he'd like to make a contribution of some kind once more and would I agree to a man staying for a while. I did, as you can see, but I feel I have a right to know a bit more about it. I'm afraid I will have trouble believing you are the cook for the group."

Dan half turned and spoke over his shoulder. "I don't want to say this wrong but it will be much the best if you don't know too much about me. I don't mean to be dramatic, but that's a fact, believe me!"

Kate rolled a pen back and forth in her fingers and stared at it as she did. "I can see where that makes some sense. Yes, I can agree with some of that, but there's one thing that is important to me and to this house and—I must ask it." She glanced at Dan and her fingers stopped and her body tensed. "You're not one of those who do the bombs. The awful things. Blowing up restaurants, department stores, the casual violence—and—oh!—I can't even say it. You're not that are you?"

Dan exhaled slowly. "No," he said, "no, I'm not. I have been involved with some tough stuff with the British Army and the so-called government in the North, but none of that other business."

Kate sighed and flipped open a notebook. "I'm glad to hear that. You can understand how I feel I hope."

Dan nodded.

"I couldn't, wouldn't feel right with someone under our roof who's—who's been involved in the—uh—the savagery—the cruel—well—oh—you know what I mean."

Dan nodded again with his back to her.

Fifteen

THE OLD MAN SAT on the edge of the easy chair, his head cocked to get full reception of the radio voice. He casually watched as the dog rose from his sprawl in front of the fire, sniffed and headed for the kitchen at a trot. When the news broadcast changed to the Irish language, Dillon rose and followed the dog's route.

"I was just going to call you, Pa."

"The smell of this cookin' was call enough, Kate."

"See how you like this, Pa." She proffered a small dish with a wedge of fish on it. "Try this piece."

He forked through the crisp cover of sauce on the fish and put a chunk into his mouth.

"What do you think?"

"Lovely, lovely."

Kate pointed at Dan. "There's the cook, congratulate him."

"Yes, it's fine, Dan," Michael said absently.

"Pa, you're not exactly jumping up and down. What's the matter? Do you feel alright?"

"I do. I do. There's somethin' I want to talk to Dan about."

"Well, talk then."

Michael looked questioningly at Dan who was placing the last of their heavily laden plates on the table.

"Go ahead, Michael," Dan said.

"Can we sit?" Kate asked.

"Shure, shure," her father grumbled.

"And say grace?" she added.

Michael Dillon's head went down and his daughter reached across the table and removed his cap. He shrugged, blessed himself with a short circular wave of his right hand and raised his head.

"Dan," he said with a rush, "they've picked up a fellow named O'Connor in the North. James John O'Connor. The English say he was in on the big fight with the army when the helicopter got shot down. It's in the news." He stared at Dan waiting for him to speak.

Dan calmly chewed a mouthful of fish and finally the old man blurted. "Is he one of your people, Dan?"

"If they've got the right O'Connor, he is," Dan said.

"The radio says he's a plumber. Is that right?"

Dan snorted. "If you can call havin' about a month's work in five years being a plumber, I suppose that's right. His brother's been starvin' at it even longer. The fact is that like most of us up there he's on the dole."

"Most of us—you mean Catholics, Dan?" Kate asked.

"Yes."

"Why, Dan? Why so many Catholics on the dole?" Kate asked.

"It's because they don't want to give us anything. If there aren't enough jobs, they get the ones there are. I'm sure if there's plumbing to be done their people get the work. If there's housing that's got dignity about it, they get it. Anything worthwhile, they grab it and hold it. Hold it with the help of the British Army like they've been doin' for hundreds of years."

"They—the protestants. Then it's a religious thing isn't it?" Kate said.

"Hell, no! Not for us it isn't. The church has done nothin' but play footsie with the establishment for centuries. It's kept our people livin' on their knees all these years—if you can call it livin'. Someday maybe we can make an offer. Get the British out and you can take the church with you."

"Ah, Dan, that's strong stuff," Michael Dillon said. "The church has comforted all of us at times when we've been desperate for comfort. Shure, over the years, the big shots have thrown their weight around and been tough on the organization, but for the little people in the parishes the church is like a warm heart beatin'. I can't agree with ya about the church itself, Dan."

"I'll bet you can agree on this food. It's excellent, Dan. Isn't it Pa?"

The old man brightened. "It is that. You've got a real talent with the cookin' eh, Dan?"

"What's the sauce on the fish?" Kate asked.

"It's just some mayonnaise with the leeks on it that is spread on the fish and baked right with it."

"That's easy. I'll remember, and these scalloped potatoes. Where did you learn to cook?"

"Oh, here and there, you know the way you pick things up."

"I never did," Dillon said with a chuckle.

"No, Pa, you certainly didn't. But it must have been more than odds and ends, Dan. This tastes like gourmet food. It's gourmet style isn't it?"

Dan shrugged and Kate pressed on.

"Where was it? The French Riviera?"

"Ah!" said the old man wiping his chin. "Was it, Dan?"

"No, no it wasn't."

"Where?" Kate asked insistently.

"It was in prison."

"In prison?" Kate breathed.

"Well, you asked. I was in prison in the North and we were planning a break-out. I went on my best behaviour so I could get kitchen work. There were things we needed I could get hold of in the kitchen. I turned out to be good at it. Ended up cookin' for the guards. It was perfect for us and I liked cooking. Still do."

"Did you break out?" Kate asked. Her father looked up from his plate.

"We did."

"Was that the affair some years ago when they shot the Sheehy lad, Dan?" asked Dillon.

"Yes, but the Brits didn't tell the truth about that."

"What happened?"

"They caught Martin Sheehy right after we got out. They banged him around to make him tell 'em what he knew."

"He wouldn't talk. Not a Sheehy, Dan. His grandfather fought with me in the twenties."

"You're right Michael, he wouldn't talk, so they took him out and shot him and said he'd tried to escape again."

"My God, Dan, are you sure of that?" Kate asked.

"I'm sure. Later we grabbed one of their people. When we got him talking he told us just what happened."

Kate stared at her plate. Dan watched her and finally asked quietly, "How's your fish?"

"Not quite as good as it was."

Michael Dillon shoved the dog's nose away from his elbow. "Stop it, Bluff, you'll get the leftovers if there are any. You know that."

Kate pushed away from the table. "I think I'll take him for a walk. C'mon Bluff," she said briskly.

The two men looked at her unfinished meal and then at one another. Michael Dillon shook his head as Kate took a slicker from the hook and went out the back door with the dog.

"You got to remember, Dan, she's never heard anything like this before. I don't talk to her about the days of the Black and Tan and the awful times of the Civil War in the twenties. The life you live, the things that go on are completely foreign to the people here in this part of Ireland, Dan. It's a different world here. Do you understand?"

"Never more than right now," Dan said, staring at Kate's unfinished meal.

Sixteen

MICHAEL DILLON SWABBED his plate clean with a thick slice of bread and then stood rubbing his lower back before moving slowly upstairs to bed, trailing a soft, "Good night," behind him.

Dan washed and dried the dishes and then after a glance at one of the rows of books he settled into the easy chair with the *Autobiography of William Butler Yeats*.

The occasional moan of the wind coincided with an expanded glow of the peat fire and a momentary smokiness in the room. The sound of the kitchen clock was a steady, lonesome lament to the passing of time.

Dan could not concentrate on the words. He read and re-read sentences. The clock seemed louder and louder, competing with the rain against the windows. He got up and centered the rod with the tea kettle over the fire. He tried to read again. He could not get Kate Dillon out of his thoughts. He thought he could smell the fragrance of her now mingled with the scent of the burning peat.

The front door opened suddenly and she was there in the room. She stood shaking her hair as she took off the slicker and when she hung it by the door he could see the contour of her breasts despite the baggy blue shirt.

"The dog ran off," she said simply.

"Off?"

"A deer or a rabbit. He does that."

She walked over to the fire and spread her hands to it in one of mankind's oldest gestures.

"I'm sorry I ran out on dinner, Dan, but you and what you represent are confusing me."

"I know—would you like some tea?"

"Yes, please."

They sat sipping tea, not speaking, not uncomfortable, staring into the fire. Dan turned his head slowly. There was a sound outside the cottage. A strange sound. He heard it again. He put his cup of tea down quickly as Kate asked, "What is that?"

He moved across the room in long flat strides and jerked his pistol from his jacket pocket.

Kate stood and stared wide-eyed at the gun; her skin seemed darker in the fire-glow.

"What do you think it is?"

Dan shook his head and brushed past her into the kitchen. The essence of her stayed with him as he gently pushed the back door open and slipped out into the night. He went down onto the wet grass on his hands and knees and waited until his eyes could deal with the darkness. He moved slowly toward a formless thicket, still on hands and knees, putting his weight on the knuckles of one hand as he gripped the pistol. The sound was close now. He came to one knee and waited and held his breath. He raised the pistol and pointed it toward the thicket.

"Come out of there!"

An animal whimpered. Dan breathed deeply and exhaled. He moved forward and with his free hand moved some dripping branches.

The animal's figure was darker than the dark. It was Bluff. He whimpered again.

Dan pocketed his pistol and gently lifted the dog. He pushed open the kitchen door with his foot, almost hitting Kate who stood rigidly beside it. She reached out a hand.

"Oh, Bluff, what happened to you? Was it Bluff, Dan? Was that it?"

"Yes," he said.

"What is it? What happened to you, Bluff?"

"I'd say he ran into a tougher dog, or dogs, from the look of him. That's a bad wound there."

"O, God! Look at that. I'll bet it was those damn dogs the O'Dwyer's keep. They're brutes. Like their masters." She stroked the dog's head and he moaned softly. "Will he be all right, Dan? What should we do?"

"Is there a vet or doctor nearby?"

"No, we'd have to go all the way to Bantry—but—oh dear, I think he might be at the cattle auction in Macroom. Oh! Bluff, you poor puppy!"

"I'm afraid we're going to have to do something right away. Look!"

"Oh, Dan, your jacket's soaked with blood and look at the floor! Oh, that's a nasty cut. Those brutes!" She continued to stroke the dog's head.

"Kate, get the heaviest thread and sharpest, fat needle you can find. We're going to have to do some sewing."

"All right. I won't be a minute."

The dog quivered and shook and moaned again.

"Easy pup, take it easy." Dan ran his hands softly down the back of the dog's head.

Kate held the needle in front of her and threaded it on the first try. "I brought this antiseptic Pa uses on the cows too."

"Good girl."

"Which one of us will do the sewing? I've never done anything like this. Have you, Dan?"

"No. Never. Maybe I'd better hold him. He's not going to like this with nothing to kill the pain—he'll be a handful."

Kate nodded her head in agreement as she tenderly fingered the tear in the dog's hind quarters. Then, still holding the needle, she went to the sideboard and lit a large kerosene lamp and placed it on the table.

"Get ready," she said somberly.

"Okay. Oh, Bluff. Sorry fella. Sorry." The dog yelped and twisted as Dan forced him flat on the table.

Dan watched Kate's hands—small fingers tensed as she punched the needle through the skin—a vein swelled blue on the back of one hand.

The dog whined.

"Easy boy," Dan said, his head down, his face almost in Kate's hair. The dog tried hard to twist off the table and Dan pressed him tighter. Kate turned her head and her face was next to Dan's. He could see tiny golden flecks in the green of her eyes.

"Just a bit more, Dan, we're almost done."

"We are?" he said hoarsely and their eyes held until she shook her head and bent over the dog again.

Finally, Kate sighed and stepped back from the table. She threw her head back and the black veil of her hair was flung from her forehead. Perspiration glistened on her skin.

"I think that does it, Dan, what do you think?"

"That's a good job, Kate Dillon, a damn good job." Dan cradled the dog in his arms. "Let's put some of that antiseptic on him and then I'll set him in front of the fire."

Kate was standing at the sink when Dan came back to the kitchen.

"I think he's going to be all right, Kate."

"Thank goodness. Lord, I hope I never have to do that again." She ran the water and laughed and held her hands out to him. "Look. Look at how my hands are shaking."

To the astonishment of both of them Dan took her hands in his, raised them to his lips and kissed them. Then he put his arms around her and lifted her up, his face close to hers, holding her tightly. Timidly she reached out a finger and softly touched the break of his nose. Then she quickly moved her hand away.

"Please! Dan, no! This whole thing has my mind in a whirl. Let's just say goodnight."

His eyes searched her face and he smiled and set her down. "I'll see you in the morning, Kate. Goodnight."

When he awoke he tossed the covers from him, rose from the bed and dressed quickly. He put on the fishing sweater from Cronin's, listening for sounds of movement above him as he did. One thought was in his mind from the moment of consciousness. Kate Dillon and he were going fishing this morning. He would be with her. Just her. In the boat. There was a feeling of freedom and excitement and youthfulness in him that made him want to shout for the pure pleasure of it. He continued to listen for sounds from upstairs that would tell him that Kate was awake and at the same time he said a word aloud. "Giddy," he said and thought to himself, "I am giddy, like a child" and then a memory filled him. A young boy running across a green meadow, running as fast as he could and continuing down a steep hill. The hill a solid mass of knee high golden flowers. And the boy's speed increased with the pitch of the hill until he was whirling, arms flailing, down the hill, out of control, not caring, shouting in total gleeful abandon as his body pitched wildly forward in a long tripping fall that left him lying laughing between gasps for breath. A golden moment—like now—and Dan remembered his grandfather growling the word to his father later.

"Giddy. Sometimes he's a giddy child," the old man said.

He went into the living room and saw the dog lying flat-out in one of the rectangles of warm sunshine the morning sun sketched on the worn linoleum. Bluff's breathing was steady and deep. Dan went into the kitchen, stood for a moment in the stillness of the house, and then took two pans down from their hooks over the sink, banging them together as he did. Then he opened the tiny refrigerator, took out eggs, cheese and bacon, and tossed two bowls onto the sideboard, hitting the pans as he did, and then slammed the refrigerator door shut. He began preparing breakfast whistling off key. The sound of footsteps overhead made him grin.

Footsteps on the stairs. Her voice murmuring to the dog. Then he could feel her presence behind him as he worked at the sink.

"Good morning," she said in a low voice.

He turned and looked at her. Her hair was piled on top of her head. Tendrils of hair clung to the curve of her neck. She was wearing jeans and a black jersey and held her heavy sweater in her hands.

"Good morning."

"Dan, what would your pals say if they found out you're not Irish?"

"What do you mean?"

"You're a fraud. You can't be Irish. There isn't an Irishman in this country out of bed at this time of the day. Unless he hasn't gone to bed yet."

"I'm an early riser. Particularly if I'm looking forward to the day."

"And you are?"

"I am. Indeed I am."

"The fishing you mean."

He grinned wickedly at her. "What else would it be, Madam?"

Her face flushed. "I've been wondering if it's a good idea—I'm expecting a guest—the dog and all—you know—"

"Hey. The dog is going to be fine. I looked at him. You did too, I think. He's all right."

"Well—yes—he seems to be."

"We're going fishing. It's on. A commitment."

"Well—all right. Back at noon though, fair enough?"

"Fine. Hungry?"

"I should be after not finishing dinner last night but I'm not really."

"Good. Me either. I'll bring a snack for us. Let's go."

They walked through the thick, wet green of the meadow. They had not spoken since setting the dog on the sun warmed wood of the bench by the front door. Kate carried her rod with a graceful nonchalance that told him she had done it many times. She walked ahead of him when they reached the stile and stopped at the top so that his next step brought him beside her.

The view held them there, side by side, on the narrow platform step. The irregular fields of green were sprinkled with bright dots of daisies and buttercups and bounded by sturdy stonewalls. Beyond the fields lay the grey-gold strip of beach and then Bantry Bay, stretching out to the Atlantic in the West. The early angle of the sun colored the sea a dark blue and the wave tips glistened white despite the morning mist. To the East, heather covered, rock scarred mountains closed upon the inner-most reaches of the Bay and hosted distant scattered sheep. The tiny white washed cottages across the bay looked neater than they ever could be.

Instinctively, Dan put his arm around Kate and a feeling of electricity went through him at the touch of her. She did not move away from him.

"If there's a God he must have spent some extra time on this part of his job," he said.

"Oh, I'm sure there is and I'm very sure he did."

She stayed close against him and then moved away with a little laugh and quick-stepped down to the ground. "Now, let's see what He did about putting some fish in the ocean for us."

He sliced the blades of the oars deep into the water, braced his feet and put his back into a powerful pull. One of the oarlocks pulled out and his effort carried him right on backwards off the seat. He grunted a curse as he looked up at Kate Dillon in the bow. She put her hand to her mouth, laughed once, then again and then exploded into laughter. Dan sat upright on the bottom of the dory, stared at her for a moment and then his own strong laughter joined hers and the boat drifted while their happy sounds drifted across the water and echoed from the rocky inlet.

The morning hours flowed like the water under the boat. Kate's casts, long and accurate. Dan's line slowly reaching out to hers and finally triumphantly exceeding hers. Kate talking of college, of books. Of her book. Her father. Her love for him and for this piece of Ireland ran like a thread through the fabric of her easy words.

The excitement of the catch. Dan missing with three swipes of the gaff at Kate's first fish and their laughter, often their laughter. Her sharp words of command and direction as Dan hooked, played and landed two large fish in consecutive casts. The continuous action left the two of them excited and euphoric as they stood precariously balanced. And then, at that moment Dan turned and looked at Kate, her face glowing with pleasure, her eyes shining a stunning green, her lips slightly parted and he put a hand on her shoulder and kissed her, long and deep and her mouth came up to him. The boat tipped.

"Careful, you'll fall," Kate said breathing deeply.

"I'm afraid I already have," Dan said somberly and they both sat and stared wordlessly at one another.

Kate broke the long silence alternately looking directly at him or watching her hand as it trailed in the water as she spoke.

"Dan, you came into my life from God knows where. I know almost nothing about you and what I do know frightens me. I have a reasonable, pleasant life here. I know it's a backwater of the world. I've traveled to Europe and England. I know what city life is. I'm not a complete country girl, believe me. But, I love this place, this lovely place. It's what I want. It's truly heaven to me. Now you show up. On the run, I'd guess." She raised a hand. "You're right about that. I don't want to know. Or at least I'm telling myself I don't want to know. Anyway, here you are, and you've got me confused. I told you that and I meant it. I'm not being coy. I'm not a kid." She smiled. "I'm considered a spinster school teacher here in West Cork. But my life is settled. I'm content. You swagger around here." She looked at him. "Ah, never mind, don't say anything, you know it. You swagger even when you don't. You probably swagger in your sleep. You're a—what are you? The British would say a terrorist. An urban guerrilla leader. And I'm sure you're a leader in a—whatever it's called. I'm aware of you. Very aware of you and I have been since we met. And I'm not happy about it and now you tell me you've fallen for me. What the hell is that supposed to mean? Wait! Let me finish. I've had a relationship, typically Irish, I suppose, with Kevin Duffy for five years now. He's very different than you are but a fine man and it's easy, it's predictable, it's pleasant. I didn't want anybody coming into my life and upsetting anything. Certainly not Dan Conway who's going to drive the English out of Northern Ireland. It's upsetting and its scares me."

"Why?" he asked softly.

"You know damn well why. I'm attracted to you and you know it. God! Next thing my father will know it and—Oh! Lord! I forgot! Kevin's coming today. He's probably already here. We've got to get back."

She swung around and looked shoreward. "You've not got a long row ahead of you Mister Conway, but maybe it will use up your extra energy."

"Not all of it, Miss Dillon," he said. And he emphasized the Miss. "Not all of it."

He rowed them back at a fast steady pace that left a straight frothy wake of water behind them.

SEVENTEEN

THE DOG WAS LYING curled up in the noon sun, his tongue working on the wound on his leg. A bearded man crouched near him, watching him closely. The man stood up at their approach. His close cropped beard was augmented by a luxurious mustache that swept away from his nostrils in a graceful arc. He wore a well fitted checked shooting jacket with leather patches on the elbows. He was only a few inches taller than Kate, and only needed to dip his head a bit to kiss her on the cheek.

"My goodness, Katherine, what's happened to this poor animal?" he said after giving Dan a quick glance with a shift of his eyes. He did not acknowledge the three fish hanging from the line in Dan's hand.

"Oh, we think he got torn up by those terrible dogs that the O'Dwyer's keep. He seems to be all right now tho'. Oh, Kevin, this is Dan Conway. Dan. Kevin Duffy."

Dan reached out and was just barely able to grasp Duffy's hand, it was withdrawn so quickly.

"Nice to see you," Duffy said and then without pause, "Well, Katherine, I've good news from up North, they are very interested in doing the book."

"Oh, Kevin! That's wonderful. Just wonderful! Pa must be delighted. Did you tell him?"

"He's not here. I went inside. He must have gone to the village."

"Oh, he must be at Cronin's. Let's go tell him and have a celebrating drink."

"Good idea," Duffy said. "Let's do it."

"Just let me run inside and get out of this sweater," Kate said and reached and took the fish from Dan. "I'll put these in the fridge."

Dan bent over the dog and rubbed his head with one hand while he scrutinized the condition of the dog's cuts.

"Here for the fishing?" Duffy was lighting a pipe whose bowl was so highly polished it reflected the sunlight.

"Uh-hum," Dan grunted out as he rose from the dog.

"Where from?"

"Dublin area." Dan fiddled with the line on one of the rods.

"Oh, I would have guessed the North. I fancy myself rather good with accents. I usually only need a few words to catch the geography."

Dan turned and stared at Duffy for a moment. "Yes, some people have that ability. I grew up in the North, in Belfast. I moved to Dublin some years ago."

"I don't blame you. I've just come back—"

Kate's arrival cut Duffy's words short. She was wearing a plain navy blue colored dress with a heavy red belt and her hair was tied back with a thin red ribbon. Her leather sandals matched the warm color of her stockingless legs.

"Well, Katherine, it's good to see you out of jeans for a change. Shall we go?" Duffy took a couple of hesitant steps and stopped. "You'll join us won't you? Mister—ah—Conway."

"Dan Conway. Yes, I'd like that."

"Fine, fine," Duffy said and turned away.

Dan gave Kate a wink and she colored and turned her head quickly.

The car was an elegant old Mercedes, its woodwork as bright and keen as the bowl of Duffy's pipe. Dan got into the back and ran his palm over the worn leather seats.

Duffy spoke to Kate without taking his eyes from the gravel roadway. He talked of the editorial ideas that had been suggested regarding their joint effort at authorship. Dan let the conversation wash over unheard as he leaned back and savored the lively beauty of Kate Dillon as she responded to Duffy's information. She turned once and met his eyes as he watched her and quickly swiveled her head back to give her attention to Duffy, raising her chin as she did.

The Mercedes added one final category of transportation to Cronin's parking area on this Saturday afternoon. There were thin tired bicycles with rusted iron seats and no mud guards. Bicycles with sponge rubber seats. Two pony carts, one wagon drawn by a massive Percheron. A motor bike fallen over on its side. Two mud-caked pickup trucks, a dusty two door Ford and a couple of tractors each with flat-bed trailers holding metal milk cans.

A steady rumble of sound was capped by the cloud of smoke on the ceiling of Cronin's. Bits of wet clay and turf from the boots of the black suited farmers who lined the bar speckled the floor. Michael Dillon sat behind a smokey pipe watching two men play cribbage at the corner table. Dillon rose to his feet when he spotted them and for one awful moment Dan thought he was going to tip his cap to Kevin Duffy. The old man did, in fact, offer Duffy his chair which was accepted with a nod. The two cribbage players mumbled an excuse and squeezed up to the bar. Duffy looked around the room, which had become considerably quieter, and after fingertipping the sweep of his moustache he greeted the old man with a smile that allowed a brief look at the excellent white teeth beneath his moustache.

"You look very fit, Michael," he said.

"And yourself," said the old man. As he spoke Mrs. Cronin came around from behind the bar with her arms spread, her breasts swinging with her gait. She threw her arms around Kate and hugged her. Kate was almost lost in the woman's fullness and her delighted laughter caused the men in the bar to grin. Duffy watched the scene with a pained expression.

"Ah! Kate, my sweet," Mrs. Cronin crooned. "How's the sweetest girl in all of Ireland?" She stepped back from Kate and although holding her by the shoulders, her chest had just barely disengaged. "And don't you look grand! Just grand! Oh, it's nice to have you back."

"My goodness," Duffy muttered to Dan. "She's been gone a week—I wonder what would happen if she stayed away for a month."

Mrs. Cronin turned to the table. "And you've brought the gentry with ya today, eh? Well, we're honored Mister Duffy. But, I'll tell ya, I'd spend more time out here with this lovely, darlin' girl if I were you. The University's doin's can't be as important as that. Don't you agree big fella?" she said giving Dan a poke on the shoulder.

"I do," said Dan clearly.

Duffy gave a quick little cough. Mrs. Cronin shot a swift, shrewd glance at the obviously startled Kate and spoke quickly.

"Well, what's it to be? What'll you have?"

"By God! About time," Michael Dillon grumbled as they ordered.

Kate rushed into conversation with her father with the news of the book and Duffy turned to Dan.

"You said you were from the North."

"Originally, yes."

"Did you go to University in Belfast?"

"No. I didn't."

Duffy seemed to be waiting for something further to be said and when Dan merely looked around the room Duffy spoke again.

"Perhaps you know the Hammills of Strabane? Wonderful people. We have a shooting lodge near them in Connemara."

"It's been quite a while since I've been up North. I'm not involved with people up there."

"You're not interested in the politics up there?"

"Oh, no. No, I'm not."

"You're lucky to be out of the place, believe me. I went up there to see this publishing firm. They're very good and I don't know how because the climate up there is awful. The moral climate, I mean." He spoke across Dan to Michael Dillon, interrupting Kate's bubbling words.

"Listen to this, Michael. I was told they recently found a dead man in Belfast—an undercover Army officer—who had been killed by having his head bashed in by a crucifix. A crucifix! Can you believe that? Yes, Conway, you're well out of that place, believe me."

Two glassy eyed young men sat at a nearby table and one of them suddenly broke into song and was soon joined by his companion. They sang a rebel song, as old as the stones in Cronin's building.

"Hurrah for the men of the West," the two chanted, rocking their glasses on the table in time to the music.

Behind the bar Mrs. Cronin lifted her eyes, in dramatic fashion, heaven-ward and shook her head mournfully. Some of the Wellingtons in the room began to tap to the martial beat of the song. Dan could feel Kate's glance on him as he sipped his Guinness. Michael Dillon's watery eyes shifted focus to a faraway expression.

"By God, for once I agree with that woman," Duffy said, banging his whiskey glass down with an exasperated grunt. "Really, this thing is a farce. No disrespect to you, Michael, or your old comrades, but this thing is a cultural joke. Look at these people. The men of the West indeed! Take a look at them! And the pubs are full of them at every point of the compass in Ireland. Singing rebel songs, if they can remember the words. Enjoying their fuzzy alcoholic fantasies of driving the British out. Signs all over the North and now they're even down here. Brits out! Ha! Who's going to drive them out, this rabble? God, they'd have to lock the pubs first to get enough men under arms. And if the British Army did invade the country from the North, all they'd have to do is come down here before noon and they'd have the country taken over before the men of the West or South or wherever got out of bed."

Duffy shook his head and the four of them formed a somber island in the midst of the room's camaraderie.

"That's quite a speech," Dan said finally. "Have you heard it before, Michael?"

Dillon's face flamed.

"Have you?"

"Well, I know Kevin's feelings on this."

"And have you told him he's talking pure bullshit?"

Dillon shook his head. "Easy, Dan, easy," he murmured.

"Has anybody out here told him that?" Dan asked, completely ignoring Duffy's astonished stare.

Kate watched Dan anxiously in the momentary silence at the table.

"Well then, maybe he's right about the men of the West, but I'll tell you this, Mis-ter Duffy—" Dan turned and looked hard at the man. "You're sure as hell wrong about some of the other men of Ireland."

Eighteen

"The big fella got the squire upset, did he?" Mrs. Cronin spoke as though Dan was not there. Michael Dillon gave her a sour look.

"You want another one, Michael?" Dan asked. The old man nodded glumly.

"Oh, Michael Dillon, don't be silly," Mrs. Cronin said sharply. "Whatever got said here I'm sure won't disable Mr. Kevin Duffy. He's so pleased with himself he'll recover very quickly. You know he needs takin' down a peg or two. That whole Duffy clan does—with their big feelin' ways. Did you hear him bark at Kate on the way out. She won't put up with that I'll tell ya."

Dan waited till she was out of earshot before he spoke. "I guess I'd better plan to get out of here."

"Ah, Dan, I dunno what to say. I'm sure Kate will be upset, the way he stormed out of here with herself followin' him. Sure—she'll be upset. Mind ya, Dan, I don't blame ya one bit for settin' Kevin Duffy straight and myself too, for that matter. You were right, I've heard that talk of his many times and I've never said a word." He turned to Mrs. Cronin as she set two wet glasses of Guinness on the table. "Bring us a bottle of Paddy's, woman, and a couple of glasses."

"Oh," she said winking at Dan, "it's whiskey now, is it?"

Dillon ignored her. "Dan, are ya married? Ya know I know nothin' about ya except you're a leader in the organization and you've been drivin' the English wild for years—but I don't know if you're a family man or what."

"I'm not married, Michael, never have been." Mrs. Cronin set the whiskey and the glasses on the table and stared at the old man for a moment, then harrumphed away when he continued to ignore her.

"Never married, eh? Well then you don't know what it's like havin' a child—and with Kate 'n me it's pretty special. There's been just the two of us from the beginning. I've watched her grow and she's brought me nothin' but pleasure. It's quite a thing. She's the happy center of my life. I see the other young people around this part of the Bay—I know their parents and I can guess how many broken hearts there are—I watch them and know how tough it can be—but, Dan, Kate has never done anything but please me. Never a disappointment. So here she is with Kevin Duffy from one of the richest families in Cork, Dan. His people are big landowners—wealthy for generations. That's why things with the English don't bother him. He was born out of it. Probably thinks of himself more English than Irish despite being a Catholic. But, Dan, he's crazy about Kate. He's asked her to marry him for the last couple of years and she's fond of him and it would give her a marvelous life—money and servants and all—it would be a good thing for her." He finished his drink, poured himself another and added to Dan's glass. "So, Dan, that's why I don't tell Kevin Duffy that his ideas are bullshit—I want Kate to have the best, and the life that Duffy offers is a fine one, as fine as there is in this part of Ireland. So, I can listen to a lot of bullshit if it means a good life for Kate—ya understand?"

"I do, Michael, and that's another reason why I better clear out."

"Well, I told ya before, when the man in the grey Ford was lookin' for ya, that it would be up to Kate. I know you're only just here, and I know leavin' can be a problem with so many eyes lookin' for ya—but it's up to Kate. I wanted to help for old time's sake but," he wiped his mouth, "I mean I want to help for old time's sake but—" He drained his glass, staring at the last stubborn drops as they slid onto his tongue, then he spread his hands and shrugged.

Dan supplied the words for him. "You don't want anything to mess up Kate's life."

The late afternoon sun balanced on the far edge of the ocean. Its last effort seemed to polish the broad leaves of the palms and lacquer the petals of the buttercups they passed as they slowly walked up the ridge to the cottage.

They had shared the Paddy's with cronies of Michael's. Their talk had been in the tumbled, quick brogue of their forefathers. Dan did not bother to do the listening necessary to understand them for his thoughts were on the cottage on the hill. They stood now by the shed. The combination of the light and the whiskey bronzed Michael Dillon's features. He rocked briefly and reached out and held Dan's arm. "Dan, ya understand I'm with you, the organization has been a big thing in my life but when Kate tells you to leave—"

"All right, all right," Dan barked, "let's go in."

"We'll slip in the back door here, no need makin' a fuss in the front room," the old man said.

Kate stood at the stove stirring the contents of a frying pan. She wore a crisp white blouse and had changed back into jeans. She watched the two men arrange themselves in front of her and brushed her hair away from her face. "You were planning to slip upstairs for a little nap, Pa." It was a statement.

"I was."

"I think we better have a little chat before your nap." She peered at him closely. "Are you all right for a chat, Pa?" She looked questioningly at Dan who nodded and said, "I'll excuse myself."

"No," Kate said decisively, "you stay right here. The tea kettle's on the fire and I've cooked some odds and ends; we'll eat and talk. You can stand some food, Pa." She took her father's cap off and motioned him to a chair.

"I'll get the kettle," Dan said.

Neither man spoke as she slid dishes and bowls of potatoes, chicken and peas on the table. She set a platter of bread, cheese and jam in front of them and then abruptly sat down and propped her elbows on the table.

"Dan, things seem to be getting out of kilter in the short time you've been here. This is my first venture into Irish politics and I didn't think it would turn out to be like a thunderstorm on a summer's day, but it sure has. I think it's about time I know more about you than I do—"

"Katey," her father said carefully, "Dan is about to tell ya that he'll be leavin', so there's no hard feelins'."

"No hard feelings. Ha! That's wonderful! Does that mean you'll forgive us for any inconvenience we've caused you—that's marvelous, Pa. No hard feelings, well, I hope there'll be no hard feelings if I ask a couple of simple questions—O.K.?"

"O.K."

"Who are you and why are you here?"

"I'm a fella who was born in Ulster into a family that's been fighting to drive the English out of this country for generations—your father can give you chapter and verse sometime if you want."

"I could, I could," the old man mumbled with half closed eyes.

"I'm here because I'm hiding out from the British and their so-called government in the North and their bully boys. I was involved in that shootout with the British Army where they lost a helicopter and a number of troops."

Kate put her hands down flat on the table. "My God! That big gun battle? Everybody in Ireland knows about it—there were lots of soldiers killed."

"They were trying' to trap Dan, that's what they were doin'," her father chortled.

Kate blinked and looked curiously at Dan. "What do you expect from all this—what's supposed to happen?"

"The British government will give up their claim to Northern Ireland and their Army will leave."

"That might mean civil war," Kate said softly, "the whole country will be dragged in.''

"Maybe, maybe not, but whatever happens the decisions will be made by Irishmen deciding Ireland's fate.''

"And that's your whole life? The North-South thing—no everyday job—no family—that's all there is?'' Her voice was full of wonder.

"It has been up till now.''

Kate shook her head gently. The house was very still, the sound of the kitchen clock was clear. She took a deep breath and seemed to collect her thoughts. "Well, let's get on with this,'' her voice rose, "drink some tea, Pa, I want you to hear this; it won't take long because I'm going to walk over to church to confession. I want you to know what happened with Kevin after Ireland's saviour here put his money's worth in.''

"Should I leave?'' Dan asked.

"It's a little late for that,'' Kate said not unkindly. "Pa, Kevin says he wants a marriage date set right away—he wants no more foot dragging on that—and—he wants no more guiding or boarding fishermen here while I'm living here—he says it's unseemly—''

The old man rubbed his eyes with his knuckles then fumbled with his pipe.

"Well, Pa, what do you think?''

"As far as the fishin' goes, Kate, I hate to say it but I'm gettin' past it—I'm no good for doin' two days in a row and—''

"Oh, stop it, Pa. You'd even give up fishing for me, wouldn't you?'' She got up and went over and hugged her father. "It's no use, Pa. Kevin spoke tonight as though we were peasants and I was some barefoot girl out in the fields. I don't want you to be upset, Pa, I know how much you'd like me to carry the Duffy name, but not at that price—not at that price, we can't. So I told him that Dan Conway's word seemed the best one I could think to use.''

"What word?''

"Bullshit, Pa. I told Kevin he was talking bullshit.'' She rose quickly and took her jacket from the peg by the door. "I'm off now. I'm not planning to ask forgiveness for bad language though,'' she said with a smile that brightened the room. "Don't be upset, Pa,'' she added.

"Do you mind if I walk over that way and meet you after I clean up here?'' Dan asked. "We could have a Saturday night drink.''

Kate nodded. "All right.'' She looked at him from the doorway. "I suppose it's been a long time since you had a Saturday night confession, Mr. Conway.''

"A very long time indeed,'' Dan said.

Nineteen

Dan stood on the brow of the hill. A full, cream colored moon softened the landscape, rounding off the harsh ledges of the hills and dappling the water of the Bay; in the distance, where the ocean rolled into the Bay, the violent tossing waves of the rip were a faint fluffy white.

He could see the church clearly, the whitewashed stone and the gold crucifix fresh painted by the moonlight.

Kate Dillon walked out of the church yard and he watched her and he thought he would stand and watch her and let the full pleasure of his feeling for her run through him in the privacy of the night. He could stand and savor this distant view of her and still time her walk to meet her in the village. A swift sailing cloud covered the moon for a moment as a car moved slowly up the church road and stopped beside Kate. She bent her head to the window of the car. The moonlight returned brighter after the momentary gloom. The car was a grey Ford.

For an instant Dan's body was frozen by the panic that swept through him. He started to run. Words, thoughts, fear all mingled in his brain. He watched her open the passenger door and get in, and it was only great effort that kept him from shouting across the distance. Twice he fell but never took his eyes from the car as it turned and headed back toward the village, and when it reached the village he panicked again at losing sight of it, but then on the Bay road heading out of town he caught a glimpse of it, its lights retreating from him at a point near Cronin's. It gave him a moment of wonder and hope. The car was headed toward the end of the peninsula. He plunged off the path on an angle that would bring him to Cronin's parking lot. He stumbled often and fell—each time reassuring himself that his pistol was still in his jacket pocket.

He raced across a meadow and through the scrub pines that covered the ground behind Cronin's; he climbed a defile and stood absolutely winded at the far end of the parking lot.

Not many of Cronin's regulars had left; the pony still stood patiently. Dan took a deep breath, crouched and ran to the nearest vehicle, a pickup truck. The door opened, the keys were not there. Then he moved quickly to a sedan, the doors were locked. He yanked hard at them, wanting to pull them off in his frustration. He spotted the motor bike still lying on its side and he bent over it and felt along the side of the front post. His fingers touched a key and he grunted in relief.

He turned the key, raised the bike upright and twisted the handle as he ran beside the bike across the gravel. The engine sputtered and caught and as he hopped onto the seat he hoped his guess on the direction of the Ford was correct. For some puzzling reason the man had driven past Cronin's and out the Bay road toward the ocean. He would have to come back the same way, through the village and then on to Bantry if he wanted to get inland. Now, unless Dan had missed him or he knew a rough road that Dan did not know, he was putting himself at the end of the peninsula.

Dan's eyes watered as he put the bike at its maximum speed. The moonlight reflected on the crushed shells mixed in with the macadam and Dan decided not to use the bike's light. A curve caught him by surprise. He almost lost control of the front wheel and clenched his teeth as the rear wheel slid out on him with a nasty whine. Then he balanced himself and sped flat-out on a straight stretch that disappeared in a dark mass ahead; as he reached the darkness he reduced his speed which softened the staccato noise of the bike. The mass was a thick stand of pines on both sides of the road blocking out most of the moonlight. There was a sharp turn amidst this stretch. As he entered the turn he saw the taillights of a car intensified by its breaking ahead of him and he reached down and turned off the ignition, letting the bike's momentum carry him further through the dark green tunnel of pines.

Ahead of him the tail lights joggled as the car went off the road and stopped beside a weathered boat shack standing alone on a rocky promontory. The boards of the small building were streaked blonde by the moonlight.

Dan jumped off and ran alongside the bike, heading it off the road into the spongy ground beneath the pines. The front wheel twisted on him and he fell across the bike in a tangle. He lay still for a moment. He heard a car door slam and then the sound of Kate's voice, high and unnatural.

"Don't touch me!"

He scrambled to his feet, zigzagged through the pines and stopped on the edge of the darkness of the grove where it bounded the stony ledge of the headland. The car and the shack were only a few yards from him now. Kate stood with her back pressed against the car. A man who seemed as broad as he was tall was pulling on the door of the shack. A powerful flashlight was on the ground by his feet.

Dan put his hand in his pocket for his pistol; it was not there!

"Get in here," the man growled as Dan stood cursing himself. The fall over the bike! The pistol must be back by the bike—somewhere in the pine needles! The man reached out suddenly and grabbed Kate by the arm. Her gasp of pain went through Dan and all thought of going to look for the gun left him as the man flung Kate into the shack, grumbling a string of curses as he followed her.

Dan stepped out from the darkness into the moonglow which was now no longer a friend. He moved in a low cautious crouch looking closely at the ground; twice he stopped and picked up rocks, hefted them and rejected them, placing them down gently. He stopped again and went to all fours, reaching out along the ground with alternating hands. He found what he needed—a hunk of triangular stone, the heavy end worn smooth by the water. Holding the thin rough end made it the club he needed.

Kate screamed and the sound exploded in his head and it was difficult to restrain the urge to run headlong across the remaining ground and through the open door of the shack. Despite hearing muffled sounds he planted each step carefully and moved silently to the dark side of the shack. The unevenly joined boards gave him a good view of the interior which was brightly lit by the flashlight. Kate was pressed against the overturned hull of a sailboat, a dirty rag in her mouth. Her eyes were large green and white circles dominating her features. A short squat man with an oversized bald head was bent over, working a rope around her body. He spoke in a voice that had the rough edge of Belfast in it.

"Just shut up! You're not goin' to get hurt if ya shut up. We're going to use you for a trade for the fookin' wild animal you've been harborin' in your house."

Dan took two slow sure steps around the corner, bringing himself into the doorway. He gripped the stone hard in his hand. Kate saw him and started and cried out a muffled shout. The bald head came up as Dan rushed in. The man swore and reached inside his jacket. Dan swung the stone with all his strength, the man jerked his head away and the rock edge clipped his ear and the force of the blow hit with a thud where the man's short massive neck joined his shoulder. The blow knocked the man to his knees and in spite of its force he managed to pull a pistol from inside his jacket. Dan swung the rock at the man's gun hand and the pistol flew across the room. Dan hit the man a chopping blow on the side of his face, the stone club tearing the skin from the man's cheek in a rectangular strip. The blow knocked the man onto his side. Dan dove and snatched the gun, a black Smith and Wesson with an evil looking silencer snout on the muzzle. He pointed the pistol at the man and then lowered it when he saw him lying face down.

For some moments the sound of heavy breathing and the waves against the rocks nearby were loud in the room. Dan went to Kate and pulled the rag from her mouth. She bent her head and gagged and coughed, the muscles taut in her neck. Dan pulled the rope down off her arms. "Can you undo the rest?"

She nodded, still gagging and retching. Dan turned and watched the man struggle to a sitting position. His face was a large slab of beef with tiny red eyes that seemed to have no eyelids.

"Get up slowly and put your palms against the wall," Dan snapped. Kate stepped out of the coil of the rope and moved beside Dan. Without speaking she took his free hand and lifted it to her lips and kissed it.

She continued to hold Dan's hand as he spoke. "Lean against the wall—move your feet away from the wall. You know what I mean." Dan did not take his eyes off the man.

"Kate, pick up the flashlight," he ordered. He frisked the man—holding his coat open to reveal a shoulder holster. Dan reached into the man's hip pocket for his wallet which he flipped open and read quickly.

"Well, Mr. Harry Carson, come down to bring some of the exciting delights of Ulster to this part of the world, eh?"

"Fook you, you papist prick," the man growled out the words with his head bent between his outstretched arms. His cheek was steadily dripping blood onto the ground by his feet but Carson ignored it.

Kate watched the man with an expression of pure horror on her face.

"I heard you say trade, Mr. Carson, and it's not a bad idea. If you behave, I'm going to see if I can trade you for some comrades of mine in the North—that's if you behave."

"Fook you."

Kate hugged Dan. "Dan, he makes me feel unclean," she breathed. "What are we going to do?"

"You go outside now, just outside the door. Keep the light on us in here, then I'll bring him out. All right—turn around, Carson."

The man turned and his tiny eyes glared at Dan. "Conway, you won't get away from us whatever ya do—that busted nose of yours is goin' to be the death of you someday."

"Maybe someday, but not today Carson. Now move outside." Dan stepped back and stooped quickly, picked up the rope then shoved the man ahead of him out of the shack.

The clarity of the night was gone. The wind had risen and was driving a low black billowing line of clouds across the Bay. The pine grove rustled and creaked.

"Kate, see if the keys are in that car," Dan said.

"They're here, Dan."

"Good! Take them and open the trunk. Carson, get around to the back of the car."

"Go to hell!"

"Move!"

"Go to hell! You papist bastard!"

"Move!" Dan pushed him hard and felt the solid strength of the man.

"Fook you, Conway. Shoot me right here in front of your lady friend who thinks you're such a goddamn hero. You're going to do it someplace or other anyway—go ahead—do it here in front of her."

Kate stood stock still, holding her breath.

"I told you we'd trade you if you behave," Dan said. "Now move!" He shoved the man again. Kate stepped to Dan's side, hugging him for a moment. Carson spun around quickly so that Kate was between Dan and him and smashed into her using his head as a battering ram, plowing over the two of them, forcing Dan backwards, he fell heavily on his back with Kate on top of him. Her shoulder hit hard on his arm and his pistol hand snapped backward sending the gun clattering over the rocks.

Carson's bull strength carried him across Dan and Kate and his toes and knees jabbed Kate painfully as he scrambled over them after the sliding gun. The flashlight had tumbled to the ground and shone steadily out onto the beach, and now the skittering gun came to rest in its aimless beam. Like an obscene sea creature, Carson scuttled to the gun. Dan grabbed the flashlight and pressed the switch to off, hauling Kate to her feet at the same moment. "Run like hell with me," he cried, and holding tight to her hand he raced into the darkness to the pine grove. The first strange pop of the silencer sounded as they felt the rubbery pine needles beneath their feet.

Dan paused for a moment to get his bearings.

"Run as fast as you can, you son of a bitch, you won't outrun a bullet," Carson shouted.

Dan pulled Kate after him, again heading in what he thought was the direction of the motor bike. They could hear Carson slamming his way through the grove behind them. Dan turned his head once to look. Kate was trying to speak through her ragged breathing when suddenly Dan's leg slammed into the motorbike. He twisted on one leg and threw his arms around Kate.

He spoke in a rapid low voice. "Get across the road as fast as you can and head for home."

"I want to stay with you, Dan," she whispered.

"No, please do as I say, right now, don't argue—go!" He pushed her away from him. "Kate," he said swiftly, "remember this—I love you."

"Oh, Dan," she sobbed.

"Go," he said hoarsely and went down on all fours and felt around the bike for the pistol. He still held the flashlight and debated using it.

Kate crashed into something behind him. He heard the snap of Carson's pistol and the crack of impact on a nearby tree. Dan turned on the flashlight and heard Carson's grunt of surprise. He swept the ground with the light as the first shot kicked up dirt near the bike's front wheel. Dan saw his pistol next to the freshly scarred earth. He snatched the gun, flicked the safety off, set the shining flashlight on the ground and crawled away from the light as fast as possible. A branch snapped and Carson swore wickedly, "What the hell are you up to, you crazy bastard." He made no effort at stealth. Dan lay flat behind a tree and listened to Carson's approach to the light. Another loud pop was followed by the disintegration of the flashlight globe but amazingly the bulb did not break and continued to cast a pale flickering light, enough to outline Carson standing a few feet away.

Dan stretched his pistol arm out full-length and steadied it with his other hand.

"Here, Carson," he said.

Carson pumped a shot in the direction of Dan's voice and turned full-on toward him, his eyes gleaming.

Dan aimed carefully and in the last glimmering of the flashlight shot Harry Carson between the eyes.

Twenty

DAN BRACED HIS BACK against the front of the car and dug his heels into the rocky soil. He pushed the car the length of his body, hooking his elbows on the bumper to keep himself from falling flat-out. He went around the car to the tip of the ledge and, shielding his eyes from the rain, looked down at a foamy whiteness far below. His ears gave him a good idea of the distance.

He pushed at the trunk handle again to make sure Carson's body was secure, then he walked around to the front of the car again.

He was soaked. His hair was plastered to his forehead. Rivulets of water ran under his collar and down his back. And in a true mixture of oil and water, he was sweating. He bowed his head and put his shoulder to the car now and gave one intense push. The car rolled to the edge. The back wheels went over. It balanced for a second, then tipped backward and disappeared. He couldn't hear it hit.

It was a long, long walk to the cottage through the furious black night. The cloud cover was low and full of rain which came in surges, each one competing in intensity.

Near the top of the hill he caught sight of a light in the front room of the cottage—a patch of wavering gold that quickened his dragging feet.

He stepped into the cottage and the warmth of the room stopped him. The fireplace was bright with a full load of glowing peat. The dog lay curled in a perfect black circle. Dan moved close to the fire, leaned his head against the wall above the fireplace and closed his eyes. Slowly he raised his head as he realized that Kate's clothes were tossed on the easy chair. He stared at them and then moved softly across the room. The door to his room was ajar and the sound of even breathing came from within.

He moved the door a few inches to get into the room and the breathing stopped. For a moment there was no sound, only a brittle tension that filled the room.

"Dan?"

"Yes."

"Thank God! Thank God you're here. Are you all right?" Her footsteps were quick sounds in the room, then Kate Dillon threw her body against him. He put his arms around her, the smooth firm naked touch of her body surged through him like a current.

"Dan, you're soaked! Let's get you out of those clothes."

Dan stood unmoving, head down, overwhelmed by the wonder of this moment; total fatique from the night numbed him and left him humbly grateful as Kate unbuttoned his clothes and removed them piece by piece and he continued to stand motionless and speechless as she rubbed and warmed his body with a furry towel. Then she took his hand and led him to the bed. She slid in beside him and he shivered for a moment as he lay there and she rolled onto him and lay on top of him and warmed him with her body and her breath. Her small strong hands moved over his skin and kneaded it and massaged it and rubbed him gently. She put her mouth on his and they held one another and did not let go and then she moved her mouth from his and kissed him softly on the broken part of his nose, and the night was full of wonder for them, wonder they would never forget, ever—for the rest of their lives there would be no night like it.

Twenty-One

"Dan." She whispered his name so quietly that it might have been said inside his head. Her lips were against his neck and he thought she said his name again because he felt her lips move on his skin.

The heavy darkness of the night was being lightened by the first dawn. The sound of the rain was now only a desultory dripping on the window ledges.

"Dan."

He put a finger on her lips.

"Kate, my love, before you say a word I want you to nod your head to let me know you promise never to speak about last night. No questions. And try to have no thoughts. All right? It never happened. Promise?"

He did not move until she nodded her head and then he tilted her chin and stared at her, losing himself in the marvel of the experience.

"Dan, I've got to go upstairs before Pa wakes up."

He kissed her as she spoke.

"I'll make some breakfast for you," he said.

She smiled at him. "It's wonderful to have a cook in the house." She nibbled his ear then jumped out of bed, standing, staring down at him. He looked at the full rich beauty of her and his mouth was dry. He reached out for her.

"No, Sir! I am overwhelmed with all of this. If I get back in bed with you I don't know if I'd get out again. Even if my father came downstairs. I don't know what's come over me."

"It's called love, Kate."

"Is that what this is, Dan?"

"It is for me." He looked searchingly at her. "How about you?"

"I think it might be," she said and spun away from him. She closed the door quietly behind her.

Michael Dillon rubbed his hands and did a little dance shuffle on the linoleum. "Ah, now this is the way of kings. A grand breakfast like this every morning. Ya' know, Dan, my Cousin Allie, worked years ago at Bantry House. For Lord Bantry himself. Oh! She could tell ya stories. Allie could. She could tell ya stories. She's gone now, a'course. They're all gone. But, the stories she could tell ya of the meals."

"Eat, Pa," Kate said with a fond smile. "Eat or we'll be late for Mass. This quiche is delicious, Dan."

"Is that what ya call it? A quiche is it?" The old man looked at the food suspiciously.

Kate looked at Dan and they smiled at one another and without thought their hands touched under the table.

"Are ya comin' to Mass, Dan?" Michael asked with his attention focused on his food.

"No, I think not," Dan said.

Kate squeezed his hand under the table and he loved her for it.

The radio was playing a soft accompaniment to Michael Dillon's snoring when Dan came into the room. Kate put her book down quickly and looked a worried glance at him as she stood up.

"I had to make a phone call," he said to her unasked question. "Damn, it took forever." His face was somber and she felt the tension grow in her as she watched him.

Her father yawned and stretched and settled back in his chair. "Ah, they're not worth havin'. The telephone's nothin' but trouble, the damn things. And they do nothin' but carry gossip."

Kate grabbed her jacket.

"Want to walk?" she said to Dan.

He nodded and held the door for her.

After they left, the old man got out of his chair and went to the window and watched them. Kate held out her hand and Dan took it, and the old man shook his head. He turned from the window and sat heavily in his chair and stared at the crumbling peat embers.

Dan held tight to Kate's hand. He did not look at her as he spoke.

"Kate, I said I love you and I do. I've never said, or felt it, before." He took a deep breath. "I want to ask you to come with me."

Her nails bit into the palm of his hand. "Come with you? Where? What do you mean? You're leaving?"

"Yes, I've got to leave."

"Dan, you can't—not now—it's not fair."

"I've got to leave, Kate, most of all for you and your father's sake. I talked to the people in the North. I agreed to a project. They don't know it but it'll be my last one. That's why I feel I can ask you to come with me."

"I can't, Dan, I can't."

"Why? Is it Kevin Duffy?"

"Kevin Duffy! Don't talk nonsense. Do you think I'd be like this if I had strong feelings for Kevin Duffy? I feel as tho' it's a hundred years ago that I knew him. In some other life. I can't go with you. And where is 'it', anyway?"

"America."

"America. God Almighty! Why not China, that's even further from me. And my father."

"It's your father," he said quickly.

"Of course it is. I can't leave him, it would be barbaric—but of course, your people would know about barbaric things. Oh!" She clapped a hand over her mouth. "Oh, God! I'm sorry! I didn't mean that. I don't care about your people. I only care about you." She turned to him and flung her arms around his neck. "I love you, Dan. Don't leave me now. Not now! Not when we've just discovered this."

He could feel her tears as he bent to kiss her and suddenly he realized with astonishment that his eyes were flooding. They stood arms around one another, he lifted her up to him and they kissed, tasting the salt of their tears.

Dan set her down and stared at her, and when he spoke, it was very gently. "I'll go and I'll do what they've asked and I'll do it well and that will be it. I promise you."

"And, what do they ask?" Her voice was bitter.

"They want me to raise money. They think I should get out of Ireland for a while anyway, and they need money badly. They always do. So it's best, Kate. You could come and—"

"No, Dan. I'll be here if you want me. I'm hooked, like one of those poor damned fish. But, if you come back it must be to stay."

"I want us to get married, Kate, now."

"When you come back."

"Now!"

"Oh, no. When you come back. We'll talk to my father. Our life won't begin until you come back."

"I'm going to talk to your father now."

"Are you really?"

"I am, I want him to know. I respect him, I'm goin to tell him about our feelings."

She looked up at him and smiled through her tears. "You are a brave man, Dan Conway. I love you so much my heart is aching already with the thought of missing you."

Michael Dillon had the dog piled on his lap. Dan and Kate stood for some time watching as he stroked the dog and murmured to him. He did not look up at them.

Dan spoke and his voice sounded loud in the room.

"I'd like to speak to you, Michael."

"Ya know, this is a fine piece of surgery that was done on this dog," Michael said, examining the scar closely.

"I just asked Kate to go away with me," Dan said.

"A fine piece of sewin'," the old man said distantly.

"And she said no. But I'm comin' back here and I'd like to marry her when I return."

Michael Dillon looked up at him and his eyes were deep set in his head.

"And what did my daughter say to that?"

"She wants your permission."

"She doesn't have it." The old man's words were very soft.

"Pa," Kate breathed.

"I have not raised this girl to spend her days in the kind of life you live. I said I'd do one last thing for the organization, but I didn't intend to donate my daughter to the cause and I won't."

"I promised Kate I'll leave that life behind me when I come back."

"Can you do that? Just like that? You've been in the organization all your life."

"I can."

"Well you're a tough customer, Dan Conway. Maybe you can. But what will you do for a livin'? You've known nothin' but fightin'."

"I'd like to do the same thing you've done. I'd like to learn the fishing from you and how to work those scallop dredges and trap the lobsters. I'd like to live here on Bantry Bay with Kate and you." Kate hugged Dan fiercely as he finished.

"You know, Katey," the old man said, "I been tellin' ya that if I could just find a strong young fella' I could be back out there again earnin' a livin'."

"Well I'm your man, Michael Dillon. Is it settled?"

"I guess it is," Michael said, staring at Kate. "I guess it is if it's what Kate wants and if you're really done and through with the organization when you come back.

"If ya come back," he added, rubbing the dog's ears.

Part Two

Twenty-Two

SENATOR WILLIAM FRANCIS XAVIER BURKE (Dem., South Boston), Majority Leader of the Massachusetts Senate, known to everyone, except his wife, as Bucky, steadied himself against the front door that he had just carefully closed. He grunted with the effort as he bent to take off his shoes. "By God," he muttered, "if the kids see this, I'll never hear the end of it." Bucky Burke was drunk, not falling-down drunk, he'd never been that way, but wobbly, slurringly drunk, and he'd seldom been this way. Later he would be upset and contrite about it. He would make an extra visit or two to St. Bridget's to pray and think and remind himself to be careful and to remember to beware the curse of the Irish. But right now he was concerned about getting into bed quietly, without Mary or any of his seven children seeing him like this. It would be hard to get past Mary's vigilance; she was particularly alert when he spent time with the old man. In fact, he knew if he put his mind on it, he'd come face to face with the fact that the times he got wobbly were almost always the times he spent with the old man and his pals, and that accounted for Mary's vigilance.

Bucky Burke winced as he tiptoed up the stairs. He was a small square man with a round cherub face topped by short blond hair. Even now, at age forty-two, he still had the face of an innocent boy. His soft blue eyes looked out at the world without the slightest hint of shrewdness or cunning or guile, all of which he had in abundance. The reason he winced was that he had done something tonight that he knew would cause him to exercise a great deal of his shrewdness and cunning and guile. Tonight in a long rambling conversation with the old man, disjointed as they always seemed to be these last few years, he had promised—he couldn't believe it even now as he thought about it, and he knew that if he had trouble believing it now it would be torment on the sober businesslike tomorrow—he had promised that he would help an Irish political group raise money. "Well," he thought, wrinkling his forehead and unknowingly mumbling aloud, "put that way, it doesn't sound too bad. Let's try that again, helping an Irish political group raise money, and—let's see now, for aid to families of prisoners held illegally by the English—O.K." He would work on that theme and he knew he would need a story, a plausible story. He knew it because Bucky Burke was a complete politician. It was his blood, his breath, his life, equal to Mary and the kids and the old man and, of course, the church. Politics was his profession. He knew its savagery and his instincts were those of a survivor in this war that took no prisoners, the war that was Boston politics. He knew the newspapers might sniff around this Irish money raising thing. Raising money for Irish political matters was not spoken well of in Boston newspapers and Bucky thought he knew why and knew he would have to be careful. Bucky Burke was a careful man, a very careful man. He knew that was the only way to survive.

He was just as careful now as he folded his trousers, trimmed the creases and caught the cuffs inside the top drawer of the bureau. He was pleased with the way he was moving, sure-footed, silent,—stealthy would be the description, he thought, as he unfolded his pajamas which had been placed as always on the top right hand of the bureau. "Ah, like an Indian or a scout outwitting an Indian, that's what this is like," he mused as he inched his way toward the bed. Bucky Burke had never experienced military service, a fact that nagged at him whenever he was listing the mind-boggling number of clubs and associations he maintained. True, he was an honorary member of the Martin J. Doyle Post 1164, Veterans of Foreign Wars, but he was not a veteran. Yet he knew in his heart of hearts that he would have been a superb soldier.

It was Bucky Burke, Marine Raider, who slid soundlessly under the covers and let his breath seep silently into the small room. He could smell and feel the warmth of his wife and longed to move beside her, to fit himself into the familiar curves of her body, and sleep, but he knew that delicious bliss was fraught with peril. It meant the possibility of waking her and that meant conversation—which meant telling her about the Irish thing, the promise he'd made to the old man. Bucky Burke, Marine Raider, would sleep on his side of the bed tonight.

"Bill."

"Ummm."

"Bill."

"Ummmm."

"Oh, I see, you're supposed to be asleep now and I'm not supposed to be awake even after you bounce off the bureau and stagger around the room. I'm sorry, Senator, I can't buy your act. So what's your father trying to talk you into doing now, a no-show job in the Parks Department for one of his drunken pals?

Or is it another promotion for one of those nitwit cousins at the Public Works Department, something like the one that almost got you in trouble before?"

"No big deal, honey, let's go to sleep, we can talk in the morning."

"No, we can't talk in the morning with seven children racing around here. You know full well we can't talk in the morning. It'll be years before we can talk in the morning. We talk at night, and we'll talk right now."

"Aw, Mary, c'mon."

"Let's have it. What's the old man want this time?"

"Nothin' much really. He just talked a lot about the old country. He does that a lot lately."

His wife's voice softened. "I know, as he's gotten so feeble in the last year, Ireland seems very much on his mind." He sensed her pull the covers up around her and relax and he gave a thankful sigh. "Wait a minute," she said, "I must be getting feeble, too. Your father always wants something for some half-baked relative or pal. What was it this time, Senator?"

"Well, it wasn't anything really."

"Wow! the way you're fiddling around with this, it must be something really wacky. Alright, William, what is it?"

Burke squidged around in the bed; even in the darkness he could feel the implacable scrutiny of his wife. "As a matter of fact, all he asked was for me to help raise money for an Irish group—kind of a charity, really."

"Oh?" The tone told him he must go further than this with an explanation if he was going to get to sleep and stop the bed from its dizzying spins.

"Well, what he wanted was for me to help this group raise money."

"You said that," said Mary, biting the words. She was wide awake now. "What group is it?"

"It's a thing called Northern Irish Aid—or Irish Aid of the North or something."

"You mean Irish Irish?"

"Yes."

"You mean the old man wants you to lend your name to helping a group from Ireland raise money?"

"Yes."

"What's the money for?"

"Ah, for families of fellas that are illegally put in jail by the British."

"What do you mean, 'illegally'?"

"Well, there's some question about the legality of what the British are doing with people they pick up in this mess of a thing in Northern Ireland—they feel strongly that they're political prisoners and should be treated as such." He yawned saying, "Honey, I'm exhausted, let's have this talk tomorrow."

He sensed his wife slide up in the bed; even so, the light surprised him when it came on, and he shaded his eyes. When he lowered his hand, he met the steady open stare of his wife's grey eyes, her face reflecting concern. She used one elbow to prop herself; the outline of one of her heavy breasts bulged under the flannel nightgown she wore and as his mind selected and discarded items to use in the impending conversation Bucky Burke was aware, as he always was, of the sexual impact his wife made on him. She was prematurely grey and her hair framed a face of round rosy-cheeked sweetness that held no hint of the vigorous sexuality that had astonished, indeed startled him on their wedding night. Their marriage had brought more to them than they had expected and their hopes had been high. They let nothing threaten it. Mary Burke was the keystone on which the family stood. Her husband and children knew it and cherished her. For her husband, she was at various times lover, mother, debating opponent, financial partner, confidante and political consultant, and always, he knew, she was on his side. Seeing her concern now, he felt a tiny ripple of guilt but consoled himself with the thought that he didn't really *know* more than he'd said.

"Bill, this could be serious business, couldn't it?"

"How da ya mean, hon?" He rubbed a hand across his mouth.

"Well, I'm thinking of things like where does the money really go? I mean is this for these people that have been shooting people and blowing up things over there—is it or isn't it? Do you know?"

"The old man says it's for families who are hurtin' because the breadwinner is in the slammer. There were some people there tonight who work on this committee of theirs and they certainly seemed legitimate."

"Irish people?"

"Sure—our own. Catholics, certainly, some from St. Bridget's—all Irish-Americans, I suppose."

"Probably like me, mothers born in Poland," said Mary. She continued, "Were they from your district?"

"Some and some I'd never met before. Not political types like we know. A couple had brogues—greenhorns, come-overs, but they aren't wild-eyed kids. One old guy seemed to know the old man from over there."

"Bill, you know I always thought it was strange that with all the gabbin' your father does, he never talked about his being wanted by the English when he came over here. When was it? A year ago you learned about it—he mentions it now after not saying a word all those years."

"Yeah, and we wouldn't have known about it now if those cousins from Chicago hadn't appeared."

"Do you think this thing is on the level, Bill?"

"You mean, is the money going to go for family aid? Of course," he waved a hand majestically, "don't worry, honey."

"You don't think he's trying to get even for things that happened fifty years ago, do you?"

Burke ran a hand through his wiry hair. "Honey, I don't know. You know how he is, he talks a lot, but he doesn't say very much."

Mary Burke sighed and gave an exasperated half laugh. "I can't disagree with that, but, Bill . . ."

"Hon, I feel rotten, can we talk about this later?"

"Well, you smell rotten, so I can believe that you feel rotten. I don't want to win the nagging wife of the year award, so just tell me what happens next and I won't bother you any more tonight." She measured her words. "And I don't expect you to bother me."

He looked at her with his much practiced never-fail alter boy expression. "Yeah, well, there's a fella arriving tomorrow night from Ireland."

"Tomorrow night!"

"Yeh, I told the old man I'd have someone meet him. This guy represents the group that's raising the money."

"That's kind of strange that your father would give you such short notice on this thing. Why?"

"Hon, I don't know what's strange and what isn't. Right now—let's go to sleep. O.K.?" There was an edge of whining in Bucky's voice and he hated to hear it. Mary snapped the light off.

He grunted and turned on his side.

Twenty-Three

IN THE MORNING Bucky lay flat on his back for a long time. He squinted as he stared at the dimpled plaster marks on the ceiling.

"Well," he mused aloud as he finally swung his legs out of bed, "I can only go by what the old man says and in America money gets raised for all kinds of things." He sat on the edge of the bed and held his head with his hands. He sat half-hearing the busy morning sounds of the house. When his mind registered the last slam of a door, he got up and walked slowly down the hall to the bathroom.

When he stepped out of his pajamas, he looked down at his belly. He sighed as he pushed at it with his stubby fingers.

He sang a few bars of "Danny Boy" in the shower and wondered what shirt and tie Mary would have laid out for him. He thought about his day today at the State House. It pleased him—every day at the State House pleased him.

Bucky Burke's State House day started immediately after breakfast—at the curb at his front door where "Jabber" O'Rourke sat in a dusty, rumpled-fender Chevy and waited for "The Senator" to come out the door. "Jabber" O'Rourke's given name was Edward John, but only his mother, the Senator and the State Treasurer's Office where his checks were written, knew it. To everyone else in South Boston—across the state in fact—he was "Jabber," Senator Burke's shadow.

Jabber sat now, as he did every morning, a long cadaverous figure, with his bony knees up, snap-brim felt hat pushed back on his head revealing hair of a suspicious blonde color, a cigarette in his mouth. The car was murky with cigarette smoke. Jabber was reading the *New York Times*. He read the *Times* every morning. He despised the Boston newspaper. He made sure people knew he read the *Times* and had no respect for the Boston paper. Bucky Burke knew that Jabber devoured every word in the Boston paper every day, but try as he did, he seldom caught him reading it.

Jabber uncoiled and reached over and shoved open the passenger's door as the Senator came down the sidewalk. The morning sun caught him as he did and accentuated the pasty whiteness of Jabber's flesh. His face was thin and long like the rest of him—his chin had a fuzzy stubble which seemed neither to grow nor go away. "Good morning, Senator."

Bucky Burke settled carefully into the front seat and sighed heavily. "Once again, I know why you gave up the grape, Jab." O'Rourke grinned a death mask smile and lit another cigarette. He looked sideways at Burke who winked at him. They understood one another so well that sometimes their minds locked as they did now with the thought that Jabber had almost killed himself with drink and had started doing odd jobs for the Senator at the old man's behest. He and Bucky had been pals from childhood and since the day, some years ago, when Burke had casually asked, "Would you like to drive me tomorrow?" Jabber O'Rourke had not had a drink.

O'Rourke reached under the seat and handed the Boston paper to the Senator, handling it theatrically as he always did, "like a new father with his first diaper," Bucky once said. Burke unfolded the newspaper as the car pulled away from the curb. They were quickly in bumper to bumper traffic. Neither man spoke; Jabber smoked without letup, while the Senator worked through the paper, marking items to be followed up by his staff. He used a fat red pencil, a few of which always lay on the dashboard. Burke checked a name in the obituary section, marking in large figures "8 P.M." and the words "send note" by the picture.

"Mrs. Cleary died, Jab."

"Yeah, I heard. Will they wake her tonight?"

"Yeah, we'll go at eight."

"Stay for the Rosary?"

"Yeah, they've always been with us."

"For sure."

The car was inching up Beacon Street, getting closer to the State House, or what Jabber referred to as the "entertainment capital of Massachusetts." "Well," thought Burke, "the 'entertainment' is about to begin."

He watched as a portly police officer wearing a large white patch proclaiming him a member of the Capitol Police stood on the curb peering closely at the traffic as it nosed up the hill. The officer spotted the Chevy just as a smartly dressed Beacon Hill matron took her cue from the traffic light and began to cross the street. The police officer hitched up the trousers that sagged beneath his ballooning belly and moved into the middle of the street. He raised one hand, palm up, in front of the startled woman, stopping her movement, and with the other hand he beckoned eagerly at the Chevy to proceed, paying no attention to the red light in front of them or the outraged look from the would-be pedestrian. "Good morning to ya, Senator," he bellowed.

"By God," said Jabber, "there's a man that doesn't know the meaning of the word shame."

"Talk to him again, will you, Jab? He's such an embarrassment."

"I will, but I'd have better luck talking to General Hooker's horse there on the statue. With that pay raise bill comin' in this session, I'm surprised he doesn't throw his body under the car to make sure you get a softer ride."

As they turned the corner of the State House, another officer standing there did a slight pirouette and a kind of genuflection on seeing the car. Jabber gave him a big wink. The Senator's head was down, engrossed in his newspaper.

The parking area beside the State House featured much hollering, stomping and finger pointing on this morning as three men in various uniforms vied for the attention of the driver of a car pulled halfway into a parking space. Jabber squinted through the smoke of the butt that hung perilously from his lower lip. "Aha! They've caught some poor beknighted taxpayer trying to use the Legislators' parking lot."

"God help him," said Burke, bending over his newspaper again.

One of the uniformed trio spotted the Chevy. He spoke sharply and grabbed the shoulder of one of his companions. The three abandoned their attack on the misplaced driver and came to a ragged attention.

"By God, look at that," said Jabber. "Just like the Italian Army." As he spoke, one of the three performed a snappy salute. Burke, head down over the paper, glanced at the scene out of the corner of his eye. He groaned softly as the group let forth a volley of "Good morning, Senator"'s. The three men turned as though on command and in shambling, jerky movements ran to undo the chain strung in front of the parking space marked Majority Leader in bold black letters. This space was only less choice than the Senate President's space just beyond, and in the progression of chairs that was the Massachusetts Senate, this would be Bucky Burke's next parking place. "You know what, Senator?" said Jabber as they prepared to leave the car.

"What?"

"If we could hire just one more of these stiffs for this parking lot, we could hold practices and get 'em to look like the Notre Dame backfield when they run to undo the little chain across the parking spaces for the leaders of our democracy."

The Majority Leader burst into laughter and it was a smiling, relaxed Senator Burke who nodded and chatted and "hiya, pal"'d his way across the lot to the State House door which was opened for them by a short sad-faced man in trousers much too long for him who performed this duty as he had for some eighteen years, with a loud, contemptuous sniffing sound.

"Some of the boys were going to give 'the sniffer' handkerchiefs last Christmas. I always forget to ask if he got them," said Jabber, shaking his head as they waited for the painfully crippled elevator operator to push the button that would take them to Burke's third floor office.

"Jabber, I'd like you to find Ruth Klein," said Burke as he bounced along the corridor in his distinctive, up-on-his-toes walk. Earlier than the rest of the staff, they walked through his empty outer offices into the ornate Chamber of the Majority Leader of the Massachusetts Senate. As usual the Senator was just a little awed by his surroundings.

It was not hard for Jabber O'Rourke to find Ruth Klein. He moved briskly along the corridors and down the marble stairs, his extra high leather heels tapping out the announcement of his arrival. He had tossed his hat on an outer office desk and now his hands were busy combing and patting his yellow blonde hair as he clicked along to the large door marked Senate Library. He opened the door slowly, enjoying the luxurious feel of the large brass knob in his hand. The mingled smell of leather, paper and dust that was the unique perfume of this room surrounded him as he closed the door. He stood motionless, feeling the special calm of the place and then surprised, as he always was, by the rush of pleasure that went through him when he saw her.

Ruth Klein sat at her favorite table by the window which looked out on Boston Common. Books were scattered in front of the pad on which she wrote, and as Jabber stood watching, she raised her head to refer to a book page and the light from the window caught her face and outlined her aquiline profile to him. Her chestnut hair was piled atop her head and as he noted the graceful line that curved down her exceptionally long, slim neck, he thought as he had before of a picture he had seen of an ancient Egyptian queen whose imperious beauty stayed in his mind.

Ruth Klein heard his first steps and swung around in her chair. Her brown eyes widened at the sight of O'Rourke, her intensity softened into an open smile of welcome. "Jabber! Good morning."

"Hi, Ruthie! Who are you after this morning?" He pulled out a chair, making sure he did not look at her superb legs which he knew would be sheathed in silk stockings. Ruth Klein pursed her lips and wrinkled her forehead which contracted the pencil-fine lines of her eyebrows.

"Oh, Jabber, don't say that. It's not so much I'm after anyone. It's just that we want to make things better."

"We?"

"The Senator—me—all of us here—and you."

"Oh, sometimes I forget."

"Ahh, Jabber, you're a fraud. I know that deep down, behind that cynical exterior, there's a heart of pure gold."

"I wish I could bank on that," said O'Rourke, lighting a cigarette and flipping the burnt match toward the No Smoking sign.

Ruth Klein paused for a moment and then shuddered. "Jabber O'Rourke, that's the worst pun I've ever heard." She raised her eyes to the ceiling in mock exasperation, giving O'Rourke a chance to flick his eyes at what he liked to think of as her pyramidal breasts. They were covered by a silk blouse that gleamed as though freshly polished under the jacket of a severe grey tweed suit.

"What's happening today, Jabber?"

"Just another day in our crusade for good government. State employees' raise is getting ready for debate. Nobody will have the guts to oppose it. Those State and Municipal Unions have turned all these pols into quivering bowls of jelly."

"All of them, Jabber?"

O'Rourke took a deep drag on his cigarette and blew a series of perfect smoke rings. "Well, not all of them. The Senator will put his head on the block if he thinks something's right, but the rest of 'em don't have the balls of a nun."

Ruth Klein smiled and shook her head. "Jabber, sometimes I think I ought to forget about getting my doctorate and concentrate on recording the sayings of Jabber O'Rourke."

"Don't do that, Ruthie. They'd never sell."

"I'm not so sure; but tell me, what's today's agenda?" She looked at him straight-on.

Jabber knew he'd gotten as much casual time as Ruth allowed in her working day, so he stood up saying, "The Senator wants to talk with you."

Their walk back to the Senator's office was, for Jabber, a secret delight of pure golden pleasure. Ruth Klein stirred people's consciousness like a large stone dropped into a still, small pond. It was not possible to be unaware of her. The headturning of men and their looks of unalloyed admiration, women suddenly conscious of their posture or smoothing a rumpled skirt, all of these were part of the waves that rippled from her. None of this she ever appeared to notice. Jabber always felt taller and dashing when he walked with her.

Sitting behind the massive teak desk in the high-backed swivel chair, Bucky Burke looked like a misplaced schoolboy, but his tone on the telephone he held was strong with confidence and authority. "I can't accept that excuse. This office asked for that information ten days ago and we've gotten nothing but a run-around from you people." He paused, waved Ruth to a chair. "I want a written report on my desk before the end of business today or I'm going to shake that department up and that means at the top. You understand? O.K." He put the phone down quick and flat. "Good morning, Ruth. How are you today?"

"I'm fine, Senator, feeling much better than whoever that was on the phone."

Burke shook his head. "Every once in a while we should get a chance to fire the top third of every department just to remind these bureaucrats they work for the people—or at least they're supposed to."

"Indeed," said Ruth sitting at ease in her chair. She was relaxed and her smile reflected her pleasure in being in this place of power.

"Jab, how about getting coffee or tea? What'll you have, Ruth?"

"Still coffee."

"Can't change you into a tea drinker, eh?"

"Not yet. My instincts are becoming more Irish all the time, but not that much."

Burke's eyes followed O'Rourke as he left the room and his hands picked up a glass paperweight from the desk at the same time. "As a matter of fact, Ruth, it's something to do with Ireland that I want to talk about."

"Oh."

"Yeah, this is a kind of personal thing. Nothing to do with legislation at all. It's something I'd like you to do for me."

"I hope I can be helpful—I'll be glad to do anything."

Burke raised a hand. "No, better listen first. This is something for my father." Klein straightened in her chair and Burke smiled. "You and Mary make a good pair; just mention my old man and you both put out an all-points bulletin."

"I didn't mean to."

"I know, but remember, most things he asks for are for little people who need help, who can't help themselves."

Ruth Klein's face registered concern. "Senator, I think your father is one of the most interesting characters—people, I should say—I've ever met. You know I've told you he is the only Irish Irishman I've ever met and I'm fascinated with his brogue, but—"

He interrupted, "But you're afraid he'll get me in a jam sometime with his favors, I know, but you've learned by now favors are what this business is all about."

Jabber shouldered in the door with cups in hand. He placed them on the desk, gave an ironic bow and said, "I hope everything is satisfactory, Senator. The tea is from the finest crop brought down by elephant from high in the Himalayas free of charge by the Sheriff of Middlesex County who wants to add two more deputies to his fat budget—but at least they're relatives."

"Thanks, Jab. Have a chat with the Senate President's people and see if he and I can spend fifteen minutes or so sometime before I leave."

As O'Rourke closed the door Ruth Klein said, "I think he's marvelous."

Burke grinned at her. "I expect the feeling is mutual." Ruth gave no indication she had heard him. "Where were we?" said Burke as he concentrated on tilting back the big chair.

Ruth Klein spoke quietly. "I'm not sure, Senator, something about your father and Ireland, I think."

"Right. Yes, Ruth, I've agreed to lend a hand to raise money for a group called Irish Aid or Northern Irish Aid, something like that. It's to help families of Irish political prisoners in British prisons."

"I see."

Burke's chair came down and he reached for his paperweight again. "There's a man coming in on today's Aer Lingus flight. I told the old man I'd take care of putting this fellow up while he's here and help in this money raising thing they're doing."

"Who is this man, Senator?"

"Hell, I don't know anything about him other than his name—which is Conroy, I think, let me see." He took a small black notebook from his jacket and flipped the pages. "Ah, here it is. No—Conway is his name. Tall, busted nose, the old man says—Dan Conway."

"And this money is for the families of the men in British prisons?"

"That's right, Ruth."

"Then this is charity, not guns."

Bucky Burke leaned toward her. His words were clipped. "I've been assured it's charity." He looked intently at her and said, "What would you say if it were guns, Ruth?"

"Senator, you haven't forgotten I'm Jewish have you? We understand guns from both ends. From what I've read of the history of Ireland, I think I might be able to live with the idea of money for guns. In fact, it's always puzzled me," she paused.

"What has?"

"The Irish thing and the American Irish. Especially the politicians. They seem to want nothing to do with the Irish troubles, and as a Jew I find that hard to understand. You people don't seem to want to identify with it in any way. I always thought that if some of you did, things over there might get settled faster."

Burke was staring at the paperweight which she knew contained a shamrock magnified by the glass around it. "That's not the way your people operate, is it?" he said flatly.

"It certainly is not. Hitler taught us too well. We'll fight and scramble and bully if necessary for what's ours and Israel is ours and is going to stay that way. We want the world to know America is going to guarantee Israel's independence and continue to guarantee it if we have anything to say about it, and we'll punish any politician here who even wavers on that. And yet look at the difference in numbers—Irish Americans versus Jewish Americans. I don't want to sound macho, Senator, but either we Jews are a lot tougher than people ever gave us credit for, or you Irish aren't as tough as you like everyone to think. You ought to be looking for the same deal for Ireland."

"Hey! Wait a minute, Ruthie. What this comes down to is that like most Irish pols I'm not interested, or at least not much, in the mess in Ireland. It's been going on for hundreds of years. Who needs it?—I'm an American."

"But you like the songs and the sentiment, Senator, is that right?"

"Sort of, I suppose—anyway, I'd like you to meet this fellow, Conway, at the airport and take him to the Coolidge Hotel. The owner owes me a favor and he'll put him up for us, I think."

"I don't think I know the Coolidge," Ruth said with a frown.

"I'm not surprised," Burke said with a grin. "It's in the South End—guy named Meyer Levin owns it—give him a call and tell him it's for me."

"Another Irishman, eh, Senator?"

"Probably somebody else who wishes he was."

Twenty-Four

THE AER LINGUS PLANE was late. Ruth sat trying to read, glancing at the arrival screen every few pages. The room was clamorous with people, running children, a few priests, young and old women and men, none in stylish clothes. These were working people. A group of nuns sat near her, plump, round white faces, easily smiling. She looked over at them now and then, her head bent over her magazine, sometimes catching the quick glances they sent her way. They fascinated her and made her vaguely uncomfortable. She wasn't sure why. She studied them closer and realized what she was looking for—lines—there were no lines in their faces! The skin of the older women was as smooth as the children's playing nearby. Her mind fastened on this until she sensed the stir around her and realized the plane had arrived.

Dan Conway disliked uniforms and there were many of them in the large room where the passengers milled about claiming baggage or waited in surly lines for customs clearance. He had retrieved his pistol from the place on the plane where the mechanic member of the organization at Shannon Airport had hidden it. The gun felt large and heavy in his pocket as he stood watching the customs officer turn over the few things in his scuffed leather handbag and pat the plastic case carrying his navy blue suit. He walked out into the cavernous reception area and looked around. The room was festooned with unknown flags of garish colors. They were the only brightness inside the soaring reaches of concrete.

A handsome woman, tall and dark-eyed, with a sulky mouth was heading toward him. He noticed heads and eyes of people in the crowd followed her as she moved. She was tall enough to almost meet his eye-level as she stood before him.

"Mr. Conway?"

"Yes."

She offered her hand. "Welcome to America. I'm Ruth Klein from Senator Burke's office."

Conway juggled his baggage and shook the slim taut manicured hand. "How do ya do?"

"The Senator is sorry he couldn't be here himself and I'm afraid I couldn't locate his father today, but you'll be seeing them both tomorrow."

"Fine." His clear steady gaze told her nothing. She couldn't sense whether he was pleased or irritated with these circumstances. She wondered about his broken nose and as he turned his head to look at the crowd, the profile of his nose and his unruly black hair made her think of a hawk. She watched his eyes as they flicked over the crowd and wasn't sure if they were blue or grey. She realized with surprise that she was disconcerted. She swung on her heel and looked around the terminal. "Is there anyone else with you?"

"No, I'm alone."

"Well," she said turning to look at him and then shifting her gaze around him, "you'll want to get the rest of your baggage."

"This is it, Miss Klein."

She put her left hand in her jacket pocket. "My goodness, you travel light."

"It's that kind of life," he said flatly.

"Well, are there any other people here whom you want to contact now?"

"No. Malachi Burke's my contact and if I can get together with him tomorrow, we'll get things started."

Ruth Klein looked at him and her mouth slowly curved upward into an open smile that she covered with a hand.

"Malachi—did you say Malachi?"

"I did indeed," said Conway.

"You know, I've worked for the Senator for three years and I never knew his father's name was Malachi. No wonder he keeps it quiet—Malachi—I don't know that I've ever heard anybody—anybody alive that is—to have the name Malachi."

"Oh, we've lots of Malachi's in Ireland. I expect they'd send you a few if you're short of 'em here."

Ruth laughed. "I'm sorry, standing here gabbing—that's what you'd call it, isn't it?—anyway, my car is outside."

"All right."

They moved through the scattered crowd. She noticed Conway's head turn and his eyes move again over the people in the room. He stood on the curb a moment and braced his shoulders. Then with a slow turn of his head Dan looked at the airport complex, the spread of black macadam, the two massive glass topped towers of jumbled salty concrete.

"Quite a place," he said.

"You've never been to Boston before, Mr. Conway?"

"I've never been to America before," he said, gazing beyond her at the acres of parked cars.

"Oh, my, then I imagine this is exciting." She looked at him with a doubtful expression, "Well, at least it would be to a lot of people."

Conway stared at her for a moment and she felt that he was not aware of her. It did not happen to her often. His face was set and rigid but now the lines around his eyes crinkled and his mouth softened into a sad smile. "I like it fine, Miss Klein, and I appreciate your comin' out here ta meet me."

She was intrigued with his speech. It was not the rolling Irish brogue of Malachi Burke. Despite its masculine depth, it had a lightness and lilt she found delightful. As they walked between rows of cars, she glanced at Conway and saw that his eyes seemed never to cease their searching. "Where in Ireland do you come from, Mr. Conway?"

"Do ya know Ireland, Miss?"

"No, I've always wanted to go there. It's funny, I've traveled just about everywhere else but never managed Ireland, and yet if someone were to ask me where I'd like to go—what place I'd like to see—I'm sure I'd say Ireland."

"I hope you get there one day."

They had arrived at her car and she watched the Irishman closely. Ruth Klein drove a glossy, blue, two-seater Mercedes convertible. The leather seats reflected the fading daylight.

"I call this my 'Blue Beauty'," she said with a smile.

Conway got into the car without a change of expression, holding his luggage on his lap. Ruth settled into the driver's seat. She stared at Conway's luggage, then pushed herself out of the car and walked briskly around to the passenger side and opened the door.

"I'll put your bags in the trunk," she said crisply.

"Oh, it's not necessary, Miss."

She put a hand out for the bag. "Please," she said with an exasperated sigh. "It isn't necessary to ride with luggage in your lap."

"Of course," said Conway. He looked at her closely and handed her the bags.

Ruth Klein got back in the car; she sat still for a moment and then laughed briefly. "I'm sorry, that wasn't necessary. I'm just too taken with my car, I guess."

Dan looked at her with a puzzled expression.

"I mean, I'm kind of nuts about this car and seeing you sitting there with the luggage in your lap, like it was a—a—well—I—you understand?"

"No, I don't. I've always thought of cars as just things for carryin' people and things."

She stared at him. "Is that the Irish way of thinking? I mean, in Ireland?"

"Oh, I don't know about that." Dan glanced out the window, his gaze moved along the row of cars, and he continued to speak. "But I s'pose—yes it is—some Irishmen anyway. Ireland doesn't see anything like this for cars—so many—or so many big ones. And I guess you could say that we wouldn't spend money like this—on these things. But of course we haven't the money, so we're not tempted."

Ruth smiled, "You mean that even the Irish get tempted by things, Mr. Conway?"

"All sorts of things," Dan said quietly and his thoughts were of Kate and Bantry Bay as Ruth Klein rushed the blue car into the traffic.

Dusk was shading the city. Lights came on in patches across the mass of tall buildings Dan saw in front of them. Ruth drove in aggressive bursts punctuated by jolting stops, the car darting into openings and swerving just in time when they closed. From time to time she muttered or groaned, as she did now on seeing the mass of cars in front of a barrier of toll booths stretched across the road ahead of them. She twisted the wheel hard right and cut in front of a highly polished station wagon. The grey haired lady behind the wheel shook her fist at them and her mouth was busy. Ruth chuckled and as she did a low yellow two-door sedan with the fattest tires Dan had ever seen recklessly arrowed in front of the Mercedes.

"God damn him!" Ruth cried.

The Mercedes stalled.

A horn blared behind them, then another and another. Someone shouted. Ruth's head bent over the steering wheel as she twisted the key in the ignition. The engine started and they jerked up alongside a coin basket. Ruth's lacquered fingernails were an amber blur in the mustard light of the toll booths as she flipped in her coin. The engine roared for the few yards that she raced the car away from the gate until forced to slow down to join the two orderly lines of traffic entering a tunnel.

Ruth glanced briefly at Dan and said, "Well, Mr. Conway, what do you think of America so far?"

"I think it's a long, long way from Ireland," Dan said softly as he stared out the window at the soot-blackened walls of the tunnel.

Ruth Klein's voice interrupted Dan's thoughts as the car emerged from the tunnel. She spoke in a tentative manner. "As a matter of fact, Mr. Conway, I've been thinking—I gather you don't know a soul here. I wonder if you'd like to have dinner with me and my father. We have our weekly dinner tonight. You might enjoy him—and, as a matter of fact," she took her eyes from the road to look at him, "since you're here to raise money, he might give you some advice. I think he might be intrigued talking with you. I'd like to try to better understand the political situation in your country and my Dad loves that kind of talk. Almost as well as business, or golf. I know he'd enjoy it. It doesn't seem right for you to be alone on your first night in America. What do you think? Are you too tired from the flight?"

"No, I'm fine and I'd like to meet your father if it's not a bother."

"Good, that's settled. You'll have to wear a tie and jacket at the Ritz," she spoke more to herself than to him. "I think we'll pass up the Coolidge Hotel for the moment. You can shower and change at my apartment."

A few minutes later she swerved expertly out of the traffic to the curb, stopping beside a no-parking sign. A uniformed doorman hustled to the car from his post under a canopied entrance. "Evening, Miss Klein."

"Hi, Steve, we'll be no more than an hour."

"Yes, M'am." He opened the door for her and she went around to the trunk which she had opened by pushing a button in the driver's seat. "These go upstairs, Steve."

"It's no bother, Miss," said Conway firmly, "I'll take 'em." He reached in and took the rumpled leather bag and the plastic suit-holder. The doorman looked at Ruth and shrugged.

The floor and walls of the lobby of the apartment building were covered in a speckled off-white marble. A straight backed bench of thick black wood stood against one wall. There was no other furniture; a spotlight illuminated a small fountain that trickled noiselessly in the center of the room. A somber-faced man dressed in a brown uniform with yellow trim stood impassively by the elevator. He gave no indication of seeing them as their footsteps sounded through the cemetery-like stillness. They walked past him, and the man turned stiffly, followed Conway into the elevator and touched a small panel of numbers. The upward movement began without a sound. No one moved or spoke. Silently the car stopped and the doors slid open. Ruth Klein moved with regal grace into the corridor. Not a glance had been exchanged. Conway mumbled a "thanks" and followed Ruth down the corridor, his thoughts on the cottage on Bantry Bay so very far away.

Dan Conway had spent many hours at the movies. They were the best place to hide, even better than libraries. A movie theater allowed one to see and not be seen. During bombing and harassment campaigns in England when Scotland Yard constantly sought out Irish guerrillas, many of them were at the movies—hour after hour.

Ruth Klein's apartment made him think of movies he had seen: the floor covered with thick carpets that muffled sound, incomprehensible paintings in strong, solid colors on the wall, modern furniture alternating between grace and awkwardness. It was immaculate and there was a certain kind of smell, perhaps the smell of opulence, Dan thought.

Ruth tossed her coat onto a frothy white couch. "There's a guest room and bath down the hall on your left—towels should be fresh. Yell if they're not. Sometimes my maid has a terrible memory."

Conway digested this as he walked into the guest room that looked as though it had never seen a guest. The room was spotless. The bright blue cover on the bed was as flat and unwrinkled as a slab of wood. The heavy mahogany bureau had a lamp on it, nothing else. A trim, white bedside table held a slim rod of brass that Dan realized was a lamp. He placed his bag on the rug and gently laid the plastic suit-carrier on the bed. He turned and was surprised to see himself staring out from a gold edged mirror that reached from the floor to the ceiling. He moved up closer to the mirror and looked into his eyes. He stood, staring like this, not moving for a long time. Then he shook his head, fingered the break on his nose, turned away and stripped off his clothes.

The bathroom was yellow and blue tile and gleaming chrome. He ran his fingers over the frosted glass of the shower door, down to the series of fat, fluffy towels lined up along the railing on the door. The tile was smooth and solid under his bare feet. He spent some time figuring the mechanics of the shower, irritated until he finally managed a heavy fall of hot water. He stood with his head down under the pulsing stream. The heat of the water never faltered; from time to time he stepped away from it and lathered the clean smelling soap over and over all of his body, then he would step again under the spray and watch the hot water redden his pale skin. He knew he was staying too long but he didn't move.

Finally he got out, toweled himself dry, and opened his leather bag. The fishing sweater lay on top of his few belongings and he picked up the sweater and held it in his hands and lost himself in the feel of the texture. He stood motionless, unaware of his surroundings, his fingers running over the pattern of the sweater's stitch, his chest tight with thoughts of Kate. It was a physical effort for him to put down the sweater and regain time and place.

He shook his head and then slowly put on his white shirt, and navy blue trousers and shoes, then searched through the plastic carrier with dismay until he found the necktie which had fallen from the coat hanger. It was a blue and white flowered tie Jerry Regan had given him years ago on a trip to England. He stared at the tie and smoothed the fabric with his fingers. After he tied it, he stood and ran the palm of his hand up and down on the tie. He searched through the bag and took out a leather clip holster which he fitted onto his belt. He slid the pistol in and put on his suitcoat, then picked up his bags and walked rapidly back to the living room. He did not glance at the mirror.

Ruth Klein stood looking out of the massive window that was one wall of the living room. She turned her head and looked at him. She had changed into a long black dress that hugged the base of her slim neck; above the neckline she wore a choker of pearls. "All set?" she asked.

"Yes. I'm afraid I got a bit taken up with the shower."

"No problem, one of the best moments of any day for me is if I can stand here at this time and look out at the city." Her glance went to his bags. "The Senator arranged for you to stay at a place called the Coolidge Hotel. I checked it out and it really is quite grim. I think perhaps we'll leave your things here for the moment and see if we can't do a little better somehow—do you mind?"

"I'm pretty much your ward at the moment, Miss."

"Well I wouldn't put it that way, I don't think, but I would like you to do me a favor."

"Oh?"

"Will you please stop calling me Miss? My name is Ruth."

"Certainly—Ruth."

She smiled—a quick brightness against her dark skin. "And do you think I might call you by your first name? It's Dan, isn't it?"

"Yes, it is."

She stared at him with raised eyebrows. "Well?"

Conway looked at her and the moment verged on being awkward.

"Sure."

She gave an uncertain laugh and said, "Well, then, Dan, let's go out and meet Gus."

As they went out the door, he frowned at her. She smiled. "Ah," she said, "I know what you're wondering—who's Gus? Gus is my father and he'll be raising hell right about now because I'm late."

Dan took long strides to keep up with her pace to the elevator. She spoke over her shoulder. "But he knows that for some reason or other, I always seem to keep him waiting. My psychiatrist has a theory about it."

She paced back and forth in short spins as they waited for the elevator. When it reached the ground floor she rushed past the silent operator the instant the door opened wide enough. Her heels rapped a warning tattoo through the lifeless lobby that sent the doorman scurrying to her car. He got the door opened just a step ahead of her. She slid smoothly behind the wheel, swinging her long legs up and in with a motion that brought a delight to the doorman that his eyes made no effort to hide. Dan watched this as he twisted his long frame into the passenger seat. The rear wheels screamed as they pulled away from the curb.

Twenty-Five

BY THE TIME Ruth suddenly wheeled the car out of the lurching traffic, Dan's feet were braced against the car floor. She drove straight toward a parking lot sign that said FULL in bright red letters. She got out of the car, leaving it sitting across the sidewalk. The parking lot attendant was a slim red-cheeked man in a black cap and jacket. He walked slowly toward them, swinging a key chain.

"We're having dinner, Bunny," said Ruth. The man tipped a bored glance at Conway, running quickly down to Dan's scuffed shoes. His eyebrows raised just perceptibly.

"Dad's already here, Miss Klein," he said in an exaggerated voice that worked at being cultured. He held his hand out absentmindedly for the keys and bill that Ruth placed there. Ruth shook her head as they walked across the street toward the hotel. A coil of her hair turned copper in the bright streetlight.

"God! that Bunny is a snob. I hate people who act like that—don't you?"
"Yes."
"I mean, who the hell does he think he is? He acts like an English lord."
"He does indeed."

Ruth stopped short in front of the hotel's revolving door. "You know, Dan, that's just a phrase to me, but is that the way it is—I mean do they act like that?"

"To the Irish they do."
"Really! How you must hate it!"
"All my life."

She looked full into Dan's eyes as he pushed the revolving door for her. He followed her across the lobby and caught up with her as she went up a wide sweeping stairway. He sensed the eyes of people in the lobby following them and knew they weren't watching him. A formally dressed man stood at the top of the stairs, rubbing his fingers back and forth across one palm. His dark eyes widened in concern as they approached.

"Ah, Mizz Klein, your father iz upset—for more than one hour hees been here."

Ruth laid a hand on the man's arm. "Don't let him bully you, Eric, I've told you that."

"He doesn't bully me, miz, but you know you get him upset vaiting like dis." He waved a finger at her, "Your fadder iz a very important man, iz not nize for you alvays to be late."

Ruth shrugged off her coat as he spoke, draped it across the man's outstretched arm, and she stalked her way across the room. Dan watched the heads lift and turn to follow her, controlled by the eternal magnetism of a beautiful woman.

Eric hurried to hold Ruth's chair at the empty corner table. Dan settled himself and surveyed the room. He would remember this place. It was a long, high ceilinged room crowded with serious looking people. The noise level was muted. No harshness of sound or spirit would be allowed in a room such as this, he thought. His eyes followed the long, wide, floor-to-ceiling windows and then to the creamy white cupid-like figures playing silently on the soft blue of the ceiling above them. The table was laid with crisp linen. The silverware, solid and uncompromising, set like sentries beside the handsome imperious plates. A number of waiters moved purposefully around the tables, hovering for a moment, then quickly reaching to take or place china or glassware. Some were dressed in black jackets, some in white, and all their eyes focused on the tables, apparently unaware of the diners who ignored them.

Through the room now came the sound of music, light and cheerful above the murmur, played by a formally dressed white haired man at a grand piano set in the far corner of the room. None of the diners looked at the man.

Ruth Klein's voice caught Conway's attention. He looked at her and followed her gaze as she said, "Well, I suppose we have to put up with his little games." She was watching a swarthy, heavy set man sitting sideways on a chair pulled up makeshift fashion to a table where two couples were dining. The man was speaking rapidly, gesturing occasionally with a long cigar. His listeners did not touch the food on their plates; their eyes were fastened on him.

Ruth observed this scene for a short time and then crooked a finger at a waiter who hurried to the table. She looked at Conway, "Will you have a drink, Dan?"

"A bottle of beer would be nice."

"Beer? Is that what you want?"

"That's what I want."

"Bring Mr. Conway a beer and I'll have Dubonnet on the rocks."

The waiter bent closer to the table. He spoke to Conway, his manner very grave, "Will Heineken beer be all right, sir?"

Conway winked at the man. "Splendid."

The man turned to go and Ruth said to his back, "Waiter, ask my father if he'd like a drink." He nodded his head in acknowledgement of these instructions and spoke over his shoulder, "Yes, Miss Klein." He walked over to the man with the cigar who continued to control the attention of the table of diners—one lady was cautiously beginning to pick at her food. The waiter stood motionless for some time waiting for a pause in the man's conversation. Ruth watched this and then in a voice that carried said, "Forget him, waiter, bring us our drinks."

The waiter turned and as he did the seated man said something over his shoulder, nodded to his audience, got up and moved quickly to Ruth's table. He was dressed in a dark suit and tie; his body was muscular, seeming to be as wide as it was short. His black hair was flecked with patches of white which was the only lightness about him. His walk was heavy and aggressive; at each step he seemed to want to be reassured of the strength of the floor's construction. His dark eyes fastened on Conway as he moved toward the table, and Dan felt the man could give a good estimate of his age, height and weight in the time it took him to reach them.

"Well, well," he said, staring at Ruth. "The late Ruth Klein."

She ignored this. "Gus, I'd like you to meet Dan Conway from Ireland."

He continued to look at his daughter. "Why the hell can't you ever be on time with me." Now he looked at Conway. "My daughter, all kinds of degrees, the smartest girl in town they say, gonna get a Doctorate from Harvard, but she can't tell time." He waved his cigar. "Can you imagine?"

He took a backward step as Conway stood and looked at Dan in an awed manner and offered his hand. "By golly they feed you pretty good over there in Ireland." He gave a quick strong shake to Conway's hand, then looked at his daughter. She reached and took his hand in both of her hands and held it to her cheek. Her father rubbed her shoulder and his face crinkled into a glowing smile. The set mouth of the stolid waiter placing drinks on the table softened into a hint of a smile.

Conway and Gus Klein sat down and as he settled himself, Klein scowled. The darkness of his features increased. "There was a call for you, Ruthie."

She looked up at him over her drink. "Oh."

"Yes, and you know who it was."

Ruth spoke slowly with mock intensity. "No, Mister Klein, I don't know who it was."

Conway drank his beer undisturbed by the fact that these two people were completely unaware of him now.

Gus Klein turned his glass in small circles on the tablecloth and looked up at his daughter with a face that had lost its liveliness. "It was that goddamned newspaperman."

Ruth stiffened. "Bill?"

"Yes, Bill Hurley. I thought that was over, Ruth."

"He's going to get a divorce."

"Yeah, when? After he has somebody make double sure my finances are in good shape?"

"Daddy!"

"Never mind the Daddy stuff, Ruth. I understood you weren't going to see that sonofabitch anymore."

"Gus, we have a guest here at this table. We don't have to talk about this now."

"Ohh! no you don't—that's probably why we have a guest. I'm sorry, baby, we do have to talk about this now. I never get a chance to talk to you except at these dinners, and Hurley's going to meet you here."

"Oh." She turned to Conway. "I'm sorry about this, Dan."

"I expect you'd feel more comfortable if I went someplace else for a while," said Conway, pushing back his chair.

Guy Klein grabbed Dan's arm, not gently. "No, no, you stay, I can use an extra hand. If it's just the two of us, I get nowhere with her." He didn't look at Conway as he spoke but continued to stare at his daughter whose eyes were focused on her drink.

"Sweetheart, listen to me, will you? This guy's got six kids and a reputation of having the fastest zipper in the East. What do you want to get involved with him for?"

"Gus, please don't. Bill Hurley is a very bright man, one of the brightest I've ever known. I admit I'm fascinated by his position as the political editor of the paper. His column is referred to—and referred to a lot at the Kennedy school. His power is immense. He's advised Presidents and U.S. Senators and—"

"Yeah, on who they could go to bed with. Meanwhile, he writes those stuttering moralistic columns of his."

Ruth's face colored and she slammed her drink down. "Dad, I don't want to have this conversation with you. I asked Dan to join us because I thought you might want to talk about things in Ireland. You've mentioned that it fascinates you. Well here is a real live Irish political figure." She turned to Conway, "I guess that's right, isn't it?"

"No, it isn't," said Conway. "I'm not an Irish political figure—I'm just taking time to help the families of some of the people in prison, raising money to help these families get through rough times. But I'm not what you'd call a political figure."

"Well, to be doing what you are you must be in sympathy with them," said Ruth, keeping her attention on Conway and not looking at her father.

"Yes, I am in sympathy with them," he said softly.

"Oh hell." Gus Klein's voice was strong; he made no attempt to lower it. Conway and Ruth looked at him. He was not speaking to them. His gaze was directed at the room's entrance. Ruth turned and looked and then swung round in her chair with a bright smile at a man in a checkered tweed sport coat who was moving toward them, shaking hands, smiling, nodding, touching an occasional shoulder.

Just before the man arrived, Ruth said with intensity, not moving her head or altering her smile, "Now, Gus, puhleeze."

Bill Hurley shot a look at Conway as he bent down to kiss Ruth's cheek, and as he did Conway saw that the man was balding and combed the hair on the back of his head straight forward to cover as much of the baldness as possible.

"Hi, Ruth, I hope you don't mind my coming over. I came back early from Washington."

"I couldn't be more pleased," said Ruth, glancing at her father. "Oh, I'm sorry, Dan—Bill, this is Dan Conway from Ireland—Bill Hurley."

Hurley put a hand on Dan's shoulder. "Don't get up—nice to meet you—from Ireland, huh?"

"Yes," said Conway.

"And, Bill, you know my father," said Ruth.

"Sure, we've met a number of times. Last time I guess was at the ceremony when one of your companies finished building the American Insurance Company building. What a building! Nice to see you again, Mr. Klein."

"Hello, Hurley. How's the family?" Gus Klein said as he watched the flame work on the end of a fresh cigar he held in his hand.

Hurley flushed; the color ran up to his receding hairline. "The kids are fine, thanks."

Ruth's lips were pressed tight. She broke the moment of silence. "We haven't ordered yet, Bill, will you have a drink?"

"I would love a nice, dry, Martini," he said, rubbing his hands and smiling up at the waiter.

"Another beer, Dan?" asked Ruth.

"Please," said Conway.

"Bring me another," growled Gus.

"Well, Conway, what brings you to Boston?" asked Hurley.

"I'm here to try and raise a bit of money for the families of political prisoners in Ireland."

"Oh, really? Which prisoners are those?"

"People the British have put away for talkin' or actin' for one Ireland, breadwinners most of 'em—or at least they attempt to be breadwinners—when they're not bein' questioned or harassed by soldiers or police. When the British lock 'em up, their families have a tough time."

Hurley interrupted, "You mean like people in the Maze in Long Kesh Prison in Belfast—the fellows that don't wear clothes or wash?"

"Yes, that's been one of their forms of protest," said Conway.

"What's the point of that?" asked Gus.

"These men consider themselves political prisoners and they want the rights of political prisoners," said Conway.

"You mean like prisoners of war?" Klein asked frowning.

"That's right," answered Conway.

"But they're terrorists, plain and simple," said Hurley. "They've been bombing and shooting and raising general hell against the British for years. What do they expect?" he added with a shrug.

"Christ, you're Irish aren't you, Hurley?" asked Gus Klein thrusting his head forward.

"My grandmother came from Ireland, as a matter of fact," said Hurley, "but I think of myself only as American. I never was very much taken with that hyphenated American stuff."

"I imagine you lost that at Harvard, didn't you?" said Klein, blowing a large cloud of smoke toward one of the cupids high above on the ceiling.

"I suppose I did," said Hurley, sipping his drink.

"So you're not much interested in Ireland's problems then, eh, Hurley?"

"Not really."

"Not even as a newspaperman?" asked Ruth.

"Yes, in that sense I am but, of course, we Americans like problems that have some kind of solution." He turned to Conway. "I mean there really isn't any solution to your thing is there?"

"There's one that comes to mind," said Dan, looking up from pouring beer into his glass.

"What's that?" asked Hurley.

"The British could get out of our country."

"Hey, my friend," said Hurley leaning back in his chair, "that would mean a hell of a mess in Ireland if the British Army moved out—probably civil war, I've heard. We sent a couple of people to cover the story over there last year, but, hell, there's no romance in any of it. Frankly, it's boring to readers here. Some bishop over there said it, 'little people from the little unlovely streets,' and too many troublemakers. England's a marvelous country, Conway. You people ought to imitate them, not fight 'em."

Dan started to speak but Gus Klein's voice cut across his, sharp and quick. "Do ya think we Jews ought to become Arabs, too, Hurley?"

Hurley laughed, "Of course not, Gus,—do you mind if I call you Gus? The

Jewish-Arab thing or Israeli-Arab thing is a hell of a lot different than this Irish business."

"How so, Bill?" Ruth asked quickly, forestalling whatever her father was about to say.

"Well, it's certainly more clearly defined. The Irish thing is so muddled. I mean, after all, the English have been in the North of Ireland for generations."

"What the hell—" snapped Gus.

"Excuse me, everyone," said Ruth, "why don't we order?"

"Swell," said Hurley, "I would like another one of these, though," he said pointing at his empty glass.

"The chef has prepared a special veal dish for Mr. Klein," intoned the waiter, holding his pencil at the ready.

Gus grunted in satisfaction through his cigar, "Why don't we all try that."

"The chef really works to please Gus," Ruth said. "I think it might be because of the rumor that you were going to buy this place. Would the veal be all right with you, Dan?"

"That's fine with me, Ruth," he said, feeling Hurley's eyes on him.

"Me too," said Hurley. "Conway, since you're here with Ruth, am I to assume that Bucky Burke is sponsoring this visit?"

"No, he's not, but he has been kind enough to offer me a hand while I'm here."

"Quite a fellow Bucky, don't you think?" said Hurley.

"I haven't met him yet," said Conway.

"It is money for families you're collecting, is that right?" Hurley peered closely at Dan through Gus Klein's cigar smoke.

Conway looked calmly at the newspaperman. Hurley's lips were large and rubbery, his mouth very mobile. He was smiling now. He was a man who smiled often, but his eyes, above the tired pouches, glinted hard and steady.

"Yes, it is. We have some families that have become favorites of the British security people and they—"

"What's that mean?" interrupted Gus.

"Well, over the years the security people seem to work on certain families and before they get through they've got most of 'em in prisons for political reasons. There's an area in Belfast called the Short Strand—I suppose the street is half a mile long. It runs along the River Lagan—twenty-five hundred people, families live there. It's a Catholic ghetto, most of the men out of work and their fathers before 'em. The security people—the Royal Ulster Constabulary, the British Army—they're in there constantly, searching, interrogating, shaking people down day and night. They haunt some houses. We've had cases where in the last twenty years the third generation of the same family has been imprisoned for political reasons. Right now, of those twenty-five hundred people, over sixty are in prison as political prisoners—and that's men, women, girls and boys. Those of their families left outside are often old or sick, or—" Dan's voice trailed off.

"Or just overwhelmed, I imagine," Ruth finished his sentence. "So they arrest a father and enrage a son or daughter who becomes political even if they weren't, is that it Dan?"

"Yes."

Ruth turned to her father. "Gus, it's the same thing with the Palestinians. I know you don't like me to say it, but Israel's doing the same thing with every Palestinian baby who grows up being told they can't have a homeland—it's a vicious circle."

Gus Klein worked his cigar around in his mouth. As usual he made no effort to moderate the strength of his voice. "Ruth, the Jewish people and the land of Israel are one, just like the Irish own their own island. It's their land, for Christ's sake. Isn't that what you people believe, Dan?"

"It is," said Conway quietly.

"What is the name of your group, Conway? Not the IRA or the Provos, I'm sure," said Hurley with a laugh.

"That's right, we're strictly helpin' the families—our group is called Aid for Northern Ireland," Dan said.

"Are you from Belfast yourself?"

Dan cut a triangle of veal, put his knife down slowly and raised the meat to his mouth to find Hurley watching him expectantly. "Oh no, I'm from outside Strabane, a good way from Belfast."

Hurley pressed on, "How did you happen to get involved in this business?"

"What do you mean?" asked Conway.

"Well you say you're just raising money for families, but even that is political action of a sort. How'd you get started in this. That might make a good story."

Conway had food in his mouth and he looked closely at Hurley as he chewed and swallowed. "I'd prefer not to get involved with newspaper interviews," he said. "I'm not a political person."

"Well, why—" began Hurley.

"For Christ's sake, Hurley, this fellow is here as our dinner guest. He doesn't have to be interrogated by the press if he doesn't want to," Gus said, putting down his knife and fork. "Goddamn. You guys never quit. How about another beer, Dan?"

Dan nodded and Gus made a circular motion to the waiter indicating another round, and as he did Hurley gave a little chuckle. "I suppose you know the joke about the Irishman's seven course dinner, don't you?" he asked, looking at Dan who stared blankly at him.

"No," Dan said.

"You know it, don't you, Ruth?" he queried, and when she frowned at him he smiled and continued. "Well, no hard feelings—I think you'll get a kick out of it, Conway. A seven course dinner for an Irishman is a six-pack and a potato." He grinned expectantly around the table. No one smiled. Ruth's color heightened and Gus Klein was staring at him and shaking his head. Hurley looked at Dan who had his glass at his mouth.

"Well, what the hell—I don't think I'm out of order with that story. I told you I've got Irish roots myself, and let's face it, the world laughs at the Irish weakness for drink. They say Ireland spends more on booze than on health care. It's a kind of national disgrace—it's no secret. It's a shame, and especially the men with their drinking. I'm sure you're aware of the problem, Conway. It's a shame," he repeated, his voice trailed off and he took a long swallow of his Martini.

"Jeezus," muttered Gus Klein, but Dan's voice rode over his words.

"Maybe it's caused by a greater shame, Hurley."

"What's that?"

"The shame of livin' under a foreign country's heel for hundreds of years, of bein' disgraced in front of our women, of losin' our language, our land, our pride. Maybe that's why the Irish drink."

Gus Klein's eyes were riveted on Dan and his mouth set in a grim smile.

Hurley moved his glass back and forth on the stiff tablecloth and spoke into the growing silence. "I thought you weren't political, Mr. Conway."

Ruth Klein spoke quickly. "What's happening in our nation's capital, Bill?"

This question to Hurley was like throwing a baseball directly over the middle of the plate to a superb hitter—Hurley socked it. He spoke of senators, ambassadors, congressmen, the Speaker, the President, first names, last names, nicknames; pending bills, due bills, dead bills, foreign affairs, personal affairs; the information, the gossip, the informed guesses were sprayed around the table. It was a masterful performance.

Conway noticed Gus nod once or twice and then shake his head just a trifle as though admonishing himself.

Ruth Klein interjected shrewd questions and comments that seemed to inspire Hurley to further revelations. Gus Klein caught Conway's eye and then looked from Hurley to his delighted daughter and rolled his eyes up toward the ever-watching cupids.

"Where are you staying, Dan?" Gus asked as he finished his coffee and rubbed a large crisp linen napkin across his mouth in a rough gesture. His voice cut through Hurley's words. The question brought the newsman to a halt in the middle of a story about the Iranian Ambassador and he glanced around the table with an irritated pursing of his lips.

Conway looked at Ruth. "I'm afraid I can't remember the name of that hotel. I know it's one of your Presidents."

Gus looked blankly at Ruth who groaned and said, "It's the Coolidge, Gus."

"What!! That dump that Meyer Levin owns? That's a hell of a way to show him America. We can do better than that—hell, you've got the guest room at your place."

"Of course—that's not a bad idea," Ruth said.

Hurley looked fast and hard at Gus and then into his coffee cup. "Would you mind staying in the guest room, Dan?" asked Ruth.

"I think that would be an inconvenience."

"Certainly not. I've an extra key and you can come and go as you please."

"Well, I—" Dan began.

"No, it's settled, Dan. She wouldn't say it if she didn't mean it," said Gus, and his face lightened with the flash of a wide grin.

Hurley got up from his chair and watched Gus Klein sign the check with a sweeping movement of his pen. From across the table one could see that his signature, a comment and the addition of a tip were a scrawl that covered the entire face of the paper.

"Can I buy a nightcap downstairs?" offered Hurley.

"Not for me," said Gus. "I've got to make an honest living in the morning."

"I hope you'll excuse me," said Conway. "Would you have that extra key with you, Ruth?"

"I forget you're just in from Ireland," said Ruth. "You must be exhausted."

They stood by the table as they talked. Heads turned to watch them. "I'll go along with you," she said.

"No, please stay and have some time with your friend."

Ruth dug in her purse and after sifting through a jumble of items she handed Conway a key. "Well, I'm going to have a drink with Bill. Gus can drop you off, can't you, Gus?" she said mischievously.

"Let's go, Dan," said her father.

Ruth took a long step to her father's side and bent and kissed him on the cheek. He looked up at his daughter, the corner of his lips turned into the beginning of a smile and he shook his head and hugged her, then turned and wended his forceful way out of the room, carelessly acknowledging some of the respectful nods and waves sent his way.

Twenty-Six

DAN STOOD QUIETLY on the sidewalk in front of the hotel, watching while Klein paced back and forth, occasionally pounding a fist into his palm.

"Goddamn, I don't like that guy, Dan. I just don't feel good about him." He paced away from Conway and then spun around and blurted out the question. "Do you think my daughter's in love with that son of a bitch?" He looked closely at Dan who was watching a long grey car pull up at the curb. A soft interior light showed the polished leather upholstery and a uniformed black chauffeur behind the wheel.

"My car," said Klein brusquely. "Well, what do you think? You haven't answered me."

"Mr. Klein."

"Make it Gus, will ya?"

"Gus, I met your daughter some hours ago. I've never been in America before; I'm not the man to be making judgments."

Klein interrupted him, "Don't worry about it, we do it here all the time. I want to know what you think."

Conway grinned. "I don't think she's in love with him."

"Ya don't, huh? Good." He turned and opened the back door and got in. Conway stooped and followed him.

"Stop at my daughter's first," he barked at the driver and then for the first time that evening he lowered his voice. "I don't believe a word of that bullshit about raising money to help families of people in prison and I want you to know that."

He stared hard at Dan. Dan gazed straight at him but did not speak. Klein continued to watch him closely; he spoke again. "I just don't want you to think

I'm a goddamn dummy, O.K.?'' Conway shrugged. "Alright, you're smart,'' growled Gus, "say nothin', but I like you and I'm gonna help you.'' He looked out the window, his voice still low, and continued. "I don't like that kind of stuff, never did, people gettin' pushed around by other people. It's never gonna happen to our people again. I'll tell ya that. That's why I'll help. I want people to respect what we want for Israel and I respect what you said up there about getting the English out of your country—that makes sense. But for Christ's sake, why are the Irish here embarrassed about it? I can't understand it. We're not. Let's say we want X millions for bonds for Israel. We say it out loud and we raise the dough publicly. What Israel buys with the money—well what the hell do people think Israel does with the money—buy cotton candy—ha?'' He leaned close to Conway, close enough so that Conway could see flecks of cigar tobacco on the corner of his mouth. "Dan, tomorrow night there's a cocktail party for heavy hitters for Israel.'' He put his hand on Conway's shoulder. "Believe me, heavy hitters. It's at 6:30 at the Harbor Club, right on top of the city's biggest bank. You see, we're not bashful. You come tomorrow. Ruth'll bring you. I'll call her. We'll put some money in your hands, cash, and you take it back to Ireland and use it the best way you know how.''

The car stopped and Klein looked out the window. His voice rose to its natural harsh strength. "We're here.'' Then he bent his head and spoke quietly again: "One thing I want to ask you, what do you think is going to happen in Ireland?''

Dan's voice sounded gentle after Klein's rasp. "We're going to keep the pressure on the British in every way and drive them out.''

Klein nodded once, his eyes fixed on Conway's face. "I figured you right. Will it be soon?''

"I wish I knew—I hope so and I expect it—but, remember, we've been workin' on it for over four hundred years.''

"Yeah, yeah.'' He shook his head. "Well goodnight, Dan.''

"It's been a pleasure to meet you and Ruth,'' said Dan, "and thanks for a fine meal. I'll see you tomorrow evening.''

Conway stood and watched the red taillights of the car until they were obscured by the traffic. The night was chilly with wind that blew in dirty gusts. Bits of paper swirled round his feet. He was surprised by the morning-after look of the sidewalks and the city streets, but even more the lights—lights everywhere. No one seemed to bother to turn out the lights in America. A siren sounded harshly somewhere close by.

He watched the uneven march of cars. Horns hammered at the night. He turned his back on this and walked quickly through the antiseptic lobby. The ritual of the elevator was unchanged. This time Dan's "thanks'' was louder but the response was just as silent.

After fitting the key in the lock and closing the apartment door behind him, he headed at once for the shower. He set the water temperature as hot as his hand could stand, then hotter, and when he stood under the jets of water, he let his mind run as free as the water that bounced and streamed from his body. He thought of Kate and he reveled in the pleasure of having no other thought. Nothing else impinged, just Kate—all of Kate—everything about her and of them together and how he missed her. He placed the palms of his hands against the warm, moist tile of the walls and lowered his head between his outstretched arms and thought of her and wanted her as the water pounded on him. He ached with this want, all through his body, from the deepest reaches inside him to the nerve ends on the edge of his skin. Now with his eyes squeezed shut he could see her and feel her. The burning water cooled his body and his mind.

He toweled himself quickly. He did not want to be further aware of his body. He turned off the light and the faint golden haze of the city's lights glowing through the windows kept the room from total darkness. He slipped under the covers and for an instant his body tensed. The sheets were silk. The luxurious feel of them against his nude body astonished him and he lay staring wide-eyed at the light and shadows on the ceiling. Then he turned over on his stomach and stretched out, his arms pushing the pillow from him. He lay still for a long time, then just before sleep he remembered. He got out of bed, poked through his clothes for a moment and got back in bed. He put his pistol under the pillow and went to sleep.

Twenty-Seven

The sounds from the kitchen woke Ruth Klein and she knew at once she'd overslept and turned and looked at the square gold clock on the night table. It wasn't the maid—she wouldn't dare make noise. Then she remembered Conway. She stretched and swung her feet out and down into her slippers, sitting up as she did. She remained sitting on the edge of the bed for some time, staring at her feet, then rose and with no wasted motion prepared herself for the day. She wore a silk print dress that shimmered and whispered as she walked into the kitchen.

"Good morning, Dan."

"Good morning."

"Oh, Dan, I am disappointed."

"What is it?"

"I expected to hear you say, 'the top of the mornin'' to ya.' Isn't that what people say in Ireland?"

"Indeed," Dan said nodding, "it's still often said."

"Ahh, good, then I can still believe in something." She looked past him at the stove. "What are you up to?"

"Just boilin' some water for tea that I found in the ice box—will you have some?"

"Not hard to find things in that refrigerator, is it?" She walked out to the hallway, still talking. "Well, I tell myself, I'm just not a kitchen person, but I'd love a cup of coffee. I'll get the morning paper in the hall and then make a couple of phone calls and be right back."

Ruth folded the newspaper and tossed it on the table. She picked up her coffee cup and leaned against the counter, watching Dan over the rim of her cup.

He leafed through the paper and sipped his tea. For a few minutes there was no sound in the all-white kitchen.

Ruth cleared her throat. "Umm, Dan?"

"Yes."

"How did you like Bill Hurley?" She put her cup down and walked over beside the table. "You know, he's a very powerful and influential man."

"So I gathered."

"Not just here in Boston, but nationally. He's one of the bosses of the biggest paper in New England and his column makes or breaks people." She pointed at the paper. "It's not in today."

"Ah," Dan said and tipped his cup to his mouth.

Ruth turned away from the table. "Well, I just wondered what you thought of him—that's all." She walked over to the stove. "You don't have to say anything if you don't want to."

"It's not that. You asked me how I liked him—he might be a good fella—I don't know, it's hard to tell. Journalists seem to see themselves as a breed apart from the rest of us—and they've good reason."

"What do you mean?"

"They can destroy people and they know it, and they don't need a gun or even a license. Your friend Hurley's walkin' round with a lot of real power and he's pleased with himself, so you'd have to get past those big feelin's of his to find out what kind of a man he really is."

"Humph! I suppose that's why my father thinks you're marvelous. Well, let's get going, you've a date to meet your sponsor, Mister Mal-a-chi Burke, at the Parker House. Ever hear of it?"

"No."

Dan thought that he'd never get used to the driving habits of Americans—the constant combative elbowing for better position in traffic, veering from lane to lane, jumping the lights, sometimes ignoring them, and the horns, especially the horns. One could drive the length or width of the island of Ireland and not hear a car horn. In England they were seldom heard. But here in the States they seemed to him to be more often used than hand signals. He watched with interest as Ruth drove into a narrow, crowded street and nosed into a reserved area in front of the green marquee of the Parker House.

A stubby man in a three-cornered hat and breeches walked across the sidewalk toward the car.

"What's the meanin' of that outfit?" Dan asked.

"It's supposed to be what the Pilgrims wore, I guess. You know, gives the place a little history. But why would anybody allow himself to be costumed up like that?"

"Why? Money, I suppose! That's a lot of what America's all about, isn't it?"

The man bent to speak to Ruth, but she was looking at Dan.

"Don't knock it, Dan. You're here, aren't you?—and so is anybody else who can get here."

The edge of the tri-cornered hat was in the window now and the man spoke. "Sorry, lady, no parking."

Ruth slid a bill under the hand he had placed on the edge of the window. "I'll just be a few minutes."

"Oh, good morning, Miss Klein—didn't know you at first. No problem."

Ruth pushed open the door and the man stepped back. "Keys are in it."

"O.K."

Twenty-Eight

They stood just inside the door of a coffee shop that was two steps up and off the hotel lobby. Ruth's gaze searched the room. "Ah, there he is over there."

Conway followed her across the room to the most distant corner. A pale man sat engrossed in a newspaper. Fragile looking, silvery wire spectacles sat near the end of his nose. He was very thin. What flesh he had was tight on his frame. The bony sides of his nose were protected by a heavy wrapping of adhesive tape on the nosepiece of his glasses. He turned his head and on his pink scalp there lay a few tired scraps of grey hair. His bright, quick blue eyes were in sharp contrast to his dry white skin. He worked his way to his feet. He was tall with no stoop or slouch. He wore a dark blue suit with a black sweater under the coat and a white shirt buttoned to the neck with no tie. His face did not show the slightest trace of ever having needed a shave.

The old man spoke to Ruth but his eyes were fastened on Conway. His voice was very low and his words had the sound of the quick, rolling brogue of the West of Ireland—probably County Kerry, thought Dan. He looked at Ruth and realized she had to pay close attention to understand Malachi Burke.

"Good morning, Miss Klein. It's nice to see you and you're lookin' grand, as always."

Ruth turned to introduce Dan. The old man had scarcely glanced at her and was staring at Conway. "Mister Burke, this is Dan Conway from the Irish Aid Committee."

Burke stood motionless, not moving to accept Conway's outstretched hand as Ruth realized with a start that Malachi Burke was immobilized by shyness.

"It's a pleasure, Mister Burke," Dan said.

"Not half that it is for me," the old man said softly. His hand was cool with the chill of age.

Ruth frowned as she watched them. "Well, I'll leave you two to get acquainted," she said and then paused. "You know that the Senator is going to meet you here for lunch?"

Conway turned his head and answered, "Yes, we'll be right here."

The old man continued to stare at Conway even as she said her goodbyes and left them.

Conway slid in on the mustard colored plastic seat on one side of the booth. The old man settled himself across from him, speaking as he folded into the seat. "I've been hearin' the name Dan Conway for years. I expected you'd be much older."

Dan fingered the break on the bridge of his nose for a moment before he answered. "I'm old inside," he said without a smile.

"Indeed ya must be after a lifetime in the movement. But by God it looks as though we might be comin' down to the wire." He paused and they both turned to look up at a waitress who slouched vacant-faced by the booth, running a pencil absently through hair that was bleached as hard and crisp as shredded wheat. Conway had the feeling that if neither one of them spoke she would spend the day in that pose.

"Will ya have tea or coffee, Dan Conway?"

"Tea."

"Ah, good. Would ya bring us a nice pot of tea, Miss, for both of us, and toast. Will ya have some toast or a bun maybe?"

"Thanks, no, tea is fine."

The girl moved woodenly away without changing expression. Malachi Burke ran a bony thumb along his jawline. "What was I—oh sure. It looks like the British are gettin' fed up with things in the North. When I heard about the helicopter full of soldiers gettin' shot down, I figured you were really pressin' the hot iron against their flesh. Sure, they got enough trouble in their own island without grief like you're givin' 'em now, Dan Conway. Lord, who'd have believed it back in 1916 when I left. They were God's darlin's then. We didn't know how much the first war was hurtin' 'em, cripplin' 'em forever."

The waitress set a teapot and dropped mugs and spoons haphazardly onto the table. The old man paused to pour the amber colored liquid into the mugs. His hand shook as he poured and he grimaced as he stared at it. The girl returned with a small aluminum pitcher containing some very thin cream.

"Dan, you won't mind me callin' you Dan?"

Conway shook his head and Burke continued speaking. "Sometimes I look around at the things that have happened in my lifetime and I can't believe it. The changes I mean. The speed of things. I mean look how fast the British lion lost his teeth." He smiled pointing with a thumb at his own mouth. "Almost as fast as I lost mine. Who'd believe it. Sure, sometimes I almost think we ought to feel sorry for 'em—almost, but not quite.''

"I've never had that feeling," Dan said, stirring his tea.

"Oh, I'm sure of that, spendin' time like ya have in their prisons. They never got me—I ran away. Had a fine Kilkenny girl waitin' for me here in America. So I ran away from the English." He looked into his mug of tea as though searching for something. "But ya know, Dan, maybe God's punishin' 'em now for what they did to us."

Conway shook his head. "It's up to us to do the punishin' and on that score you've helped a great bit all these years. They tell me you've always helped with money and information."

The old man colored, a blush that moved from his cheeks up to his scalp where the pink flared brighter. "I thank you for those words, Dan Conway. I hope we can help some more while you're here and, by the way, is it true this is your first visit to America?"

"It is," said Dan.

"And what do you think of it?"

"I've not had a chance to see much really, but what I've seen is pretty rich for my blood."

"The Klein girl's lookin' after you, is she?"

"Yes. I had dinner with her and her father last night at a fine hotel, the Ritz Carlton it was. So I guess I'm not seein' bread and butter America yet."

"You had dinner with Gus Klein? By God! That's amazin'—first night in America and dinner with one of the richest men."

"He's invited me to an affair tonight and says he'll raise some money for us."

"Holy Mother, if he says it, he'll do it and his friends have got a helluva lot more money than we'll ever have." He looked closely at Conway. "He thinks this is aid for families, doesn't he? He doesn't know where the money goes?"

Conway stared cooly back at the old man until he could hear him shuffling his feet in agitation under the table.

"Ah, Dan, forgive me. Here I am a sparrow, givin' a hawk advice about flyin'. Anyway, I've a meetin' for ya tonight, too. I'm hopin' my boy Bucky will go with us. Wait 'til he hears Gus Klein's goin' to help you. He'll feel better."

"What do ya mean?" asked Dan.

The old man rubbed his jaw again. "Well, I think he's afraid that this money might not be for helpin' poor Irish families. If it got out that it was for somethin' else, guns maybe," he winked at Conway, "he's afraid that it would be a bit of a hassle. I think that's in the back of his mind. He hasn't said anything, but I know him pretty well. He's a good boy—but awful cautious."

"Nothin' wrong with that," said Dan.

"How would you be knowin' that, Dan Conway?" the old man asked with a chuckle.

Dan grinned back at him, then leaned back against the booth and stretched his legs out. Malachi took off his spectacles, breathed on them and carefully wiped them with a wrinkled spotted handkerchief.

"Have ya spent any time in the West of Ireland, Dan?"

"I have."

"D'ya know the town of Dingle?"

"Yes."

"Shure, I grew up near there on a farm in Annascaul. Hugh Greany was our man in the organization, I wonder—"

"He's dead now."

"Ah, and the old lady at Brennan's, she'd be helpful when she could."

"I never knew her. Some Yanks own Brennan's now."

"Ahh."

"Malachi, it sounds like you haven't been home in a long time."

"God help me, I hate to say it, I've never gone back." He gazed off past Dan's shoulder. "Lots of reasons I s'pose but—" He broke off. "Anyway I've done whatever I could from over here. I never told my kids any of it. None of 'em. The wife knew but she died when the kids were young." Now his pure blue eyes searched Dan's face. "Bucky knows almost nothin' about this."

"Why not? Are you ashamed of it?" asked Conway. His flat fingered hands cradled his cup. He looked straight back at the old man, who spoke quietly, almost to himself.

"I think you wouldn't understand this thing, Dan. I'm not sure I understand it myself. I s'pose it's a kind of shame. God forgive me. You've lived your life strong and proud. I've heard stories of things you've done, but for most of us, we carry this feelin' around with us that's been passed on maybe for hundreds of years. It's the feelin' of bein' less than we should be. Ya know, Dan, ya might wonder, lookin' round at what ya've seen so far, but America, oh—there's nothin' quite like it, I don't think—and we Irish when we get here—and start livin' this American life—well we don't want to be reminded about the bad times in Ireland. I guess we like to show a different face in America than the way people think of us in Europe. We know what the English did to us and we don't want our kids to know it, to see that part of us, and we don't want other Americans to know it either." He stared blankly at the middle of the table for a moment, then he raised his head and looked at Dan. "Do ya know what I'm tryin' ta say?"

"Some of it, I guess," said Dan.

The old man traced a thin, nearly transparent finger on the smooth plastic tabletop. "America has a bad problem, it's bad and gonna get worse—with the colored. The courts and the national government are in it and Bucky gets into it in the Senate now—schools and all that—very emotional. People in our part of the city, oh, they're wild over the whole business. A lot of 'em doin' the talkin' are our own. I listen to 'em and it's 'nigger' this and 'nigger' that. And they don't realize what they're sayin'—they don't know that's where they come from, too." He paused and waited.

"I don't understand," Dan said.

"Well, Dan, I'll tell ya I've thought about it all these years since the English chased me out of my own country." Malachi leaned back against the booth and exhaled. His eyes followed his tremulous hand as it moved up to rub his jaw, then he placed both hands flat on the edge of the table, thumbs braced underneath. "It's a kind of theory I have. It comes to me watching the blacks here."

Conway looked obliquely at the old man without speaking.

"We're the niggers of Europe, Dan."

Dan pursed his lips.

"Sure, think about it," said Burke. "Think what hundreds of years of occupation by the British have done to us—the men especially. Shamed in front of our women and children by the English masters—our manhood ridiculed. Few jobs worth the name—and the drink, always the drink—to kill the pain and shame of it. I think of it now when I see the blacks sittin' on the doorsteps in the sun with a jug, or two or three of 'em on a street corner passin' a bottle round. I know what's goin' on in their minds. What do they care? They know there's nothin' else. And the chatter they have, it's like us. The English took our language away. Imagine, a hangin' offense to speak Gaelic. So we work out a way of talkin' that's English but almost isn't and we add as much jargon to it as we can to confuse everyone else. And there's more. We love music, so do the blacks, and, like us, their women run the families beneath all the noise and swagger of the men. It goes on and on," he concluded somberly.

"That's quite a theory, Malachi," said Conway. "And they're religious, too, or were. Isn't that so, especially during slavery?"

The old man nodded sadly.

Conway said sharply, "It fits perfectly. Keep the people doped up on prayer and booze and they never have the wit to resist. I'd say the blacks had only one piece of luck in the whole thing."

"What's that, Dan?" inquired Malachi.

"They didn't have a Catholic Church to deal with."

"Ah, Dan, easy, easy."

"Malachi, you know—" Conway broke off and said, "I think we've got visitors."

The old man turned gingerly and gave a nod. "Right, it's my boy." Then with the edges of his mouth working at a grin he said, "I hope you'll be your usual cautious self. And remember, he's a daily communicant and a cautious man, too—like yourself—and for the love of Almighty God don't mention my theory."

Conway laughed out loud, a quick rolling laugh that was gone so fast Senator Bucky Burke was not sure he'd heard it as he came to the table. He wore a well pressed, grey, three piece suit with a fat modish necktie.

"Well, Pa, you must be in heaven with someone from the old country to talk with. Hi, Dan Conway, I'm Bucky Burke." He took Conway's hand as he started to rise. "Stay where you are—say hello to Jabber O'Rourke." Jabber raised a hand, palm up, and said, "Hi," through the cigarette in his mouth.

Senator Burke slid in beside his father. Jabber grabbed a chair from a nearby table, dragged it a few feet and sat down near the end of the booth. He lit another cigarette and watched the Senator and Conway appraise one another.

Senator Burke spoke first. "Well, this is a pleasure," he said and smiled a boyish grin which was the currency he used whenever a quick exchange was needed. It seldom failed to make a purchase.

"We appreciate your help," Dan said gravely.

"Glad to help," said the Senator, looking out at the room and beckoning to a waitress. "Are you being taken care of all right?"

"Fine, thanks," said Conway.

"Yes, well—" He fingered his tie and glanced sideways at his father. "I'm sorry, Pa, something's come up and I won't be able to have lunch. We're busy as the dickens at the State House today, but I did want to stop and have a chat with Mister Conway."

The waitress was beside them continuing the work on her scalp with the pencil.

"Will you have some more?" asked Burke. "What is it, tea?"

Conway nodded.

"Bring a couple pots of tea for us, Miss. Coffee for you, Jab?"

"Yep," said Jabber. He was tilted back in his chair and looking out the window that formed one side of the room and gave some customers a chance to eat in the public eye.

"Buck, I'm sorry you won't be able to have lunch with us," said Malachi and his voice strengthened. "And what about tonight, you said you'd come to St. Bridget's."

"I will, Pa, I will. I promised you and I will."

"Well, they're expectin' ya, ya know. I told 'em ya'd introduce Dan Conway."

"I said I will and I'll be there." He poured some tea. "I'm really sorry to be so rushed but you know how these things are. By the way, say hello to my friend, Meyer Levin, for me."

Conway looked puzzled as Burke drank his tea.

"The fellow at the hotel you're staying at. His name's Levin," said Bucky.

"I'm not stayin' at a hotel," said Conway.

"Oh," said the Senator and looked at his father who raised his eyebrows and stared at his son.

"Where are you staying?"

"Miss Klein was nice enough to put me up," said Conway.

The front legs of Jabber's chair settled back on the floor.

"I'm afraid her father pushed her a bit."

"Her father—Gus Klein? He pushed her? You know Gus Klein?" The Senator put his cup down.

"Yes, we had dinner last night."

Burke looked at Jabber who was looking with raised eyebrows at Dan.

"I didn't know you knew these people," said Bucky, looking quickly at his father who was drinking his tea with apparent disinterest.

"We met last night," said Dan.

"Oh, I didn't know. I didn't get a chance to say much to Ruthie this morning. Well that's fine—it sure is fine—glad you had a good first night in America. It *was* your first night, wasn't it?" He looked at his father with a frown. "Didn't you say that, Pa?"

Malachi was sitting very erect. "Sure I did, and it's a fact. This is Dan Conway's first time in America and I'm sure he's greatly honored that such important men as yourselves have found time in your busy schedules ta spend five minutes with him. You might want to mention other matters in reference to Mister Gus Klein, Dan, although I know you boys are in a fearful hurry to get back to your big doin's at the State House."

Jabber O'Rourke's laughter swept across the table.

Bucky Burke's lips were tight. He breathed noisily through his nose and shook his head.

"Jeezus, Pa, you are something. Dan, I think I'd better back up a bit—Ruth took you to dinner with her father?"

Conway nodded.

Jabber put out his cigarette and directed a remark to the ashtray. "Not your usual talkative Irishman."

Bucky continued, "Anyone else at the dinner?"

"Yes, a fella named Hurley, Bill Hurley."

"By God," said Jabber, "you had quite an opening night, Champ."

"Ah, he did indeed, indeed," intoned Malachi.

Bucky gave him a sharp glance. "Dan, I don't want to sound like an interrogator, I didn't know you met those people. They're both very big names in my business. Especially Hurley. Do you understand the role of newspapers here in America?"

"I'm not sure I understand much at all about America."

"You're not alone," said Jabber.

"Well, one place to start is with the newspapers," said Bucky. "Did Hurley have much to say?"

"He did," said Dan.

"I mean, to you, Dan. Did he quiz you about what you're doin' here?"

"He asked if you were sponsoring me. I told him you are not."

The three men watched him closely.

"You explained the Irish Aid thing? He knows that's what you're here for?"

"Yes."

"Dan, you know, sometimes there's a question in people's minds when Northern Ireland comes up. So much violence for so many years. There's lots of talk in the papers and television here about the money raised goin' for guns."

"Yes, Gus Klein and I talked about that. He's very strong for Israel and helps with their fund raising."

"I'll bet," interjected Jabber.

"And for your information, Senator Burke," said Malachi, "Gus Klein has invited Dan to a fund raisin' affair tonight and is goin' to raise him some money for our cause."

"Your cause, Pa. Not my cause. That's a surprise, Dan. Klein invited you to—what?—an Israeli fund raising affair to give you some help?"

"That's right," said Dan.

"Why the hell would he do that?" Jabber asked to no one in particular.

Their eyes stayed on Conway.

"I think it's because he feels that the independence cause of both small countries is similar, and—"

"You don't think it's because you're such a charmer over dinner?" asked Jabber.

"I don't think so," said Dan.

"But that's what you think, eh?" mused Bucky. "You think he identified with the 'one Ireland' idea, huh? Well he's a tough guy with a *lot* of dough, and I guess he can do what he wants with it."

The four men sat still and quiet, their minds so full they were scarcely aware of one another. Finally, as Jabber put a new cigarette in his mouth, Bucky Burke spoke. "This business with Gus Klein confuses me, although the hold Israel has over American Jews has always amazed me. I guess he's built up sympathy for the Irish thing because of the Jews' history of being pushed around, too."

"They sure as hell aren't pushed around here," said Jabber reflectively.

"Well, the world changes," said Bucky.

"Everywhere but Ireland," said the old man, tearing his paper napkin in bits. "Don't you have any feel for that, son?"

Bucky Burke and Jabber O'Rourke were shocked. Their faces showed it at once. Jabber had never heard the old man refer to Bucky as son, and Bucky's mind raced to remember when he had last heard his father use the word.

Dan's voice came through the muddle of emotion. His words were clipped, his voice was hard, there was little accent. "Malachi, one way or another, we'll get the job done."

Burke stared at Dan. When he spoke he sounded weary. "Look, Conway, I don't know exactly what the hell you do for a living—and I don't want to know. My father asked me to help raise money to aid Irish families in the North. I agreed and, for the record, that's what I'm doing. I'm sorry if I disappoint my father in not caring about this Irish business, but I don't. For my money it's a merry-go-round that never stops and I don't want to get on. I'm an American—a Boston politician. My business is getting re-elected—and anybody fooling around with the Northern Irish thing would get in big trouble with the papers here, and in this country trouble with the press is disaster, especially for a politician. Gus Klein, he can afford his enthusiasms. Politicians can't if the newspapers don't share 'em and the newspapers in this country, and especially in this town, don't have any enthusiasm for the Irish business. Boston may be an Irish town, but it's in spite of the newspapers."

Jabber ground a cigarette into an ashtray and spoke as he did. "The bastards who run the newspaper here would love to be English country gentlemen, so they never want to see a bad word written about England."

"I don't know about that, Jab, but they obviously aren't interested in the rights or wrongs of what goes on in Northern Ireland. I'd guess they're bored with it cuz it seems it'll take more than a thousand-word editorial to find the right answer." He watched Dan closely. "The IRA or the Provos or whoever it is settin' the bombs off and killin' soldiers—and civilians—are not popular with the press here. They don't see 'em as freedom fighters."

"Shure, that's the press for ya," Malachi said, shaking his head.

"Lookit, Pa! for God's sake, I'm trying to tell ya something—the two of you—Hurley scares me! He's a dangerous guy; he'd trade one of his kids in for a one-day news story that destroyed somebody's reputation—that's the way these guys are."

"Ah, Buck, Dan's doin' nothin' but collectin' money for poor families that are bein' harassed by the English, that's all."

"I know, I know, but remember, Conway, the newspapers are the government now in this country. The politicians know it and, unfortunately, so do the newspapers. So be careful because I can't help you if they get on you."

Jabber got to his feet. He winked at Dan. "Well—see you tonight, Champ."

"I think Gus Klein planned to have Ruth bring me to this affair. It's at a place called the Harbor Club," Dan said, getting to his feet.

"O.K., I'll check with you there," said Jabber. He looked at the old man. "Can I give you a ride back to your home turf, Mal? Those beer sippers in

Southie must be sendin' out search parties for you by now."

"Would ya like to come along with me, Dan?" asked Malachi eagerly.

"Thanks, Malachi, I think I'll walk a bit. I'll see you tonight."

"Shure, shure, I understand. Jabber'll get everything set up. He always does."

Jabber gave the old man a fond grin. "I hope ya heard that, Boss."

Bucky Burke tossed a bill on the table and stood looking down at his father. "I'll see you tonight, Pa. I hope this hasn't set wrong with you, Dan." He put a hand on Dan's arm.

"Not a bit of it," Dan said.

Twenty-Nine

DAN STOOD UNDER the hotel's marquee for a moment looking right and left. A man and woman brushed past him as they left the hotel. The man held the woman's arm. A battered taxi pulled up to the curb. Most of the taxis he'd seen in America were scarred—fenders crumpled, windows cracked, handles missing, paint fading. He wondered why. He thought about it as he watched the man hold the car door for the woman. She bent her head to enter and her hair swung in a cascade of black. Then the thought of Kate was part of him and all other thoughts were gone. He started to walk, aware only of the strange feeling of loss within him. Now he knew what Moira meant when she said she ached for him. A wave of emotion rolled through his belly. With profound wonder he knew that it was loneliness and that he had never felt this way before. There was a hollow urgency within him, of wanting to be with Kate. A need. Not just for a woman—he knew that pull. This was simply, totally a need for Kate, to be with her, to be in her presence, to see her, to hear her, to touch her. He hoped he could raise a respectable sum of money quickly in Boston and leave. Gus Klein was a lucky find, a strong man whose financial help could be significant—beyond the usual modest sums he and his comrades struggled to raise. He would clean the slate with the organization. Others had done it. He felt no reservation or doubt. He thought of his father and the old man, pictured them in his mind and still felt no regret at his decision, and then strangely through the sounds of the city he could hear Jerry Regan's voice echoing off the stone walls in the barn, dreading the loss of heaven and the pains of hell, asking God's forgiveness as his life drained out onto the dirt, and Dan knew with an overwhelming certainty that he must be with Kate in the cottage overlooking Bantry Bay.

His thoughts propelled him and the city was a blur of movement and noise.

"Good afternoon."

The voice tugged at him and he turned and saw the doorman of Ruth's apartment. He stopped and rubbed the crooked bridge of his nose. He glanced at the traffic. A young man in a bulky two-toned sedan was leaning forward on the horn and making a middle fingered gesture at the car in front of him. Dan walked through the hollow lobby and stepped into the elevator.

A jangle of music was hammering through the apartment. The air was gritty with smoke. A girl sat on the couch near the window. She wore a starched uniform that was pure white against her black skin, her hair was a mass of glistening black coils. She didn't take the cigarette from her mouth when she looked up from the magazine she was reading.

"You Mista Conway?"

"Yes."

"Ruth left me a note sayin' you'd be here, and a Mista Burke—I couldn't get his first name—he call sayin' everthin' is all set for tonight. He talk kinda funny."

"Thank you."

The girl resumed her reading.

Dan walked to the window and looked out at the city. The music made him wince and he turned to look at the girl. She looked up at him and rose and walked slowly to a silver faced stereo in a corner. She snapped a switch and the music stopped.

"Well, I got things I gotta do," the girl said as she opened a closet door. "I gonna leave a little early today." She draped a fur trimmed leather jacket over her shoulders and gave Dan a quick white smile. "So long."

Goodbye," Dan said. he walked down the hall to his bedroom and took off his shoes and jacket and stretched out on the bed. He took the pistol out of the holster and held it in front of him. His hand fitted easily into the indents on the hard rubbed wood of the butt. He ran his index finger over the blue-black steel and thought of Malachi Burke, of all the Malachi Burkes he'd known, of their lifelong humiliation by the English and their desperate need for revenge. He sighted along the short barrel of the gun, but then Kate's face was before him. He could see the dusting of freckles across her cheekbones and he closed his eyes and tried to conjure the exact green of her eyes.

The sound of the door closing startled him and he realized he had fallen asleep. He heard Ruth Klein's voice humming a tune. He put on his jacket to cover his holster and went down the hall in his stocking feet. Ruth was dumping the contents of an ashtray into a wastebasket.

"Hi, Dan, did you get a chance for a nap?"

He wrinkled his forehead and squeezed his eyes shut. "Can you tell so easily?"

Ruth laughed, a bright sunny sound that made the room cheerier than it was. "Just as easy as I can tell that that fraud of a maid was here." She placed the ashtray on a side table, took a step back from it and then moved it a few inches toward the center of the table. "I don't know why I put up with her," she said speaking as though to herself.

"Why do you?"

Ruth grimaced. "I'm sure it's guilt."

"Guilt?"

"Yes, for the way we've treated blacks here. I suppose it's my way of doing penance. You people do penance, don't you?"

"Not me."

"Not ever?"

"Not since I was a wee child; my grandmother believed in it."

She cocked her head and grinned. "So you're not sorry for anything you've ever done, Dan?"

"No."

Her grin disappeared. "I think it must take a very strong man to say that." She paused and then smiled again. "How about a drink?"

"That's a fine idea."

Dan followed her toward the kitchen and she spoke over her shoulder. "I've been delegated by my father to bring you to this affair tonight."

"I know."

"Gus is amazing, isn't he? He never fails to surprise me. He's so impulsive. I don't mean that I disagree with his helping you, it's just that it surprises me. He's always surprising people."

"I can imagine," Dan said as she poured a beer for him.

"Bill Hurley called me today," Ruth said, watching the head of foam rise. "He's back in Washington—just for the day. What a life he has—so exciting! He's talking with someone in the White House and then coming back tonight. He asked me to have dinner with him and the Mayor later—after the Harbor Club thing." She looked up from the beer. "I told him about the Harbor Club meeting when he asked me to dinner, and, well, he was surprised, too, I think."

"What did he say?" Dan asked softly.

"Well, you know—he was curious, so I explained to him that my father is a fanatic about Israel and the rights of all small countries—and people really, minorities. Gus believes people should be able to determine their own destiny and not be pushed around and I told Bill that's what this is—plain and simple, my father's feeling for people—and yours." She put a polished nail on a front tooth. "That's all right, don't you think, Dan?"

"I hope so."

"I know my father would be furious if Bill came to the meeting—and even more if he knew he found out about it from me. I wish he didn't mistrust newspeople so."

"Well, we'll see what happens," Dan said.

"And, Dan, one more thing I should tell you. Bill asked questions about you. How much we know about you—your background—exactly where you're from—that kind of thing. Of course I told him nothing. I hope you won't say anything to Gus about this; he'd get mad as hell—so would the Senator, I'm afraid."

Thirty

ONE HOUR LATER, as lights were being lit in the city, Dan and Ruth stepped out of the burnished wood and polished bronze elevator car onto the thick pile carpet of the Harbor Club. A man and woman, each in suitably conservative uniforms of starched white and modest brown, stood near the elevator. The man greeted them and gave a quick appraisal of Conway's lack of topcoat and watched the woman take the fur coat Ruth Klein wore. He led them through the gently lit foyer onto a small landing that offered a view of the main room of the club and the view that room enjoyed of the city and harbor spread below, a dark velvet blanket studded with sparkling gems of light.

"Your father is expecting you, Miss Klein."

"Thank you," Ruth said and took Dan's arm as she stepped down the stairs into the well of the room. The room's walls were mostly window, and as they moved through the modest lights Dan could see their reflection in the glass on one side. He drew Ruth's attention to it. "Now there's a very handsome lady," he said.

She looked at him with astonishment. "Dan Conway, I didn't think you had a bit of blarney in you, so I'm going to accept those words as a very meaningful compliment." Her colored heightened and in the muted lights of the room she was exceptional looking. She wore a tailored grey suit over a black silk blouse and a string of pearls that just caught the dim light.

Conway ran his fingers through his tousled hair as he looked at her and as he did he heard the rasp of Gus Klein's voice at his side.

"How'd you like to have her in charge of getting you to meetings on time in Ireland?"

Dan smiled and said, "Frankly, we Irish aren't well known for our promptness, either, but I don't think Ruth would feel very much at home over there."

Ruth did a little stamping movement with her foot. "I think you just took back the compliment you gave me, Dan, but just wait, I might surprise you in Ireland some day."

"You're full of surprises, Ruthie," said her father sharply. "Including having Hurley pick you up here—is that right?"

"I don't know how you find out these things, but don't worry, Gus, he's been told to wait downstairs. I know how you are about the newspapers and money for Israel."

"Goddamn right," he gestured with his ever present cigar at the room. "How do you think these guys would like to see their names in the paper as big givers for Israel or anything else? No way! Could be lots of trouble—badgered by all kinds of nutcakes, kidnappers, crooks—or worse, the I.R.S."

Ruth burst into laughter.

Gus looked at her with a frown and then turned to Dan. "I understand you got another affair to hit so we'll get the job done for you right away. First have some food—a drink or something—c'mon." He led Dan to a table covered with a variety of dishes and bowls, some being heated. Presiding over this were three blacks dressed in crisp white outfits, wearing tall chefs' caps. One looked with concern at Dan as he said, "No thanks," and moved past this encampment to the small bar where two bored, ruddy faced bartenders wearing brown uniforms with the yellow block H of the Harbor Club were dispensing drinks.

Dan looked at Ruth. "I'd like white wine on the rocks," she said.

"And a beer, please," added Conway.

"Yes, indeed, sor," said one of the men in a thick Irish countryman's cadence. He and Conway looked closely at one another.

"Roscommon," said Conway.

"Right," said the man uncapping the bottle of beer. "You from the old country?" he asked, peering up at Dan from under bushy black brows.

"I am," Dan said. "And how does it go?"

"Good enough; there's plenty of work for those that'll do it," said the man bending to the sink.

"Good luck," Dan said and moved away.

"Thanks," said the bartender, not raising his head.

"Still our biggest export," said Dan as Gus and Ruth watched him.

"People you mean," said Gus.

"Yes, it's been like a hemorrhage to our island—losin' our people," Conway said quietly.

Ruth shivered and rubbed her hands together. "It gives me a sad feeling to hear you say that, Dan."

"Well, we're going to change it."

"By God, I hope so," Gus said tersely, "and now let's see if we can help." He raised his voice. "Folks, this is my friend from Ireland that I spoke to you about."

As Gus continued speaking Dan watched the people gather. The women were dressed in long formal gowns, none underfed, all past middle age he guessed. They displayed an awesome amount of jewelry. The men, and there were over twenty in number, were dressed conservatively—blues, blacks, greys were the colors he saw. All these men had a quality that he sensed. Tall or short, fat or not, with or without glasses or hair, they had assurance, a strong sense of self that seemed to fill the room. They stood quietly and listened to Gus Klein. No one fidgeted or shuffled. They looked at Conway with undisguised interest. Dan's eyes moved from person to person seeking each one's glance. He met no embarrassment or shyness. Gus Klein's voice bored into his thoughts.

"And if we believe that Israel has a right to its own determination, as a people, as a culture, without other nations or groups making decisions or interfering or just butting their damn noses in, then I think we should support a country like Ireland that's been trying to get control of their own island for a hell of a long time. They want the right to their own religion and culture—like Israel. If we expect people in this country to respect our position on Israel, then we have an obligation to support other countries with the same goals as Israel."

He placed the cigar in the corner of his mouth, clamped his teeth on it, and then removed it and whistled a billow of smoke into the air around him. "If you get a sense of what I'm saying, if I haven't confused myself and everybody else, Dan Conway is raising money for families that are destitute—their breadwinners are held in prisons, with serious questions of the legality of it, by the British Army. Real injustice and bigotry is going on in Northern Ireland, and as your chairman for, oh, these too many years—" He raised his eyes heavenward, turned his palms upward and held this dramatic pose long enough to rouse a chuckle from the group, "I remind you that I have always felt that we American Jews make a big mistake if we are seen in the eyes, minds or whatever of our fellow Americans as just pro-Israel. We know we have been the traditional heartbeat of liberal thinking here in America, but we are too often thought of as caring about justice only for Israel when it comes to foreign affairs. Let's put some money in Dan Conway's hands for Ireland. Let it be however you want to give it." He paused and grinned, "But I think cash might be a good idea."

The group reacted with laughter and smiles. He looked around the room with his head thrown back. Ruth whispered to Dan, "Isn't he a ham? I think he's forgotten you're here."

Gus's glance came around to them and he grinned proudly at his daughter. "Now, Dan, I know you've got another meeting, but why don't you say a few words to these folks before they do the right thing by you."

Dan waited a moment until the room was very still. He pushed his hair back from his forehead. Over the heads of the people he could see the bartender from Roscommon moving from behind the bar to the outside edge of the group. When the man stopped, Dan spoke.

"Gus Klein has said it very well for me—for us. We're a small island, a small place—like Israel. We are a people from a very old culture—like the Jews. We want the right to determine our own destiny as you want it for your people. England is still holding part of our island, our country, by force of arms. We want them to leave, to let us settle our own problems—the way you Americans did and do.

"The families involved in our efforts go through difficult times. There are many people in Ireland who will be grateful for what you do here tonight. For them I thank you." He waited a long moment and then said, "I can assure you the money will be used effectively."

There was a lengthy silence not broken until the group realized he was finished. Then an elderly man in the front moved to Dan's side and said in a strong but unsteady voice, "I'm glad to do this. Some Irishmen—I expect friends of your friends—helped us run guns against the British before the birth of Israel in 1946." He placed a sheaf of bills in an envelope, wrote his name on it and handed it to Dan. This man was first in a line of people that moved past Dan with a few words or a handshake and money. He spoke briefly with each and then it was done.

He stood alone for a moment, thinking about this thing that had happened. He had collected more money here in these few minutes than his entire group could raise in months of proud begging.

Ruth Klein touched his arm. She was standing very close to him. "I'm glad my father did this, Dan. I hope it helps." Her eyes were bright.

"It will, Ruth." He felt her slide something in his coat pocket.

"That's from me, Dan."

"Thanks, Ruth, you've been very kind." She stayed close to him and smiled. The smile was full and open and warm and meant for him. "Remember I told you that I might surprise you some day in Ireland."

"I think you'd enjoy it, Ruth, although it's a different world, especially in the West of Ireland. Maybe someday you'd come visit us."

Her smile diminished. "Is there an us, Dan?"

"There's a girl named Kate."

"Who is she?"

"She's a schoolteacher in the West of Ireland."

"You're going to be married?"

"Yes, when I get back."

Ruth's smile was gone now, her eyes darkened, and her voice was gentle. "I'd like to meet her—she's a lucky girl."

"Who is?" Gus Klein's voice cut away their conversation like a chair scraping in a library.

Ruth spoke in a rush of words. "A girl named Kate that Dan plans to marry when he gets home to Ireland." She smiled at Dan again, a different smile. "Have you known her long, Dan? The Irish sometimes have those long engagements, don't they?"

"Some do, but this happened quickly."

"Oh! That sounds romantic. You surprise me, being a romantic," she said, watching him closely.

"It surprised me too."

"And what do you do for a living over there," Ruth continued. Her father studied his daughter as he relit his cigar.

"I'm going to be a fisherman."

"A fisherman," Gus said, exhaling a cloud of cigar smoke. "Is there any money in that?"

"I hope so."

"Somehow I don't quite see you as a fisherman," Ruth said.

"I think it's not quite the kind of work you're used to," Gus said shrewdly.

"Quite a different life than raising money for political prisoners," Ruth added. "It sounds like a lovely life, though."

"It will be," Dan said flatly.

"Ah—well, good luck to ya both, you'll work it out, Dan," Gus growled as he led them by force of his presence across the room toward the landing. "I know you've got another meeting, but, listen, call me tomorrow." He took a pen and wrote rapidly on a business card. "My private number—hardly ever give it out. I think other Jewish groups around the country ought to get behind this thing. Let's face it. It could be a good way to cover our flanks." He shrugged. "You understand, Dan. What the hell. Life is tough." He reached inside his suit coat and took out an envelope. "I hope you use this effectively, too."

"Thanks, Gus—for everything. I'll call you tomorrow."

Klein slapped him on the shoulder and went down the steps back to the group, most of whom were watching him respectfully. Dan waited as the woman helped Ruth on with her coat and as he gazed across the room, the Roscommon bartender, a hazy figure in the soft light, gave him a thumbs-up sign. Dan returned it and walked with Ruth into the waiting elevator.

Thirty-One

Bill Hurley and Jabber stood talking in the lobby. Hurley wore a belted camel haired coat and had his head back laughing at something Jabber had said. Dan watched the two men as he and Ruth walked toward them. Hurley's eyes fastened on Ruth. He made no attempt to be casual. Jabber shot a glance at Hurley and then looked at Ruth. Dan saw what he thought was a flash of painful intensity cross Jabber's features before he pushed his hat further back on his head and flipped his cigarette toward the trash cylinder.

"All set, Champ?" Jabber asked, ignoring Ruth as Hurley kissed her on the cheek.

"Well, Conway," said Hurley, "You're certainly starting off in a big way here in America. The Ritz last night and now the Harbor Club. I imagine this is quite an experience for a man from Strabane. That is where you said you were from, isn't it? Strabane?"

"Yes."

"How'd it go upstairs? Did you do well?" Hurley asked.

Dan stared at him.

"Come on, man, Gus Klein was helping you raise money from those pro-Israeli hawks up there. That's no secret. I just wondered if it went well. Did you raise a lot of dough?"

Ruth took Hurley's arm. "C'mon, Bill, this is supposed to be a social evening."

Jabber spoke quickly. "Let's go, Champ, we should get a move on. See you tomorrow, Ruth. G'night, Bill."

The seats in Jabber's car were so much used they seemed form fitting. Dan leaned back and sighed in comfort as they moved carefully along in the traffic.

"Hurley and Ruth are havin' dinner with the Mayor tonight, eh?" asked Jabber.

"That's what she said," responded Dan.

"There's a great pair, Hurley and the Mayor," said Jabber without explanation. "The Mayor's another Irish Catholic that prays, if he does pray, that he'll wake up some mornin' a Beacon Hill Yankee."

"Oh?" said Dan, making an effort to show interest.

"Sure, it'll be something when Hurley tells him about you at the Harbor Club."

"Will he do that?" asked Dan.

"Oh! He and Hurley swap every bit of news and gossip they stumble across."

"But Hurley's a reporter, a columnist—one of the editors, isn't he?" said Dan.

"Yeah, but he wants to be more than that," said Jabber as he rolled down the window and whipped his cigarette out into the street. "He wants to make policy. He wants to be the government. These guys get carried away, believe me. Ya know—the sports writers want to manage the team. The political writers want to run the country." He turned to Dan with a frown. "Not so in Ireland?"

"No so much," answered Dan.

Jabber chuckled. "Wow, I tell ya it'll be somethin' when the Mayor hears Gus Klein sponsored you at an affair at the Harbor Club with all those Yankee Jews. He'd give his left ball to have that done for him." He grinned and then shrugged at Dan. "Although I guess he's traded in whatever balls he had a long time ago."

"Not a friend of yours," said Dan.

"Not a friend of anybody's from what I can figure," Jabber said. "But, anyway, not for publication—how'd it go, all right?"

"Jabber, between you and me, it went very well. My people are going to be very pleased."

"Well, Champ, I'll tell you something. I'm not going to ask who your people really are."

"You know—" started Dan.

Jabber interrupted, "Hey, Malachi Burke's got somethin' that's been burnin' inside him for years. He's been like the father I never had. I know him well and you're somethin' special to him. I can tell. So whatever you're doin' or whoever your people are, it's O.K. with me. I'll help you any way I can, but—," he took a hand from the wheel and raised a finger, "always protectin' the Senator. He's goin' places and we don't want to embarrass him."

"Why should this kind of thing embarrass him?" Dan asked.

"It shouldn't," said Jabber. "I don't know, maybe we Irish are born afraid of being embarrassed."

"Not just in America," Dan said shortly.

"Well," Jabber said slyly, "can you change that?"

"We'll see," said Dan.

They pulled into a partially filled parking lot. Dan noted the cars. There were no Mercedes. Jabber turned the ignition off, but it took a few seconds for the motor to get the message. They sat for a moment until the car hiccoughed and went still. Jabber spoke into the quiet of the car.

"Dan, my grandparents came here from Ireland. I hope good things come to the place from whatever you're doin'."

"We're going to try."

"Good luck," said Jabber, uncoiling himself out of the car. "Now let's watch Father Mike put the arm on his people for ya."

"Father Mike?"

"Sure, Father Mike Martin, a great football player at Boston College. All American. He was a rock in their defensive line and he's a rock in this neighborhood. A great pal of Malachi's and the Senator. A good guy. What the good Father says around here has a lot of clout and that's what people get if they don't pay attention to him— a clout."

Dan waited while Jabber lit a cigarette. He turned to find Jabber watching him as he surveyed the neighborhood. The houses were identical in the street lights. Three story, wood frame, built on a postage stamp patch of land, with cigar box porches, their only personality a preference of color.

"To paraphrase that great American, Spiro Agnew," said Jabber as they walked toward the long brick building that was St. Bridget's Community Hall, "if you've seen one three decker in Southie, you've seen 'em all." He continued, "I've never been to Ireland, Champ, what's it like?"

"Well, places like Derry and north of Belfast have the same charm as this place," said Dan.

"Then that's a trip I can postpone for a hundred years or so," Jabber cracked.

"Ah, but don't do that, Jabber. You'd be missin' the rest of it. And there's a beauty to parts of Ireland that'll get in a corner of your heart and stay with you forever."

"Is that guaranteed?" Jabber asked with a mocking grin.

"It is indeed," Dan said softly.

The fact that the building was a community hall was apparent as they entered the door. Young children bounced a basketball around one of the hoops that were at either end of the long, high-ceilinged building. A stage with a few wooden chairs and a piano ran along the far end of the room. Directly off the entrance was an open doorway that produced sounds of babies crying and as Dan watched, a toddler made an erratic dash for the door and was grabbed by the back of its sagging diaper by a young girl in bright red slacks.

"Go get 'im, Maureen," said Jabber without stopping. "That babysitting job's good training for your future."

With a word, a slap, or a wisecrack, regardless of age or sex, Jabber moved Dan through the hall toward the bar.

Conway looked at the crowd, which seemed to number well over a hundred, and at their clothing, and he knew he had come a long way from the Harbor Club.

Behind the bar was an enormous man in a short sleeved black clerical shirt and Roman collar. His face was fleshy and very mobile and now as he saw Jabber he broke into a wide grin. Taking a towel and wiping his hands, he moved with surprising grace out from the back of the bar and positioned himself like a prize fighter. His fists looked like rib roasts of beef and the thick, wiry dark hair on his arms seemed an extension of his black shirt. "Alright, O'Rourke, let's get at it," he growled.

Dan watched with amusement as Jabber contorted his fragile body crab-like and moved in a sideways motion around the priest, flicking out jabs with his almost feminine left hand. Suddenly Jabber stopped, pivoted and swung a roundhouse right hand. The big man tipped his upper torso back slightly, opened his right fist, caught the punch and spun Jabber around. It was done with such ease as to appear to be a practiced dance step. The priest gave Jabber a hug with one log-like arm. "How are you, Jab?"

"One of these days, Father Mike. One of these days I'm gonna flatten you," said Jabber, shaking his head while the faces of the group gathered round beamed with delight.

"Don't I know it," said the priest and looked squarely at Dan. His handshake was a quick surge of power. "This is a pleasure and an honor, Dan Conway."

Dan looked into the priest's wide green eyes and believed him. "I'm glad to meet you, Father."

"Malachi and Bucky are on the way. How about a drink? We won't start 'til they get here."

"A good idea, Father."

"Jabber, Minny Ryan says she's getting bounced around somethin' awful by the Social Security people."

"Since Tim died?" asked Jabber.

"Yup, that's it. She's here somewhere."

"I'll find her," said Jabber.

The hall was intensely lit by thin stacks of fluorescent lights lining the walls and large bright globes hanging from the ceiling. Three husky bartenders who looked like brothers worked with fast hands behind the bar, their faces gleaming with perspiration as they responded to orders from kids and grownups. All ages stood along the long black formica bar that was littered with an assortment of beer bottles, drinking glasses, potato chip bags and soft drink bottles. The bar was buttressed at either end by large Coca Cola coolers, their paint chipped and letters a faded white. The crowd gave the priest and Dan respectful room even while a number of them shuffled about and subtly positioned themselves to remain in earshot.

Father Martin set his rump against the edge of the bar. Only the neck of the beer bottle was visible in his massive hand. He and Dan savored their drinks before they spoke.

"You make me feel like a small man standin' here with you Father," said Dan.

The priest's face was grave as he listened. "You should never feel like a small man with anyone, Dan Conway. I've spent my summer vacations for the last dozen years in Ireland. I've been all over the place and I've heard your name often. I know the risks you've taken and the guts you've showed. No, Dan, you're a big man in every way to me and lots of other people. It's quite a thing for me to have you here having a drink in our Parish Hall."

"I don't always get this kind of welcome from the clergy, you know, Father."

"Ah, I know that. I know how some of 'em are over there. You know that story of the Irish Bishop who was tellin' the Pope about how things ought to be in the world and how he carried on 'til the Pope interrupted him and said, 'Remember, Father, that we here in the Vatican—we are also Catholics.' Yep, too many of the Irish clergy are only interested in perpetuating the priest class, but you'll see, they'll come around. They'll follow the power; let's face it—there's got to be one Ireland. What the devil do the English think we are, Santo Domingo and Haiti?"

Dan smiled, "Our friend Malachi has a theory that that might be incorporated into."

"Oh, Malachi's marvelous, Dan. He never gives in and he's awfully good to those in the parish that need a hand. When all is said and done, Bucky's well served by him."

"His father says the Senator's cautious and that seems accurate," said Dan.

Father Martin laughed. "Accurate indeed, but he has good reason. Politics here is a jungle and too often seems to be a case of survival of the unfittest. Buck's got a great future if all goes well. We'd like to see him Governor or United States Senator. He's a fine family man, but," and the priest shook his drum of a head, "of course, like too many Irish-Americans, he's got no sense or feel for the history of our own race." He slapped a palm on the edge of the bar and the entire length of the structure quivered. "But, Dan, a man like you can change all that. A man to make the Irish proud of their country. I think you could be the man, Dan. Keep doing what needs to be done and, God forgive me, I know what that means, I know precisely what it means, but keep it up and there'll be a better world—a more decent world for our race. And isn't it about time? Look what the British have done to our people in Ireland for so many hundreds of years. It's a sin. Absolutely a sin. We're not tough enough. Irish men and women treated like animals. No!—worse than animals. The English are fonder of animals than they are of the Irish, and they treat them better. By God, they get more upset about the fox hunting than they do about the treatment of our own Catholic people. Look at this illegal jailing of people. It's terrible! And, as always, a few good men must carry the burden of changing things—just like our Blessed Lord did and the Holy Apostles." He paused and breathed deeply. "I hope we can be of help here tonight."

Dan moved a finger along the bridge of his nose. "Whatever you do, Father, we'll appreciate it."

The priest looked at him with his thick lips turned into a proud smile. "You're surprised I know who you are, Dan, I'll bet."

"I'd have to say you're a big surprise, Father, a big surprise in every way."

The priest threw back his head and a low rumble of laughter came from him, the sound rising in intensity until it filled the air around them. Dan noticed heads turn. Faces lit with grins. Then Father Mike's head came down and he looked down at the young boy standing looking up at him with big blue marble eyes. "What is it, Danny?"

"Can I get my picture taken, Father?"

"What are you talking about, son?"

"There are two men here. They say they're from the newspaper and one of em's got a camera. Can I, Father?"

Father Mike and Dan exchanged a quick glance. Dan shook his head slightly. The priest's glance swung around the hall. "Where are they, Danny?"

"Near the end of the bar, Father, over there."

"Well, we're not going to be having any pictures or press here—you run along now while I go have a chat with them."

Jabber O'Rourke sidled up to the priest as he finished speaking. "The press is here, Father," he said, hardly moving his lips.

"So I'm told. Ah! And here they come."

Dan turned and saw two young men moving along the bar towards them. One of the men was tall with dark horn-rimmed glasses and short clipped blonde hair. He wore a blue blazer and his expression was very serious. The other man had stringy black hair and a walrus mustache. His eyes were almost closed. His narrow shoulders sloped out to wide hips. He waddled as he walked and was a step behind his companion. A camera and two small leather boxes hung from straps around his neck and bounced off his hips as he moved. The man in the blazer did the talking.

"You're Father Martin?"

"I am, boys, and you're from the newspapers are ya?"

"That's right, Father, we're here to cover this fund raiser," said the man in the blazer.

"Well, boys, I'm sorry there are no Kennedys here. This is a private get-together. I'll have to ask you to leave," the priest said with a smile.

"What a minute, Father, this raising money for Irish political prisoners is not exactly private."

"What do you mean?"

"I mean it's the public's business," the man said firmly. The photographer seemed to be falling asleep.

"It's what?"

The photographer lifted the camera and aimed it at the group. "It's a matter the public has a right to know about."

"Hey," said Jabber, "we don't want any pictures."

"That's right," said Father Martin, "no pictures."

Dan turned and looked toward the far end of the hall. He heard the click and whine of the camera and Jabber's voice.

"Goddamn it, who do you guys think you are!"

Dan turned his head to watch.

"We know who we are, mister," said the reporter, "and we think the public has the right to know who the people are that are giving money that may be used to continue terrorism in Northern Ireland."

The bartenders had stopped serving and were clustered at the bar watching. The cameraman clicked off another shot and even as the whir sounded, Father Martin's massive arm shot out. "That is a fine looking camera—do you mind?" The cameraman's head snapped forward and his mustache flapped as the priest jerked the camera out of his hand, snapping the leather strap.

"Oh, dear, I've dropped it," said the priest.

"Fumble Father," said Jabber.

"Fer Chrissake," cried the photographer. His eyes were wide open.

"I'll get it," said Dan as the camera bounced on the floor, and as he moved his foot hit the camera, sending it crashing against the brass footrail of the bar.

"Well, this is an awkward group, I must say," said Jabber.

"This is outrageous," snapped the man in the blazer, his face flared.

"It is a shame," said the priest.

"You won't get away with this bully-boy crap, Father," he hissed. "We'll get you for this."

"I'm sure we'll have to pay for the camera—it was clumsy of me, but now will you please leave?'' Father Martin said.

"You just—" started the reporter.

"C'mon, Sam, let's get the hell out of here," interrupted the photographer.

"This isn't the end of this thing, Father," the reporter said over his shoulder as he followed the photographer toward the door.

"And I'm afraid he's right," murmured Jabber.

"I know, I know, but they're so damned arrogant," said the priest.

"Of course you're right, Father, but wait'll Bucky finds out."

"Oh, I know. What is it now, Danny Boy?" he asked with a sigh.

"Senator Burke's here, Father. Shall I get the colors?"

"Go get 'em, Danny," said the priest, and the boy ran twisting through the crowd toward the stage at the end of the building. Father Martin reached over to the bar and grabbed a bottle of beer. He opened his mouth and poured the liquid down his throat without pausing. He wiped his mouth with the back of his hand.

"Let's go greet Senator Bucky Burke, Dan. Jabber, we'll say nothing about this for now."

"That's fine with me, Father Mike."

The priest grabbed Jabber's shoulder and gave a squeeze. Jabber's eyes popped wide open. "A wonderful night for this parish," said the priest solemnly as they moved through the crowd.

Thirty-Two

Senator Bucky Burke and Mary stood inside the entrance, a small crowd around them. Everyone was talking at once. Malachi was a tall thin presence by the door, his eyes bright behind his glasses which, Dan noted, had fresh adhesive on them, his face lit with pleasure as he watched Father Martin and Dan move toward him through the crowd.

The group around the Burkes parted before the priest. "Mary, Bucky, I'm glad to see you here." He reached a long arm between them toward Malachi. "And you, too, you old tiger." With his other arm, he grabbed Dan and pulled him forward. "Mary, this is Dan Conway." As Mary and Dan shook hands, the priest continued talking. "Bucky, you should be very proud of your old man for giving us this opportunity to meet Dan."

"Sure, sure, Father," said Bucky.

"You're pleased with all this, Father?" asked Mary.

"I certainly am, Mary. You know how I feel about the Irish situation."

Mary Burke colored. "I'm not sure, Father. I know you and himself," she tilted her head at Malachi who was whispering to Dan, "talk about it, but, to tell the truth, I never paid enough attention I guess."

"Well, Mary Burke, you're married to a political man who's Irish. You should know the politics of Ireland."

"I guess so, Father. Anyway we're here to help tonight."

"Exactly," said Father Martin and, turning, looked toward the end of the hall and waved a hand in a beckoning gesture. He herded the group together, Malachi, Bucky and Mary and Dan, somehow managing to keep a hand on Dan's elbow. "C'mon now, everybody, we must get up on the stage."

As he spoke a file of four young people in green and white uniforms marched onto the stage from behind the curtain. They did a smart facing movement and stood at attention. There were two girls—one carried a large American flag, the other an equally large flag with the green, white and orange colors of the Irish Republic. They were flanked by two boys carrying short wooden rifles with white gun slings.

The crowd's attention focused on this group. By the time Father Martin had his charges self-consciously assembled on the stage, the screeching sound of a needle being misplaced on a record poked at everyone's ears. The notes of the National Anthem boomed through the hall. Father Martin's voice was strong and vibrant in the vigorous, ragged singing which accompanied the music of the Anthem. There was chattering and movement in the crowd at the conclusion of the music. Scratchy bits of fumbling could be heard over the loudspeakers.

Then the impact of stirring music reverberated through the hall. Dan's eyebrows raised and he braced himself. It was the "Soldier's Song"—the Anthem of the Irish Republic. As the music swelled, Father Martin burst into song with gusto, then softer as a few others picked up the words; then the reedy voice of Malachi Burke cut through them all. The other voices trailed off as the old man carried the sense and strength of the words across the hall in his wavering tones. "Soldiers are we whose lives are pledged to Ireland."

Father Martin's voice was a whisper now, "Sworn to be free. No more our ancient sire-land. . . ."

The husky cracking voice of Malachi Burke cast a spell on the group with its undisguised passion. Right now, in this place, this was Malachi Burke's unembarrassed love song. His old voice wavered but did not quit. ". . . Shall shelter the despot or the slave . . . ."

Every eye was now on the old man. Dan could see the Senator and his wife standing beyond the old man. Bucky had pulled himself up to a version of attention, his mouth clamped so firmly shut that Dan could make out muscles in the side of his jaw. Mary took a small handkerchief from her purse. She did not look at it but pressed it at the corner of her eyes as she stared at her father-in-law.

Malachi sang with his eyes gazing into the distance over the stock-still crowd and found a younger voice somewhere within himself as he ended in strong throaty tones:

> "In Erin's cause, come woe or weal,
> Mid cannon's roar and rifles peal
> We'll chant a soldier's song."

The crowd stood silent and motionless. Children watched the adults with wide eyes. There was no sound until Father Martin cleared his throat. The group broke into applause. The color guard did a facing movement and departed.

Malachi Burke stood easy now, but his mind was full with long, long thoughts. He heard only parts and pieces of the events and speeches around him. Father Martin's voice was roaring and gentle, thunderstorm or dew on the grass.

"First, congratulations and thanks to Malachi Burke, a man who is a patriot, for his native land and for his adopted country . . . many reasons for the people of St. Bridget's to thank him." Applause, whistles. ". . . grim, somber life for our people in Ulster . . . Purgatory . . . the North of Ireland . . . Catholics treated like dirt, second-class citizens, generations of oppression, injustice..." Malachi vaguely heard the rage in the priest's voice. ". . . Jail without trial, suffering families subjected to Protestant bigotry, no jobs. Remember it when you speak too quickly in our own beloved land." Now Father Martin's tone was full of pride. ". . . the struggle of the modern martyrs in the North . . . struggle worth the cost. Heroes, real men, patriots . . . honored to have one here tonight. A man who has suffered in their jails, knows the need of the suffering families . . ." An apologetic softening. ". . . but it takes money. Do what you can to help . . ." Vibrant again. ". . . to introduce him, our own Senator . . . worthy of our respect, yes, even our love, a man of the present and the future. . ." Applause, cheers. ". . . his lovely wife, Mary." Applause, Mary smiling, bowing her head. The old man's thoughts were a fuzzy mixture of sights and sounds—images of strong green fields edged with grey stone walls, hills brushed with soft rain, hissing peat fires. His son was introducing Dan and the phrases rolled past him. ". . . Christian charity . . . hearts go out to all oppressed people . . . poor families, denied the political process . . . your money will go to help families like yourselves . . . Now, from Ireland, Mr. Dan Conway."

Malachi left his dreams of what might have been and stopped cutting himself with the knife-edge of sadness. He would listen carefully to Dan Conway.

Dan spoke in a quiet, measured cadence. "Thank you for being here and for whatever you can do to help, in any way. We need money. If you are able to contribute, what you give will be used effectively. We are grateful to Malachi Burke for his lifetime of help and to his son, the Senator, and very much to Father Martin." The applause was punctured by whistles.

Father Martin and Malachi led Dan down the steps to the crowd. They stayed by his side, their backs straight, tight smiles on their faces as Dan moved among the people. Malachi nodded from time to time as Dan was asked about people, places, relatives. Money was passed in modest amounts, a dollar, an occasional five or ten, and one man opened his wallet with unsteady hands and leafed out three ten dollar bills while a woman by his side glared at him. Then Jabber was standing in front of them.

"Father, Bucky heard about the hassle with the newshawks. He wants to talk to us."

"What's that?" asked Malachi as the priest and Dan turned toward the Senator and his wife.

"Some news people were here, tried to take pictures, we tossed 'em out," Jabber growled rapidly.

"Good, damn troublemakers!" said Malachi as he came up beside his son.

"Sure, Pa, sure," said Bucky as he turned to the priest. "Father, suicide is against the laws of the Church, isn't it?"

"Of course, Buck."

"Well, let me tell you fellas that for a politician to be involved in what you guys did here tonight is to commit suicide. Do you understand?"

"Senator, your name wasn't even mentioned, believe me," Jabber said anxiously.

"I'm sure, but, goddamn, what goes on in your mind—and, Father, you?"

"It's me," said Dan quietly.

"What do you mean?" Bucky asked.

"I think it's that fella, Hurley."

"You're goddamn right it is," said Jabber.

"Well then that's all the more reason not to have a fracas like that—you know he's a big feeling bastard and I know it, but I don't want a fight with him over this kind of goddamn nonsense."

"Careful, Buck," said Father Martin.

"I'm sorry, Father, maybe I'm overreacting—I hope so." He leaned around the priest and crooked a finger at Mary who was nearby, trying to listen to three women talking at her. "Mary and I have a retirement dinner-dance to make an appearance at," he said.

"Want me to come along?" Jabber asked.

"No. I'll see you in the morning—but thanks," he added.

Thirty-Three

MALACHI AND DAN WATCHED Jabber light a cigarette. The tip flared as he took a long deep drag. Malachi rubbed his hands against the chill of the spring night.

"Well, whadda think, Jabber boy?"

"It'll be all right, Mal. Bucky's upset but he'll be all right in the morning—I hope," he added in a low tone.

"Well Father Mike is after havin' another do in Dorchester day after tamarra."

"Good! That's good, Mal," Jabber said. "Let me know the time and place and I'll be there with the Champ here." He gave the old man a broad wink. "Now, can we drop you off?"

"No thanks, boys, I think I'll stop on the way and have a jar with the lads and talk a little insurrection. Good night to ya, Dan Conway."

"Good night, Malachi. Perhaps you'd give me a call tomorrow—and thanks."

"Ah, gowan with ya."

Jabber's car coughed and jerked as they sat at the curb in front of Ruth's apartment. The doorman looked at the car for a moment and then turned away.

"Jabber, I think it would be a good idea if I stay someplace else after tonight."

"Hurley?" Jabber snapped out the name.

"Yeh, he's got his eye on Ruth and he doesn't like the idea of my stayin' here."

"That figgers—and you think he'll lay off if you move."

"I hope so."

"O.K., Champ—I think you're right. We'll do somethin' tomorrow." He put a hand on the steering wheel and turned to Dan. His face was still. His glance slid past Dan and watched something outside. His voice was hesitant. "Do ya think Ruth is falling for him?"

"No, I don't think so, but she's taken with his job and the people he's with—it's strong stuff, I'm sure."

"Christ," Jabber burst out, "she's not swallowing that crap, is she? I mean, she's heard the stories about Hurley—not just the women, but he's a goddamn whore in the newsbusiness, he'd do anything for a story. Ruth isn't—"

"Ruth has got good judgment, Jabber, and so has her father. She'll work this out right, you'll see."

Jabber gave Dan a lopsided smile. "Sure—well, I better get goin'. Goodnight, Champ."

Dan emptied his pockets onto the bureau. The bills, crumpled or folded, made a jumbled pile. He dumped the contents of the envelopes from Gus Klein's group on top of it. He separated the currency into denominations and then counted it. He stared at the uneven rectangles of money. He'd never seen that much money before. He grunted. He'd never had much to do with money. He wondered if it was possible to be around money and remain a Marxist. He shrugged and turned away from the bureau and got ready for bed.

He lay stretched out on his back. His eyes were just barely open and through the fine gauze of his eyelashes he watched the blurred light and shadow patterns the city brightness and the night sketched on the ceiling. Now was the time—the time he had been waiting for—the time to think of Kate. A delicious drowsiness settled on him and the thought of her was such pleasure—a moment full of secret delight. There had not been many for him ever, and he remembered then how it was with those few cherished times when he was small. The noise and smell of the flat in Belfast came back to him, and the damp—he thought of the damp as he fingered the silk sheet across his chest. His grandmother would save honey and bake tiny little honey tarts for him. She would tell no one and he would tell no one and she would give them to him quickly when no one was looking—one at a time. He would suck on the tart and feel it diminish in his mouth until there was only a tiny piece, and he would push it up into the roof of his mouth and press against it with his tongue until his jaw ached and the sweetness would flow down his tongue and into the corners of his mouth. His grandmother would look at him sometimes when the old man would be cursing the English and slamming the edge of his fist on the table. Dan would keep his mouth closed tight, tasting the secret sweetness, and she seemed to sense his pleasure. Her eyes would flash bright and young for a moment, the corners would crinkle and her toothless parchment face would lose its worn sadness. He could see Kate's face, could see the outline of each exquisite freckle, and he felt the same secret delight. He turned over on his stomach, his mind and body full of her. Then he pushed the pistol and the pillow up against the headboard and slept.

Thirty-Four

THE RATTLE OF RAIN against the window woke him. He pulled the cool edge of the silk sheet and the puffy comforter up over his shoulders. He tried to gauge the time by the light at the window. He dozed for some fuzzy minutes, then got up, put on his slacks and went into the kitchen.

He was sipping tea, watching the jigsaw puzzle of rain on the window change its forms, when Ruth Klein surprised him with a sleepy hello. She was leaning against the door frame, wearing a full length black dressing gown that served her well. Her chestnut hair fell free and long and her face was still soft with sleep.

"I'll bet you're thinking about home, Dan."

"You'd win. It'd be hard not to be thinking of Ireland now. I've two of the mainstays of our life right here—rain and tea."

"Does it rain a lot?"

"In the West the old people say you only notice it when it doesn't."

Ruth laughed and for a moment she looked young and vulnerable. "I'll get the morning paper for you Dan, if it's here yet." She grinned over her shoulder at him as she went down the hall. "I'll bet that's the way it is in Ireland, too."

"What?"

"The women fetching for the men."

"You'd be right again," he said. His chuckle followed her as she went to the front door.

"Oh, Jeezus, that bastard!!" Ruth's words came into the kitchen and the lacework pattern of the rain on the window dissolved in Dan's eyes. He got up from his chair and had taken but one step when Ruth came into the kitchen. Her eyes were wide and shocked, her face drained of color.

She held the newspaper out in front of her away from her body. "Oh, Dan, this is awful. I can't believe he'd do this. He knew this was personal! That he'd take advantage of us like this—God!"

She spread the newspaper on the kitchen table. The front page headline letters seemed blacker and larger than usual to Dan as he looked at them. **IRISH TERRORIST IN BOSTON**

Beside the long column of the article were two photographs. One, obviously taken with a long-distance lens, was of him on the street yesterday afternoon; the other was a prison mug-shot used by the British Army.

Dan could feel Ruth's eyes flash from him to the story as they read. Hurley's name was not on the story. Two reporters' names were listed and they wrote in broad lurid language: "Dan Conway, legendary Irish guerilla leader thought to be responsible for the recent slaughter of a British Army patrol and the destruction of a helicopter gunship . . . in Boston to allegedly raise money for the families of so-called political prisoners held in the North . . . lifetime terrorist . . . brains behind anti-British activities in England and Northern Ireland . . . shootouts and bombings . . . sought by British Army since breaking out of . . . rumored to be a Marxist . . . sources close to Scotland Yard and British Army Intelligence indicate . . . sponsored by Senator William Burke (D-South Boston) . . . turn to page seven."

The telephone rang as Dan and Ruth, both their hands on the paper, turned to page seven.

"Oh, my God," Ruth breathed the words as pictures of Senator Bucky Burke and Father Mike Martin smiled at them from page seven. The phone continued to ring. Ruth stared intently at Dan, the side of her fist in her mouth.

"Better answer that, Ruth."

"Oh—oh—yes." She walked woodenly to the phone. "Hello—yes, yes, Jabber, we're reading it now, yes—I know—I know—all right, I'll tell him—thanks.

She set the phone down and stared at it, then spoke, still looking at the phone. "Jabber's talked to the Senator. The Senator wants him to talk to you. He's on his way down here. He'd like you to wait for him."

Dan was reading page seven. "Alright," he said, his voice soft and low.

For the first time and in that single word, Ruth heard the pure sound of Irish speech from Dan Conway. The phone rang again. She looked away from it and spoke. "Is it true Dan—what's in the paper?"

"Yes, mostly. I've spent my whole life fighting the British and what they've done to my country—it's mostly accurate."

The phone continued to ring. Dan pointed at it. Ruth picked it up. Her voice quavered. "Hello. Oh, Dad. Oh, God, do you think so? I know, I know! Jabber just said it, too. No, he's coming over—I don't blame you—I don't think he'd have the nerve to call here—You know I was with him last night—No, never, not a word. He never let on. All right, I'll tell him—Yes, I will. Goodbye."

Ruth dropped into a chair. Her hair spread fan-like in front of her face. She pushed it away with hands that shook. "My father thinks someone may bug this phone, if they haven't already, and he says—"

Dan interrupted her. "Your father's right. Is there a pay phone inside this building?"

"Yes, on every floor of the parking garage, there's one near the elevator."

"How do I find it?" He walked over to the phone and took it off the hook.

"Turn right, first corridor on your right, all the way to the end. There's a single elevator door—you'll need a key—it's there on that hook."

"I'll be a couple of minutes. Keep the phone off the hook 'til I get back."

"Dan."

"Yes."

"I'm so sorry."

"No need for that. It's not your doin'."

"Well, it's Bill Hurley's doing, and if it weren't for me, Bill Hurley wouldn't have known you were here. I can't believe this has happened, and the Senator—" She put her hands over her face. Dan left the room without speaking.

Ruth sat motionless in her chair. She suddenly began to hate the sterile kitchen. She wished she could scream, yell, stomp her feet—something, anything. Yet she felt unable to move. A weight had settled inside her. The nerve needling dat-dat-dat-dat noise of the phone off the hook punctured the sounds of the rain rushing against the windows. She thought the sound obscene. She stared at the newspaper headlines, not moving.

Dan's face told her nothing as he entered the room. He went over to the phone and settled it onto its receiver. "Ruth, I'm going to take a shower and pack. I think—"

His words were stopped by the ringing of the phone. The sound was very loud. It continued. Ruth did not move. Dan lifted the phone and, extending the cord, handed it to Ruth. Her voice shook.

"Hello." Her mouth set in a grim line. "I can't believe it—that you'd have the nerve to call here." Her words were clipped. Color came back to Ruth's face. Her nostrils flared. "Wait a minute, listen to me, Bill—No, I don't care what you have to say. No!—Is Dan Conway here?" She looked at Dan who shook his head and pointed out the window. "No, he's gone, but if he were here I'm sure he'd tell you he's not in the slightest bit interested in giving an interview—No, never mind. You've done enough damage. My father's right—you people are in the wrecking business, aren't you?—I'll give you an interview though, right now. I'll tell you that my father was wrong about one thing—that's right—yes, he said you were a no good son of a bitch. He was wrong on that—you're worse than that! You're a fucking bastard!'' Ruth took three long strides as she spoke and smashed the phone into the receiver and then leaned against the wall. Her body was shaking. "I've never done anything like that before."

"I'm told it's pretty good medicine once in a while," Dan said.

"Don't you lose your temper, Dan?"

"I learned early on that I couldn't afford it. You know, our people have a saying. Don't get mad—get even. But in your case this morning, getting mad makes a lot more sense."

The lobby-connected phone buzzed. "That will be Jabber, I hope," said Ruth. She pulled the belt of her gown together and pushed back her hair. Her face framed a question at Dan.

"If it's Jabber, have him come up," he said. "I expect he's by himself—I don't want to meet any new people right now."

Dan waited to listen to Ruth's brief exchange with the doorman.

"It's Jabber—alone," she called.

"I'm going to take that shower. Tell him I won't be long."

Jabber and Ruth were at the breakfast counter when Dan came back to the kitchen. The room was cloudy with cigarette smoke. Dan noticed Ruth smoking in an amateur fashion, repeated, quick, awkward puffs. Jabber's voice stopped the instant he saw Dan. His eyes stayed on Conway, wide and unblinking. Ruth's head swung round. Her eyes took in the suit carrier and leather bag that Dan set on a chair.

"Dan, you're leaving right now?"

"Yes, Ruth. I've talked to some of our people and it's time to see other parts of America." He took a folded piece of paper from his pocket and handed it to Jabber. "This is a note for Malachi."

"He and Father Mike asked if they could meet with you someplace today," said Jabber.

"No, this is the best way," Dan said. "Tell Father Mike that the next time he visits Ireland I want him to pass the word for me. I'll hear it and I'll see him. Tell him that for me, Jabber. That goes for you and your old gent, too," he said looking at Ruth.

"What about me, Champ?" Jabber asked solemnly.

"You, too, my friend."

"Oh, Dan," Ruth said. There was anguish in her voice.

"Listen, Miss Klein, I'm not lettin' you off the hook just yet. Is your car in that concrete fort you folks call a parking garage?"

"Yes."

"Fine. I'd like to ask one last favor—a ride to the airport."

"Good thinking, Champ," exclaimed Jabber. "Into the car in the parking garage. Nobody sees you leave, then up, up and away!"

Dan winked at him.

"I'll get ready right now," said Ruth.

"Fast," said Dan dryly.

Jabber chuckled as Ruth tossed her head and hustled from the room. "I'll come along, if you don't mind," he said.

"I want you to," Dan answered. "Ruth needs a good friend right now—one she can really trust."

Neither man spoke during the brief time that Ruth was gone. Dan gazed at the trickling rain on the window. Jabber stared into his teacup. Ruth rushed in wearing white slacks and a black sweater, her hair under a multi-colored kerchief. She buckled on a raincoat. Her appearance seemed to pull Jabber up from his seat. "I'm going to come along with you," he said.

Ruth took his hand. "I'm glad."

The elevator opened directly onto the long low-ceilinged mass of concrete that was the parking garage. Rows of massive fat, round trunks of cement supported the waffled ceiling. Long garish tubes of fluorescent lighting illuminated the walls and ceilings, insuring that every scar and blemish in the concrete could be seen. Dan assumed that the lights were lit day and night in this temple to the automobile goddess. A pickup truck with its hood raised was parked near the elevator. Two men in coveralls were bent over the motor. The loud sound of their hammering bounced back and forth off the solid walls. Dan took Ruth's arm. Jabber slowed to light a cigarette. The hammering stopped.

"Conway!"

Jabber turned to look at the men. At the same moment he realized they had guns he felt a tremendous smash in his shoulder and heard the shot and Ruth's screams. He felt himself fall as though in slow motion and saw Conway push Ruth down, dive to the floor himself and then pull her with him behind a column. He heard more shots and could see chips of concrete flying off the column as he tried to slide his body under a car. He inched along the floor but then gave it up. His body was too heavy now. It hurt too much.

He could see the men in the coveralls. They ignored him and fired toward what he now thought of as Conway's and Ruth's column. One of the men pointed, then made a sweeping motion with his arm and with a tiptoe stalking movement worked his way along the far wall. The other man drove a shot at the column and then raced to the front of a car parked just a few yards from the column. His pistol pointed unwavering in the direction of Dan and Ruth. He turned and looked casually at Jabber, who quickly closed his eyes and tried not to breathe. The concrete was sharp and rough. He could feel blood soaking his coat.

Pain started to flood his body. He was going to throw up. He couldn't help it. Panic captured him; he would throw up and the gunman would kill him. "Christ," he thought, "I'm going to puke myself to death." He willed himself not to throw up. He squeezed his eyes shut, then found himself peeking out between the lids. The gunman moved without a sound toward the column. He had thick rubber soled shoes on. "The son of a bitch," he thought, "he's planned not to make a sound. I won't either—I won't throw up."

Now the pain became terrible. He hated himself, but he knew that what he wanted was that they leave him alone, not shoot him again. He wanted to live. He was cold. He felt the bile coming into his throat, up to his mouth. He gagged; his stomach emptied; he could not stop it. His mouth filled to bursting. He vomited. The gunman turned his head at the sound. He looked at Jabber.

Dan Conway jumped from behind the column in a low crouch. Before the gunman knew what happened, Dan's bullet caught him full in the neck. The gunman dropped his pistol as his hands went toward his throat. His body pitched backward. Jabber winced as he heard the short awful strangling sounds of the gunman as he fell, his life over before his body smashed against the unforgiving floor.

Ruth was on her hands and knees next to the column. Her head was down, eyes wide open, staring unseeing at the grey pebbled texture of the concrete. She willed herself not to blink so that nothing could interfere with her hearing. Her entire being listened. She had scarcely noticed the men in the coveralls. She thought there were two of them. She was terrified. She was not sure what was happening. Now her concern was her breathing. Her mouth was wide open. She did not want to make noise, but she knew noises were coming from her mouth. She could not get enough air; if only she could breathe and not make any sound. She heard Dan move away from her side. Panic swept through her. She did not want him to leave her. She could not be alone with this fear. It was too much.

A strange sound. What was it? Retching? She puzzled on that. There was a shot close by. She had never heard shots before but now she knew their distinctive report. A terrible cry cut short—quick steps—she closed her eyes. Every fiber in her body tensed. She was terrified. Then Dan's voice in her ear, and she began to cry. Tears flooded her eyes. She couldn't stop. Heavy wracking crying. Her body shook.

Dan placed a hand on the back of her neck as he whispered, his breath warm. "There's one more of them. Now you and I are going to get under that car right there." His strong fingers turned her head sideways. "You see that blue car?"

Ruth was surprised to hear her voice. "It's a Cadillac."

"That's the girl. That's the one. When I take a shot at this bastard, I want you to move as fast and low as you can."

As he spoke his fingers rubbed her neck going deep into her muscles. She began to get her shuddering body under control.

A shot cracked through the air knocking chips off the column, snapping against a car. Dan's fingers stopped and he squeezed hard. "Get well under that car. I'm comin' in after ya—move."

He pushed her and rose up into a half crouch and fired. His bullet exploded a fluorescent tube which cracked and hissed. A return shot smashed a window in a nearby Jaguar. Dan bent over as low as he could and in two long strides was beside the blue Cadillac, then he dove flat-out on all fours on the concrete, feeling the floor cut him as he did, and quickly hauled himself under the car. His hands and knees hurt. He was vaguely aware that they were burning and bleeding. Ruth's eyes were pressed tight. Her knees pulled up. Dan whispered very softly, "Lay out flat, girl." Her eyes opened and widened. His face was right beside her. "I think he's over that way, but you watch there," Dan whispered, pointing a finger. "Punch me if you see him, but don't make a noise."

As he finished speaking, Dan slid up past the top of Ruth's head. He noticed, without feeling, the raw meat on the edge of his left hand as he brought it up to steady his pistol. His cheek scraped on the sandpaper texture of the floor as he sighted into an open field of fire between a row of cars and rank of tires.

Suddenly at the end of the row, near the wall, he thought he saw the toe of a rubber soled shoe. He watched it intently—forgetting everything else. It was a shoe. It moved. Dan breathed deeply and exhaled slowly. One hand braced the other as he sighted along the barrel at the shoe. It lifted and as he breathed and exhaled the shoe and ankle and the bottom of coveralls came into view. It set down and did not move. Dan squeezed the trigger gently. The ankle jumped. A voice cried out. Dan rolled quickly out from under the car, scrambled to his feet and ran in a zigzag crouch toward the gunman who had fallen on his side out between the row of cars. The man was holding his ankle, his pistol still in one hand; cries and grunts of pain echoed off the wall. The man saw Dan and swung his pistol up. His hand was shaking as he fired. Dan pumped a bullet out as he moved. The man screamed as the metal tore into his stomach. He dropped the pistol and cried out—"Ahhh!" Dan stopped and brought his pistol up to eye leve and aimed.

"No, no, please, no."

The slug hit the man in the chest and drove him back against the floor. His arms flew out from his body, his mouth opened, and he looked at Conway. His eyes were wild. He tried to speak. His head twisted and the breath shuddered out of him.

Dan watched him—then yelled, "Ruth, it's all right. Come out."

Ruth heard Dan's voice. She could see his legs. She had watched them run toward the man on the floor. Rigid with fear, she'd watched the gunman twist and fire his gun at Conway. A scream had started inside her then, but no sound came from her mouth. Now she was exhausted. She became aware of all of her body and her face flamed. She had lost control of her bladder. Her crotch was soaked. She could feel the sopping wetness in her pants and on her slacks. She was lying in a puddle of urine. She could feel it spreading beneath her. Dan's legs moved out of sight. She heard urgency in his voice.

"Jabber, Jabber. Ruth, come here—quick, girl."

Ruth worked her way out from under the car. She would not look down at herself. She glanced at the body lying on the floor near the column. She felt her heart pumping in her chest. Dan was kneeling beside Jabber, putting one of his arms under Jabber's right arm. There was no color in Jabber's face. He lay in a sticky puddle of dark blood.

"Ruth, grab my bags and get that elevator. We'll take him to your apartment. Can you walk, man?"

"I'll make it," said Jabber through paper thin lips.

"Sure you will. O.K., hold on, we'll get you up now."

They saw no one on their way to Ruth's apartment. Conway spoke an occasional encouraging word to Jabber. Ruth felt as though she was in a trance. She wondered if she might be dreaming. Her mind was blurred.

"Get the key ready, Ruth. We want to get him right into bed and under all the blankets you've got."

When the apartment door opened, Jabber's weight slid toward the floor. Dan grunted as he grabbed him tighter. Jabber moaned. The woeful sound cut through the fuzz of Ruth's senses. "Put him in my bed, Dan." She ran ahead, pulling blankets from a closet.

"Ruth, call your father. Tell him we must have a doctor here at once."

Ruth dialed the phone with one hand as she helped pull covers over Jabber. His eyes were open now and he looked at Dan as he piled warmth on him. A faint smile curved the corners of his mouth. He spoke in a soft cadence. "I've called lots of people Champ—just a name—for everybody. I'll never use it again, unless it's you."

"Hey, don't get serious now, Jabber. We'll have a doctor here soon and you're goin' to be all right."

"You sure, Champ?"

"Absolutely."

"I believe you." His eyes closed and he started to shake.

Ruth's voice cut in, "Dad, we've got to have a doctor at my apartment. Well, it's—"

The covers on the bed quivered and jumped. Dan took the phone from Ruth. "Gus, this is your Irish friend. Ruth's fine but we need a doctor here right away—all right—I'll hold on." He covered the mouthpiece. "Ruth, if there are no more blankets, it would help if you got into bed beside him, close to him. We've got to keep him warm."

Ruth became aware of her wet clothes and unbuttoned her blouse. She put her arms behind her and undid her bra. Dan uncovered the phone. Ruth stripped off her slacks and soaked pants with no wasted motion and slid under the covers. She put her body half across Jabber's. He winced and she took his face in her hands and pressed her lips against his throat. Dan stared at them for a moment. Jabber's body was less and less electric. His breathing became easy and even.

"I'm back, Irish, and the doctor's on the way."

"Good. We've had some big trouble, Gus. O'Rourke, the guy who works for Burke—"

"Yeah."

"He's not so good, but he'll be O.K., I think, and—"

"What?"

"Don't ask. You're better if you don't know, but I need a big favor from you."

"Let me talk to my daughter."

Dan put the phone toward Ruth as he spoke to her. "Your father wants to talk to you."

Ruth tensed for a moment. She brushed the hair from her ear. "Gus, we should do anything this man wants for the rest of our lives." She started to sob. "I wouldn't be alive if it weren't for him." Her voice broke, "Oh, Daddy."

Dan took the phone from her. Klein's voice was savage. "Did that fuckin' newspaper thing cause this?"

"It sure helped, though maybe it was in the stars, but now I need a favor and you're goin' to have to put yourself in some jeopardy. I need a ride."

"You want me over there?" barked Gus, and before Dan could answer, "good, cuz I was comin' anyway." The phone banged off.

The doctor, elderly, stooped, with wild white hair and bushy black eyebrows, arrived within minutes. He spoke in a thick German accent and explained that when Gus Klein called he came—"Wheneffer, whereffer." He shook his head in admiration when Ruth moved from Jabber and got out from under the blankets. "Marvelous—marvelous," he said as she glided in regal nudity to a closet and knotted on a robe. He'd exposed Jabber's wound and pinched his cheek. "You vill be fine. A stiff shoulder maybe, maybe not if you hexercize. Ya, ve fix you up, at da hospital."

Gus arrived—grim and calm. He barked a few questions.

Now Dan stood in the kitchen. Gus and Ruth sat watching him closely—their eyes never left him. "I'll need a ride to the airport."

"And if you haven't any here, some clothes," said Gus.

Dan looked at his suit which was torn and spotted with oil and blood. "Yeah, and a hat," said Dan.

"What will you do, Dan?" cried Ruth.

"You're both better off if you don't know."

"Oh! But you can't spend your life like this—there's got to be a better way. What about Kate—the girl in Ireland—you can't ask her to share this kind of thing."

"I'm going to get out of this kind of thing."

"Can you get out?"

"Yes. It's not too late. I can get out and live a quiet life in a quiet place."

"Oh, I hope so, Dan. I really hope so." Ruth stared at him with tear-filled eyes.

"Do you have another passport, Dan?" Gus asked.

"In my line of work it's a must," Dan answered matter-of-factly.

"Who were those men, Dan?" Ruth asked. "Surely not from the North of Ireland."

"No, paid guns. People who will do anything for money."

"You figure it was the newspaper, Dan?"

"Yeah! I think what happened, Gus, is that the reporters talked to the British and the Royal Ulster Constabulary and someone passed the word and all it took was a few phone calls and the Red Hand of Ulster reached out to me."

Ruth shook her head. "God, it's Red as in blood, isn't it?"

"Always," said Dan. "Folks, I've got to go. I'm surprised this place isn't swarming with police already."

"Where, Dan, where will you go—please tell me where," Ruth pleaded. She glanced at her father. "I'd like for us, Gus, Jabber and me, to know what happens to you. You'll always be part of our lives now, Dan."

"I'm goin' home, Ruth—to Ireland."

"What's the name of the place, Dan?"

"A village called Ahakista in the West, but you must both promise not to reveal that."

"Oh, I won't, Dan," said Ruth breathlessly. She reached out and held his hand in both of hers and pressed it to her cheek. "After today I know why."

"I can't even pronounce it, so don't worry about me, but maybe someday we'll surprise you," said Gus gruffly. He took a small black address book from his pocket. "Let me write it down. How do you spell it?"

Dan spelled the letters slowly. "A-H-A-K-I-S-T-A."

Thirty-Five

The plane dipped a wing into the edge of the plateau of rumpled white clouds that extended as far as one could see. For a few minutes the majesty of the great silver machine was enhanced by a cloak of ermine. Then the plane broke through the bottom of the clouds and it was there spread out below them—Ireland—so green it might be artificial. He had forgotten how abundantly green it was. Rain began to speckle his window. He shivered. The plane was not chilly. It was Kate, the excitement of Kate.

A stewardess leaned over his shoulder and shared his view. She spoke as she stared out the window. "I make this trip often, but every time I do, when I first see it, I feel strange—sad—kind of. I'm not sure why, but I'm drawn to it, it's so beautiful and powerful somehow. One of my grandparents came from here, I think. I'm not even sure." She stood up and smoothed her skirt, "Excuse me, I didn't mean to intrude on your morning privacy."

"It's all right, Miss. I understand."

The customs man was tall, heavy-footed with a uniform that was shiny with years of service. Dan looked past him as he approached. The man stared at him for a moment before he spoke, then cleared his throat.

"I'm a believer in the goal of the or-gan-i-za-tion and I've a message for ya, sor."

Dan's glance swept the room. "What is it?"

"There's a young fella waitin' for ya in the car park. Says his name's Rooney." The man shifted his bulk from foot to foot.

"Got a scar on his head?"

"He does indeed. He's waitin' in a black car—Cortina—last two numbers 76."

"Thanks."

The man raised his voice now. "Right out that way, sor, yes, indeed, sor." He raised a two-fingered salute to his cap.

Dan jammed his bags through a doorway and was out into the soggy morning. He walked quickly around the side of the building and then moved along the back side of the car park. He spotted the Cortina and came up on the passenger side.

Eddie Rooney was slouched down behind the wheel; a cigarette hung slack in his lips. Dan looked down at the doorlock and pressed his thumb against the button on the handle. He jerked the door open. Rooney's head swung and one hand went into his jacket.

"Gotta learn to keep your doors locked, Eddie."

"Bloody hell! You scared me, Dan."

"You'd better get used to a lifetime of it."

Rooney searched Dan's face with his shifting dark eyes. "Yeah, yeah," he licked the edge of a scraggly moustache, "you know they got James John."

"I know," Dan said curtly as he tossed the suit carrier into the back seat.

"I been hidin' in Dublin for a while—things are too hot up North right now—I was glad ta get outa there to drive here ta get 'cha."

"I'm not goin' to Dublin."

"You're not?"

"No, I want you to give me a lift up to Galway."

Eddie stared at him, his eyes were still. "To Galway?"

"Yes." Dan unzipped his leather bag and took out the package of money. "Give this to the Leadership in Dublin. You see the amounts written there."

"You're not comin' with me?" Rooney asked in a thoughtful voice.

"No. Just give me the ride. We'll stop in one of the villages for some Guinness and bread and cheese, but that's it—I want to go straight through."

They turned out onto the highway and Eddie spoke in a quiet voice.

"How was America, Dan?"

"Just drive, Eddie—just drive."

Dan stared out the window at the uneven beauty of the countryside, the neat stone wall-edged patchwork of fields of turned earth, green meadows whiskered with white spring flowers. He turned his head to watch two smooth brown colts nuzzle one another across a narrow white watered brook.

A tinker's wagon was parked on the verge outside the village of Clarecastle. Its hooped sides were painted a harsh purple decorated with strange yellow curlicues. Handsome, cherry-cheeked blonde children circled around a pot hanging over a ragged wood fire. Laundry was laid on the hedgerow to dry. The children turned and waved at the car.

"Lucky little shits," muttered Eddie. Dan narrowed his eyes and looked at him. Rooney shrugged. "They're so free, that's all."

Fat-bellied black and white cows milled about the square in Clarecastle. A Celtic cross rose in the center of the area. Rubber booted farmers in dark suits stood near it, chatting, smoking, watching the cattle. One man slapped another on the back and laughed loudly. Some of the men grinned.

Two cars stood waiting for the cows to move. A man got out of the lead car and walked into a storefront marked "P.J. O'Brien" in bright blue letters. He came to the doorway with a bottle of Guinness in his fist and leaned against the doorjamb and watched some high-hipped rust colored cattle move ponderously into the square from a side road.

Eddie Rooney rubbed the steering wheel, round and round. "Market day here, eh?" he said. He got out of the car, lit a cigarette and leaned on the hood until a quick-footed bushy-tailed dog drove the cattle into the far corner of the square.

They slowed behind a mud-spattered truck on the outskirts of Galway. There had been no conversation since Clarecastle.

"I'll get out here, Eddie. Deliver the money straight away. Tell the lads I'll be in touch, understand?"

"Yeah—I think I do," Rooney said nodding.

Thirty-Six

THE BOATS TIED UP along side Claddagh Quay in Galway Harbor were a dispirited lot; aging and battered, they groaned and creaked as they were jostled by the dark grey waves. Dan stopped by a fat-hulled half moon-shaped trawler painted a bright red. He couldn't understand the Gaelic script on the bow. A fat man sat mending a net amid the litter on the deck. His pipe was set upside down in his mouth and from time to time he would lift his head and gaze out toward the horizon. When Dan spoke, the man turned eyes the color of the sea on him. He listened and then answered slowly, "To the coast of Cork is it, to Bantry and Dunmanus—and no questions asked, I expect? You've picked the right man, Mister. Come aboard if you've got the cash with you. Shure we could leave with this tide. I can make that trip single-handed."

He rose from the crate he was perched on and hoisted the belt of his trousers which hung below his pumpkin belly. His thick nimble fingers worked over the bills Dan gave him and then folded them into a greasy black wallet.

"It's Captain Matthew O'Malley of the good ship *Blessed Redeemer* at your service, and I won't be needin' the burden of knowin' your name."

The wind came at them in gusts from the west as the *Blessed Redeemer* trudged its way out of Galway Bay. Captain O'Malley turned the bulldog nose of the trawler south as they passed the Aran Islands and the sky lost its few patches of blue; a grim greyness seemed to press down on the muscular little vessel and the wind picked up strength as it moved around to the southwest.

Dan sat in the wheelhouse, his legs braced against the far corner. He had accepted O'Malley's offer to "go below for a snooze," but one look and smell of the foul, greasy disarray of the sleeping quarters sent him topside to stay. A small gas-fed ring of flame kept an inexhaustible supply of hot water for tea at hand. Occasionally water was added to a mish-mash of ingredients which O'Malley referred to as "fine Irish stew" and the crusted cast iron stew pot would replace the tea kettle over the flame until a bubbling of the mass indicated to the Captain that the specialty of the house was ready.

Dan had accepted the offer of a heavy, moth eaten, turtlenecked sweater from the fisherman as the wind increased and then was proffered a large spoon and a mug. O'Malley glanced at the spoon and gave it a fast wipe on his sweater. "This will be fer yer grub," he said. As Dan watched the Captain he learned the spoon served double duty—stirring tea or ladling strange looking items from the stew pot.

The sea was well at them now, an endless procession of rolling heaving waves, some swelling to eye-lifting heights. The trawler shuddered and trembled. When the orchestration between the boat and the sea faltered, the bow was buried under a momentary mountain of grey-green water. Then the *Blessed Redeemer* would rouse herself and, quivering from the effort, work her way up the side of the always-coming next wave. Occasionally at the top of a wave the boat would react as though under the control of an uncertain elevator operator trying to come even with the floor.

O'Malley sat on a high stool directly behind the oversized burnished brass wheel. The small round surface of the stool had been expanded by the addition of a large pillow whose grimy corners drooped down its sides.

The Captain held the wheel with one hand, the other usually being busy with his mug of tea, poking in the stew pot, or fingering the chart. His voice was seldom still, for Captain Matthew O'Malley liked to sing. He sang almost constantly. His songs were of Ireland, rich and varied, popular and obscure.

Occasionally, with a big grin and without speaking to Dan, he would tap the chart and then, pointing out a particular spot on the map, proudly break into a song memorializing the area.

He began with "Galway Bay" which he sang repeatedly until the Aran Islands were behind them. Dan was able to follow their progress against the pounding sea, even as he dozed, by the lyrics of the tenor voice that filled the cramped wheelhouse. O'Malley moved them south to the sounds of "The White Cliffs of Moher." "Where the River Shannon Flows" was sung over and over as they crossed the mouth of the Shannon. The next announcement was a mournful "Rose of Tralee" as they ploughed through the empty night and the sea at the outer edge of Tralee Bay.

There was no moon. The only color in the wild black world they could feel and hear outside was the dim glow from the running lights on the mast above them. The compass light and the cheery orange flame on the gas ring that leapt out from under the tea kettle gave a sense of coziness to their tossing, tilting, plunging compartment.

O'Malley's repertoire of songs was extensive and Dan listened in a drifting half sleep to the "Wild Rover," "Maid of Fife," "The Beggar Man" and others of the apparently endless assembly that flowed from the Captain.

O'Malley finished a rendition of "The Kerry Man" and "The Dingle Puck Goat" and spoke for the first time since they left Galway. "D'ya mind drivin' a bit while I go below for a little nap? We're just past the Blaskets off Dingle Bay. Keep her on this headin' and I'll be up when we're off the Kenmare River."

He slid off his stool, turned and grabbed the top of the hatchway and swung his bulk down below with surprising ease. Soon a harsh, rasping snoring mingled with the noise of the engine.

Settling himself on the pillow, Dan alternated between glances at the compass and staring into the blackness beyond the window. Now, alone with the boat and the sea and the night, he could savor thoughts of Kate. He hoped that doubling back to Ahakista by sea would cover his tracks back to her. Kate was always in part of his mind. Sometimes the intensity of his thoughts of her were so powerful that he could feel her presence and then there was nothing else in his consciousness, only the look and smell and the touch of her. That was how it was for him now, in this no longer lonesome place, as the ocean grudgingly gave way to the *Blessed Redeemer.*

When O'Malley's hand reached past him and tapped the compass with an oil lined finger, Dan blinked hard to pull himself out of his revery. He had not heard the man come up beside him.

"I'll take her now," O'Malley said with a wink.

Dan Conway was in a deep sleep when Captain O'Malley leaned from his stool and said, "Hey, Bucko, I've no song for it right now but it's Bantry Bay dead ahead. Where is it you'd be wantin' to go ashore?"

Dan's eyes were open and seeing at once. It was early morning and the sun's rays had the beginning of summer in them. A narrow strip of fog was suspended just over the water. His gaze searched along the rocky shore of Sheep's Head up into the highlands of lush green meadows with their occasional flamboyant palm trees. Sheep and cattle moved slowly in and out of patches of morning mist.

Captain O'Malley pointed the *Blessed Redeemer* at the shore. Dan removed his shoes and socks and trousers. He sat on the edge of the bow. His pistol and clothes were in his bag. He held all his gear under one arm and pushed off from the boat. O'Malley put the boat in reverse as Dan dropped into the water which was breath-stopping cold. His feet moved unbidden to keep his balance as he worked his way toward the shore. O'Malley leaned out the side of the wheelhouse as he backed into a safe depth and bellowed, "Good luck, Bucko, I hope you find whatever it is you're lookin' for."

Dan turned, ankle deep in the ocean. He was smiling and waved at O'Malley. He sat on a rock feeling its warmth from the sun come up to him and dried his legs with his shirt. He put his clothes on and looked out at the boat which appeared very small now heading out to sea. Tiny waves made modest sounds as they died against the rocky beach. Gulls wheeled above crying peevishly. The sound of the engine came over the water and, just faintly, O'Malley's voice singing, words too muffled to hear. Dan jumped from the rock, clenched his fists and flung his arms out. He threw back his head and as the sun fingered his face he opened his mouth wide and let out a long soft moan of delight.

He walked up the coast road. The landscape sparkled with the reflection of the morning sun from still wet leaves of the oak trees. He felt as good as the day. There were shimmering moments of magic when a sunbeam was caught in the wet lace of a fern. He left the road and climbed through the thick wet grazing land, past bulky, deliberate cattle and skittish sheep, up to the dirt track that zigzagged along the spine of the ridge. He reached the top and headed for the cut to the Dillon Cottage. He had no interest in the view.

There was a powerful urgency in him. A rabbit raced out from a patch of yellow gorse beside the path, a black dog behind it, breathing hard. Dan called and the dog slid to a stop, looked, wheeled and rushed to him. Dan dropped his things as he went to one knee and wrapped his arms around the animal as it bounded against his chest.

"Ah, Bluff, Bluff." He roughed and scratched and patted the ecstatic dog. They were calm for a moment while Dan examined the healed wound on Bluff's leg. He thought of the night that he and Kate had stitched and bandaged this dog and of how he had touched Kate then for the first time. A drumming intensity throbbed in him now to touch her again. He stroked the dog's head, then picked up his bags and moved on, the dog beside him jigging and yelping.

They started down the way to the cottage. The dog's sounds brought Michael Dillon around to the side of the house from his bench by the front door. He stood well defined in the morning sun, his hand shading his eyes as he looked up at the man and the dog.

"Is that Dan Conway?" he shouted. "Is it you, Dan?"

Kate rushed round the corner of the house past her little car. She was barefoot, wearing jeans, her shirt hanging out. She didn't speak as she raced up the path to him. Dan started to run. The dog leapt and barked and barked. Kate stumbled, put her hands out and kept on towards him. Dan's momentum carried him forward; he lost his footing and slid into Kate. She fell on him. They clung to one another, lips searching for lips, for eyes, cheeks, hands, touching, pressing, holding. There were no words. The dog whined, pushing his nose against them. Harder and harder he burrowed until he pushed between them and they parted laughing, heads back, spread out against the moist, sweet smelling grass, looking up at the sunwashed blue sky. Dan turned and looked at Kate. Laughter was bubbling from her, tears coursing down her cheeks. The dog went to the side of Michael Dillon who stood looking down at them.

"Well, I see ya came back," he said dryly. "And I expect that means she's glad to see ya."

Thirty-Seven

THE BLACK TEA KETTLE hung in the fireplace and was whistling a demanding tune. Kate lifted a tattered pot-holder from its hook and pushed the iron bar that swung the kettle away from the busy flames. The dog collapsed on the hearth. Dan and Michael sat at the table and watched this. Kate laid a plate of soda bread next to the ever present chunk of butter. She looked from Dan to her father. She cut a wedge of cheese and placed it next to the bread and lined up three mugs on the table. She returned to the table carrying the kettle. She looked at the two men again and set the kettle down hard on the table.

"In the name of all that's holy, have neither one of you anything to say?"

"I have," said Dan.

"Well," said Kate fixing her hands on her hips.

"I was waitin' 'til you sat down."

She looked at her father stuffing his pipe. "Pa, will you leave us alone for a bit?"

"No," said Dan.

"No?" Kate echoed.

"I want your father to hear this. I said I'd quit and I have—I'm through—and I'm back—I want to marry your daughter and I want to learn the fishin'—just like I said."

"Well," said the old man, "I told you there's a livin' to be made here on Bantry Bay—do ya still have that in mind?"

"I do," Dan said.

"Shure, I could show you what I know. We could work together," Dillon said, leaning back in his chair. He lit a wooden match with his thumbnail and watched the flame. There was the edge of a smile at the corners of his mouth.

The smashing sound of crockery breaking jerked the two men's heads around. The dog yipped and bounded to a corner. Kate stood with her arm back holding a tea mug in her hand.

"Oh! I beg your pardon, I hope I didn't interrupt you two gentlemen in your deliberations."

Michael Dillon pushed back his chair and headed with quick steps for the door.

"I think I'll take that silly dog for a walk," he said.

Kate shook her head and burst into laughter. "The old hero, himself." She looked at Dan and the laughter was still part of her. "Dan Conway, do you have any idea how many romantic dreams a spinster schoolteacher in the West of Ireland has about being asked to marry?"

Dan stood up and moved toward her. "Ah, Kate, I'm sorry. I just wanted to be sure that—"

Michael Dillon waited, half turned, in the doorway. Kate glanced at him.

"All right, Pa, all right. Have a nice walk."

She looked at Dan and started to speak. He put a finger across her lips.

"Will ya marry me, Kate Dillon?"

"I will indeed, Dan Conway," she said and held up her arms to him.

After a while Kate stirred and took Dan's hand in hers.

"We can't stay here, Dan."

"Why?"

"Ah, my love, you know why. Pa will be back soon—let's go outside and calm down."

"All right," Dan said. "Let's go catch our supper. I'd like to do that my first day back."

"If we could, it would be a sure sign of good luck for us," she said.

They ran through the sun dappled meadow, fishing rods swinging at their sides. Dan rushed up the stairs of the stile and waited for Kate on the top step. He tossed his fishing rod forward onto the grass and when Kate reached him he grabbed her and whirled her around in a wide happy circle watching her gleaming face as he spun her. Then they kissed long and hard.

Finally Kate broke from him, smiled and said, "Come on, Mr. Conway. We don't want to starve, you know," and leapt from the platform and raced down the hill, across the beach to the boat.

The fishing rod felt good in Dan's hands. He snapped his wrist back and forth and watched the whip action of the tip. He looked at Kate. Their eyes met and they smiled—a smile full of comfort and caring. She wore her thick oversized fisherman's sweater, sleeves pushed above her elbows. Her hair was piled in a glistening black mass on her head.

Dan laughed, easy and gentle.

"What is it?" asked Kate, and then she added, "I don't think I've ever heard you laugh like that."

"I was just thinkin' that I might move down there and we'd do some kissin' and huggin' right here in the middle of Bantry Bay."

"And tip the boat over, too, Mr. Conway. I think not," Kate said with a bright grin. She pushed the handle of the oars in front of her. "I guess I'll need these for protection, but—" She heaved the blades of both oars up into the boat. "The truth is, I really don't want protection." She darted to where he sat in the stern, kissed him on the mouth, their lips lingered a moment, then backed quickly to her seat.

"By God, Kate, you're like a wizard in this boat. I didn't realize that before. The fact that you were writing a book impressed me. I didn't know you had all this talent, too."

"Of course not. I wanted you to see me as a weak, defenseless creature needing the protection of a strong, handsome older man like yourself. Now you can learn some of my other strengths."

"I already have, Madam," he said with a wicked leer.

Kate's face flamed. "Ah, Dan, do I frighten you?"

"All you do is please me, Kate, in every way." He turned and worked the line into his hand and cast it out. "I forget easy, I guess," he said. "Do I have it right?"

Kate put down the oars and picked up her own rod. She spread the fingers of her right hand. "The hand this way makes it easier." She snapped the rod and the line darted out. The splash on the glassy water was a long way from the boat.

"We're going to make a good team, Kate, when I get better at this. And speakin' of being a team, let's talk about marriage."

"All right, let's."

"What do ya say to goin' to see Father Devoy tonight?"

"I say marvelous, but he's away to Cork for this weekend. He's due back Monday."

"Well, let's see him then."

Kate smiled, "For somebody who avoided it for so long, you seem very comfortable with the idea of marriage now."

Dan spoke slowly. "I guess—I guess—I want to try and catch up for all the years we didn't have."

Kate's eyes were bright. "Oh, Dan, I love you so."

"Ahh," he said, "Ahh, Kate."

He ran a finger across the break in his nose and then spoke briskly. "Now let's see if we can find some fish. I want to be able to feed us tonight and all the nights to come."

"You won't be able to do that with rod and reel alone, love."

"Oh, I know, but I want to be really proficient with this so that we can do some guiding for the tourist fishermen."

"And women," she added, whipping the line way out.

"And women," he amended as he watched its flight.

The afternoon slipped by as smoothly as the water under the boat. The dog was lying patiently on the pier, watching their approach from between his outstretched paws. When they tossed the three firm silver mottled fish up from the boat, he rose slowly and sniffed the catch.

They walked hand in hand along the coast road. The dog made nosy excursions into the thickets and pasture land along the way. The drowsy warmth of the spring day reached inside Dan. He squeezed Kate's hand gently. "Ya know, this must be what the poets and philosophers are always searchin' for. I think this is what life's all about, girl."

She slowed her pace and turned to him and brought his hand up to her mouth. "It has to be. This feeling must be the essence of life and it can't ever have been better than this for anybody, ever." She stopped and looked up at him with a furrowing of her eyebrows. "Have you ever felt like this before, Dan?"

"Well, let's see," he scratched his head. "Let me see if I can recall exactly."

The green of Kate's eyes seemed to increase in depth; her lips formed a small round O. Dan fingered the break on his nose and looked sorrowfully at her; then his face wrinkled into a broad grin which turned into a full throated laugh as Kate's eyes widened.

She dropped her fishing rod and swung a roundhouse punch which missed completely. She moved after him and swung again as he tossed the fish and his fishing gear down and sprinted up and over the low stone wall beside the road. He ran laughing into the knee-high green meadow.

"Dan Conway, you are a terrible, cruel man and I'll punish you for it."

He turned suddenly as she clambered over the wall and scooped her into his arms. Her fists beat a tenuous tattoo on his shoulders. He squeezed her to him, holding her so he looked into her eyes. Her arms went tight around his neck. He spoke with his lips against her neck.

"Katey, I never did and never will love anyone—or anything—the way I love you."

With one arm holding her, he lowered her beside the mossy stones onto the trembling stalks of glistening grass and smooth varnished buttercups. They became part of the day and of the earth, the heat of the sun warming the moist black soil, the whisper of the breeze rippling the tips of the rich pasture, and then the sharp cries of gulls, gliding, swooping.

Michael Dillon was dozing in his chair. The turf smoldered and smoked on the grate. Kate placed a lump of peat on the fire and spoke softly as she brushed her hands. "I don't suppose you plutocrats in the North have to worry about such things, but we peasants in the West have to remember to keep the turf fire burning. It's a sign of bad luck if it ever goes out."

"We'll keep it burnin', Kate."

A luxurious deep sigh came from the old man. He pushed his cap back on his head and rubbed his eyes. "Did ya have any luck?"

"Better than a meal, Pa," said Kate.

"And did ya leave a bit with Mrs. Cronin at the Pub?"

Kate turned back to the fireplace as she felt her cheeks color.

Dan spoke. "No, we came up through the meadow."

"Well, then, perhaps that gives us an excuse for us to make a little visit after dinner." He got up from his chair and slapped the palms of his hands together and did a little shuffle. "What do ya say to that, Mr. Conway?"

"I'd say that's a fine idea, Mr. Dillon."

The early evening sky was an infinite purple that softened to blue in the west. The air was still and their easy voices carried clearly as they walked leisurely down the hill toward Cronin's, the dog trotting beside them.

"I've got dredges in the shed, Dan; we'll get them out and start workin' on 'em tomorrow or Monday. There's a livin' to be made on the water here with the scallopin' and the lobsters. It's a two-man job, though. I've needed younger arms the last few years—and there's guidin' the tourists at the fishin'. Shure, things'll be grand, you'll see. And of course there'll be money comin' in to Katey besides her teachin' if that book gets published."

"Perhaps, Pa. That's only perhaps now."

"Ah, don't you worry. I know it will, Katey. But you've no call to worry. It's only a livin' the two of you need. You don't want to get captured by money like the Yanks," said the old man as he knocked ashes from his pipe.

Mrs. Cronin nodded and flashed a black-toothed smile as she watched Michael Dillon lay the wrapping of fish on the bar, then she looked up at Dan.

"You're back, I see."

"I am," Dan said formally.

"Will you be stayin' long?"

"I will," he said.

"I thought as much," she said and she took Kate's hands in hers. "God bless ya both—and ya know you're gettin' the loveliest girl in Ireland."

"I do," Dan said and she smiled broadly at him and he forgot her bad teeth.

"Ya know, I believe ya," she said. "Well now, I was hopin' you might bring some fish tonight. I'll just pour for ya now and go back and do a bit of fussin' with it. My Jack is feelin' poorly. This'll pep 'im up." She looked around the crowded room and raised her voice. "Help yourselves, all, while I'm gone."

Kate rolled her eyes toward the ceiling. "What Jack needs is a good swift kick," she said.

"Or a punch," said Dan.

Kate's face lit up in a bright smile. "Yes, or a punch. A lot of you big feeling Irishmen could stand a good whack."

Two men shuffled close by, Wellington boots speckled with grey mud below their dark trousers. Pints of Guinness were at their lean leathery faces; they giggled at Kate's comment.

Michael Dillon eyed them sternly and took his pipe out of his mouth very slowly. "Billy, you and Joe Michael must have a bit more than this to occupy your time with on a Saturday evening." With a quick nod and a mutter, they moved erratically across the room.

Kate giggled. Her father and Dan smiled. Then, as though on cue, they raised their glasses to their lips. Dan paused, put his glass toward them and murmured quietly in the Irish language, *"Slainte,"* the toast of a hundred thousand turf fires, of glasses of Guinness or whiskey or poteen without number, of small victories and horrendous defeats, of generations of sadness, of unremitting humiliation, of hope.

Thirty-Eight

HE AWOKE. There was no noise, no softening of the night. The room was dark. Something inside told him dawn would come soon. He eased his breath out, lying very still, not to wake Kate. He thought of other times, of moments of silent breathing.

"Dan."

"You're awake."

"Yes, just now." She moved against him, her body warm and firm, her skin smooth and exciting. He was shaken for a moment by the privilege of her nakedness here for him.

Now the room was light. Kate nuzzled against him. "I've got to go upstairs. Pa and I are going to Bantry to Mass. I don't suppose you'd like to come with us?"

"No, I'll keep the home fires burning."

She brushed her lips across his. "We'll come straight home. I don't like to be away from you."

He watched her drop her flannel nightgown over her head and help it work its way down her body. She looked steadily at him and smiled gently, her face full of love. "I'll go upstairs and dress now." Then she left him.

The human sounds of morning came to him from upstairs. He got up and dressed. The turf fire was a crumbled glow. He put a chunk of peat on and watched until the edges flamed. He swiveled a look around the room for the dog, turned toward the kitchen and gave a low whistle. He waited a moment and then went outside, leaving the door open. The brightness surprised him. The sun was already in charge of the day.

He walked down the slope in front of the house, the grass wet and sticky against his legs. He whistled for the dog. The Bay was spread out before him, spotted with white tufts of waves. The slam of the car door and Kate's voice reached him and he turned and looked back at the cottage.

Michael Dillon was seated in the car, his cap firmly set, a thin signal of smoke drifting from his first pipe of the day. Kate was standing in front of the car waving. A black dress outlined her clearly against the whitewashed cottage. Dan swung his arm over his head, turned and climbed up onto a stone wall.

The dog was lying on the far side of the wall. His neck was at an awkward angle and a mass of blood and tissue was in his fur. Dan's mouth went dry. His heart hammered in his chest. He twisted on the rocks almost losing his balance and screamed, "KATE, STOP!" He raced back up the hill toward the car shouting wildly, "Don't start it. Stop! Kate! Get out! Get away from the car!" Her head turned toward him and her puzzled eyes met his.

The car lifted up off the ground. The noise smashed in on his head. A searing wave swept by and knocked him off his feet. A roaring, hissing fire covered the jumble of metal and leapt high in the air.

He scrambled to his feet and ran to the torn ugly wreckage. Flames caught at him. He pulled at a part of the car. Screams tore at his throat. "Kate! Kate!" His hands were burning. The awful smell from the wreckage gagged him. Pain drove him to his knees. He crawled away and shoved the burned palms of his hands against the wet grass. His shirt and trousers were smoking. He rolled over and over, rubbing his shaking hands on the grass.

The fire was the only sound. He got to his feet and with his head down moved unsteadily into the house. He picked up the slab of butter from the table and smeared it over his hands. He awkwardly lifted his leather bag and took out his pistol and put it in his pocket. He walked out of the house. He was crying.

Nantucket
May 28, 1982